THE SHADOW ELEMENTAL

THE BINDING TRIALS BOOK 1

D.K. HOLMBERG

JASPER ALDEN

ASH
PUBLISHING

CHAPTER 1

When the surge of fire bloomed in the distance, Lathan aimed the crossbow. Hitting one of the elementals from this distance, even a slightly larger one like the foxlike creature in front of him, was difficult at the best of times. It became harder when it suddenly burst into a fiery explosion of heat, as if it knew they were there.

"I bet you won't even get close," Jef said from where he lay on the ground next to him. "You can't even raise that thing high enough without drawing its attention. How do you think you're going to be able to hit it from here?"

His voice was little more than a whisper, but loud enough that Lathan worried the elemental might hear them. They were on the edge of a small grassy hillside, looking down on the creature. Better that than for it to look down on them. It wasn't moving. Lathan wondered if the elemental knew they'd been following it.

"I don't need to kill it. Just pierce it."

He touched the flinty tip of the crossbow bolt. It wasn't designed to kill the elemental—that wasn't anything he wanted to do—but if he could get it close enough, he *might* snare some of the power from it. Stored elemental power could be useful. It was hard enough to get this close to them, which Jef knew but obviously didn't care.

Lathan traced his finger along the trigger. His father had made the crossbow, using wood from a tree burned by an elemental that was much like the one in front of him now. It made the structure strong. The string was supposedly pulled from the whisker of another elemental—this one a large wolflike creature that his father had told him about but that Lathan had never seen.

The hyza started to turn. Then it looked toward him.

Lathan froze.

An elemental like this could attack from a distance. With the heat inside it, the elemental could not only send fire burning across the ground, likely catching them before they had a chance to draw out the cannister of infused water to counter, but it could scald the air—and their lungs—before they had a chance to react. Lathan had seen the remains of elemental hunters thinking they could trap one like this.

I'm not trying to trap. Just take a little of its power.

That was what he told himself.

Let him watch me.

He pulled the trigger.

Jef sucked in a sharp breath. "I can't believe you're trying to do this."

The bolt flew straight toward the hyza.

Fire surged along the surface of its body. It looked something like a red fox, though instead of fur it was covered in flames that licked it from head to toe. It had a long, thick tail that swished at the air. The exploding heat made him think that it wouldn't work.

But it will. I know it will.

The bolt flew straight... then hit the heat.

The wooden shaft wasn't made of element-infused wood. It burned with a bright flash and another swish of the hyza's tail. Its ears twitched, then it turned away, racing toward the rocky hills, where it disappeared.

Jef let out a long breath. "That was stupid. I can't believe I let you drag me out here. As if *you* were going to catch anything from one of them. Your bolt barely even got to it."

"It wasn't about the bolt," Lathan said, getting to his feet when he was convinced the elemental was gone. The air held some of the heat from the elemental, enough that he started to wonder how long the heat would linger. Lathan rarely managed to get close to an elemental like that.

There were some that were smaller—and less power-ful. Those were easy enough to track, even if it wasn't any easier to take a bit of their power. That was the harder part. He'd been working on getting better at snagging some of the elemental power and thought that this one would work, though elementals were hard enough to find, let alone catch.

Jef hurried after him, slowing at the top of the hill and looking around. "You didn't want to hit it? How would you hold some of the elemental?"

Most people believed you had to hit the elemental in order to take some of their power. That was what Lathan had been taught. And he believed it. He'd been chasing elementals his whole life, storing some of that elemental power so that it could be used—or better yet, traded—at another time.

An elemental with as much power as this one seemed to have should have been easier to draw power from. They didn't need to strike the elemental to get some of that energy from it. All he needed was to get *close* to the power.

Which was why he'd chosen the tip of his bolt the way that he had. That should let him call enough power from it. If he got close enough.

And if he could find it.

It was a test. Not that he'd tell Jef that he'd brought him along for a test. Jef would get mad, tell him that he used him again for an experiment that he wanted nothing to do with, and then go storming off the way he had the other few times.

Lathan reached the spot where the hyza had been standing. There was the residual heat in the air, but there was something else here. Lathan felt it as a tension that came through his boots, squeezing his legs. Power.

It *was* here.

"What are you looking for? Don't tell me that you want to follow that thing up there." He motioned toward the rock.

The stone was a deep black enough that Lathan wouldn't be able to follow the hyza in that direction, though he wondered if he *might* be able to follow the heat he felt. That wasn't the way that he wanted to go, though. What he needed was to find the stone.

"See if you can find any part of my crossbow bolt," he said.

Jef gaped at him. He was tall and thin, and when he looked at Lathan like that, his mouth practically touched his chest. "You did see what happened to it when you shot it at that thing, right? I can't be the only reasonable one here. Fiery Skies, I *am* the only reasonable one. You convinced me to follow you all the way out here. 'I'm just going to trap a little fire, Jef. I've got it covered, Jef. Yes the stone will hold something as small as the little ara sprite. Of course the touch of udilm on the stone will make sure it's safe'."

"Are you done?" Lathan asked.

"With what? I think I do a pretty good impression of you. The key is how you start to speed up the more you talk. Your mother seems to think it's nearly perfect."

Lathan sniffed and turned back to trying to find the stone. He *had* dipped it in some of the infused water of udilm. That residual water elemental should have been enough to inactivate anything the hyza would have done, *and* should have been enough for him to capture some of the hyza. "My mother has been talking to you far more than she needs to be."

"That's just because she's worried about what you might do. She knows when you go after other elementals you let the idea of a big score get into your head. It's not healthy, Lathan."

He ignored him, crouching down to try to figure out where the hyza would have come through. With the way the crossbow bolt had flown, it should have come through here, but he didn't see any sign of it. Lately, the number of elementals had increased, and Lathan wasn't sure why that would be. If his father were still around, maybe Lathan would have better answers, as he had always seemed to know more about the elementals than almost anyone else.

A shadow flittered across the ground, and he froze.

"Don't move," he whispered.

Jef had knelt down and was crawling along the grass, running his fingers through the grasses as he looked for the stone. "Why? Because you found where that elemental came through here? Don't tell me—it *didn't* destroy your bolt. And you struck it in the side and managed to draw off enough fire to power up an entire —"

"Shadow. And it's moving."

Jef froze.

That was good. There were times when Jeff got it in his head that he didn't need to listen. Thankfully, this wasn't one of them.

Shadow that moved like that suggested an elemental. They were rare—and nearly impossible to snare. It was the one thing that his father had always chased, and the one thing that Lathan had never seen. Of all the possible elemental types, shadow was the one that Lathan was most intrigued by.

"What are you doing?" Jef hissed.

"Just give me a moment," Lathan said.

He had reached into his pouch, still staring at the space on the ground where he'd seen the shadow moving, looking for one of his other pieces of binding stone. He didn't have many free pieces, and normally wouldn't even attempt something like that, but shadows were *rare*.

And rare meant valuable.

"You can't be serious. That's not going to work."

Lathan didn't dare even look in Jef's direction. With elementals, one learned to be careful while tracking them. They could be skittish. Lathan never hurt them— the binding stones he used didn't do anything more than tap into the power the elemental possessed—but that didn't mean they liked being shot at. Shadow was different.

He'd never managed to see shadow elementals, let alone even give some thought to the idea of targeting one. His father had always tracked shadow, though had never mentioned anything about attempting to capture it. Maybe his father had never truly wanted to capture it. Not like he had wanted to use other elementals. And this one might be nothing more than a fleeting cloud drifting across the sky, not an actual elemental, but if he didn't try to capture it, he would never let it go.

"Just be ready."

"You're ridiculous." Jef started to turn and head toward the rock.

When he did, the shadow slithered.

That was the only way that Lathan could describe it. It seemed to slip along the ground, like some serpentine creature clinging to the grass, slipping toward...

The black rock.

If it reached the black rock, it would blend in, and he'd never see it.

Lathan held the binding stone, then dove.

There was no guarantee this technique would even work. He didn't know whether he would hit the elemental or the ground. And if he *did* get to the elemental, there was the very real possibility that it would attack.

Hold the binding stone against the elemental.

That was one of the first lessons of hunting elementals that his father had taught him. The stone would pull the power of the elemental through, and as it did, it could be stored. The stone was neutral, not bound to any element, which made it a perfect conduit for storing power. They were hard enough to find, but Lathan knew where to look.

The ground seemed to slide beneath him.

So much for doubting that this was an elemental. It moved—and Lathan was pulled along with it.

"Is it working?"

"Maybe you could help, and we can figure it out together," he said, barely managing to get the comment out as the elemental pulled him toward the rock.

All thoughts of the hyza were gone. That power could have been a prize, but this...

This *was* a prize.

His hand went cold where he held it against the elemental. There was another surge of cold that washed through the stone. Lathan hoped that meant it was pulling on some of the shadow elemental, but there wasn't any way for him to know with any certainty.

As he neared the rock, Lathan had a decision to make. Hold on and risk crashing into the rock—and with an elemental guiding him, it was possible that it would not only crash him into the rock, but might do so with real force. Elementals could be real shits at times. Or let go.

He pushed down, forcing the binding stone toward the shadow elemental for another moment, then rolled off.

The shadow slipped to the stone, where it disappeared.

He got to his feet, breath heaving out in anxious gasps.

Had that just happened?

There was a part of him that worried about how his father might've felt about him capturing a shadow elemental, even if only a portion of it.

The stone was cold. The temperature didn't always mean much, especially as the power got stored inside and didn't make much of a difference. In this case, though, he thought that it *did* matter.

"Did it work?" Jef asked. He hadn't moved, and still stood near where they'd first spied the hyza.

Lathan held out the stone. The flat gray looked no different now than it had before. That might mean it hadn't worked. When a binding stone was used on a fire elemental, it often took on a hint of color. The same with water. Wind didn't do much, but then wind was fickle and difficult to catch.

"I hope so."

Jef looked around before making his way over to him, eyeing the stone carefully. "That really *was* a shadow elemental. I saw the way it was pulling you." His voice was hushed. Awed. "How did you even see it?"

"There was nothing more than a flicker of movement. That was it."

And had he not been focused on looking for the *other* binding stone, he might not even have seen it. How often did shadow pass by and they weren't aware?

Some claimed shadow was more common than most thought, though still rare like all elementals. It was a difficult claim to make—or to prove. They were so hard to spot. The conditions had to be just right. Then catching one was another matter altogether.

"Help me find the hyza stone."

Jef tore his gaze away from the shadow binding stone, then started to grin. "You're getting greedy. And I'm pretty sure that stone isn't going to be found. I saw the way that hyza burned your stone. You'll be lucky if you—"

Lathan bent over and plucked a gray stone off the ground. Unlike the round binding stone that he'd used on shadow, this one had been shaped to a point. There was nothing of the rest of the crossbow bolt to it, but there was no doubting that this was *his* stone.

"You were saying?"

Jef grabbed for it, and Lathan let him take it. The stone was warm, which told him that it *had* taken on some of the hyza power. At least he knew one of them worked.

"You actually hit it." Jef looked up. "I didn't think you did. Or if you did, I didn't think the elemental would let you—"

"Let me?" Lathan snatched the stone from him and stuffed it into his leather satchel. "There's no letting me. That's my hunt. My stone."

Jef looked toward the black rock. "Do you want to see if we can find more of the shadow?"

Lathan followed him, making his way to the edge of the rock and pausing as he looked out into the dark stone that climbed gradually upward. Blackstone was a strange place, one that most believed had once been filled with the power of the elementals, but time and the natural movement of elementals had changed it so that it was empty.

"Up there? The only thing we *might* be able to find would be hyza, but I'm not risking that search on Blackstone."

"You've got the shadow——"

"Which we can bring back with us."

He wasn't accustomed to being the practical one of the two of them, but there was no way that he was climbing the mountain. Not with what might be there. Hyza would be able to slip along the rock and hide. If they were lucky, they'd have time to prepare for whatever the elemental might do to them. If they were unlucky, they'd be surprised. And burned.

Shadow was another story.

Lathan knew next to nothing about shadow. There were supposedly different kinds of shadow elementals, much like there were different kinds of other elementals, but no one had ever been able to see them well enough to differentiate them.

It was best to take the prize and get back.

"How much do you think it's worth?" Jef asked.

"I'm not splitting it with you."

"What? I was here, wasn't I? That's the code, you know. Share the profits."

"And share the risk. Who was the one who jumped on top of the shadow?"

"Someone with not enough sense."

"You know how I feel about this, Jef."

"So you plan on selling it, and keeping me out of the cut?"

"Not this one," Lathan said, his voice trailing off.

Jef turned away in a huff and started stomping off toward town. Any hope of hunting other elementals on the way back disappeared with his heavy stomping. That would scare away any earth elementals, and it would probably even send the wind skittering away. Fire wouldn't care, but they'd be able to follow fire easily enough anyway.

When Lathan caught up to him, Jef paused. "You realize that we can't prove it."

He nodded slowly. "I know. We need to prove what we have."

The problem was that he wasn't entirely sure *how* to prove it.

With a capture of any of the other elementals, it was fairly straight forward to claim that they had something of earth or fire or water or wind. Shadow... that was something that couldn't be tested, which meant that it couldn't be proven.

Not in town, at least.

"I don't like that look," Jef said.

"Which look?"

"The one that tells me that you're going to make me go with you on whatever crazy thought you have in mind. It reminds me of when we were wrestling when we were younger."

"You're just mad that I always won."

"A little. You have a strange knack for fighting. So what terrible thing are you going to do now?"

Lathan flashed a smile as he slipped the binding stone into his pocket. He kept it separate from the others, not wanting it to contaminate them. "I don't have any idea what you might mean."

Jef took off, shaking his head. "You're going to get me killed."

"But you'll have fun doing it."

CHAPTER 2

A trail of smoke drifted up in the distance as they headed back toward Gorawl. It was faint, little more than a thin line that could have been nothing, though Lathan recognized the dust that hung in the air. When he pointed it out to Jef, he just shrugged.

"It's probably nothing. We know that there are others like us out searching, especially with how frequent the elementals have been moving these days. Maybe somebody else caught shadow."

He watched Lathan, and there was a hint of amusement in his eyes.

"Or maybe they just went after hyza."

"Fiery Skies, that one is bad enough," Jef said.

"Only if it catches you."

"Right. When you're firing your crossbow bolts at that thing, you don't think it's going to catch up to you?" He snorted and pitched his voice to mimic Lathan's again. "'Oh, don't worry, Jef. It's nothing my binding stone can't hold'. I think we saw what your binding stone was capable of holding."

Lathan smirked at him. Jef wasn't *completely* wrong. The binding stone usually worked well for him, and he didn't have any hesitation in trying to use it like that. Most collectors did so with smaller stones—and chased after smaller elementals. The two of them made a living finding something of a bit more power.

"What are you doing now?" Jef asked.

Lathan laughed. "You're only now realizing what I'm doing?"

Ever since leaving the black rock, he'd started toward town but had changed course when he saw the trail of dust. It *might* mean another elemental, as impossible as it was to believe that they'd come across a third elemental in a day. That was rare enough to find in a month. There were a few wind elementals that would create a dust cloud like that, and he still had a few binding stones that he'd like to try out. If it worked, and if they managed to use them to hold the elemental, he wanted to have a chance to bring back a few different elementals that would be valuable. Hyza *should* fetch a fair amount, especially as the binding stone was still warm enough that he thought most who would understand what they'd done would recognize the power of the stone, but if they were to grab a bit of wind...

"No. Not another elemental," Jef said, finally understanding.

"We don't know what's out there, and I figure that we can take a look—"

"You take a look. I'm not going to get caught up in some blast of ciran, or maybe a torand, or—"

"Or it's just ara."

A common wind elemental. Or had been. It was notoriously difficult to capture any of their power, mostly because of how difficult it was to even see the wind. It was why Lathan had started to look for the traces of remains left by the wind. In the case of most of the elementals, there was a hint of color when it swirled. Out here, where it had been dry the last week, a bit of dust kicked up from the road and from the grasses. Most of the time, the ground was damp enough that it didn't leave much of a trace.

Jef looked like he wanted to head back to town, but he let out a frustrated sigh before following. "We're just taking a look. That's it."

"That's it." Lathan started forward, then cast a glance back at Jef. "Unless we see something that gives us a chance to do more. We couldn't pass up that."

He hurried forward before Jef had a chance to complain even more. It was likely that he still would, but if Lathan could get him close enough to the wind elemental, at least he'd be drawn in. With wind, it would be useful to have someone else with him. Jef was skilled at helping corral the wind. More so than many others that Lathan had been around. He didn't have the same skill creating binding stones, but that was something that Lathan had learned from his father, who had been a skilled collector before him.

They neared a small ridge where the grasses were a

duller green and took a narrow path that wound through it. It was easier to follow the path than to stomp down a fresh one.

"What *is* that?" Jef whispered as they stopped.

The ground sloped down from here as it headed toward the shoreline in the distance. They could *just* make out the waves crashing toward the rocky shore down below. A few gulls circled overhead, but they were far enough out that he couldn't hear anything. Every so often, the gulls would be pulled quickly upward—the effect of a wind elemental, he was certain—before they caught a different current. The gulls circled the trail of dust that he'd seen, but it wasn't a wind elemental. Now that they'd gotten closer, he could see how it was denser than he'd thought. No wind elemental would make a trail like that. Maybe an earth elemental, but even that wouldn't be pure earth.

"Nothing that I've ever seen before." Lathan had already started forward when Jef caught his arm, pulling him back.

"Which seems to me a good reason to hold off, then. What do you think you're doing racing down there?"

"I'm thinking that I want to see what's coming toward Gorawl."

If the trail continued in that direction, it would make its way toward the town, though it could just as easily veer away and keep heading toward the west. Travel far enough, and they could get to Ombal, a smaller inland town, or even to Arendal, which was the next real city, though that was far enough away that Lathan had never even bothered to try reaching it. Anything he needed was found in Gorawl. Or around it. If he went too far inland, everyone knew the elementals were rarer, wanting to avoid mankind.

"You think that's some elemental?"

Lathan shrugged. "That seems the most logical answer."

But as they got closer, logical didn't fit anymore. The trail of dust turned into something else entirely.

Men.

There had to be nearly a dozen. All of them were dressed in deep gray leathers, though the leather wasn't like anything that he'd ever seen before. It was hard to make out from a distance—and he wished that he had his spyglass to make it easier to see, though he only brought that along when hunting elementals that needed more stealth than the trail of hyza they'd seen— but most of the men looked to be carrying swords on them. There was something else with them, but he couldn't *quite* see it.

"Where are they from?" Lathan whispered.

"I've never seen anything like that."

Lathan motioned for Jef to get down. Standing where they were would put them out in the open. Until they knew what this was, and who they had coming toward them, they didn't want to be too visible.

Crouching low, he stared through the grasses, trying to make sense of what he had seen. Soldiers. That was what they had to be. Gorawl was a part of the Iradaln kingdom, though they were far enough from the center of the kingdom that they rarely felt a part of it. The only evidence that they *were* a part of the kingdom came from the taxes paid to the local baron, and that was something that men like Lathan managed to avoid. How would the baron ever know what a simple collector like him managed to snag—and then sell?

"They don't look like Iradaln soldiers," Jef said, as if thinking the same thing.

"Colors are wrong."

They got occasional patrols of the maroon-clad soldiers through Gorawl, mostly small contingents of soldiers recruiting. The pay was good, and there were quite a few men in Gorawl who wanted nothing more than to get away from the town. There really wasn't much out here.

"We should get back," Jef said.

"Before we even know what we're dealing with here?"

Jef looked over to him. His face was drawn, and there was an edge to him that wasn't there very often, a seriousness that he rarely displayed. "Soldiers? We are going to go deal with that. At least, I'm not going to go deal with that. You can do whatever you want."

He started to back away and then got to his feet.

Lathan had been watching the line of men snaking their way forward when Jef moved. Had he not been, he wasn't sure that he would have seen what happened.

The trail seemed to shift.

It was subtle, but he was certain that was what he'd

seen. The dark trail lifted—then began to drift in their direction.

Lathan grabbed Jef and pulled him back down.

Jef started to argue, but Lathan clamped a hand over his friend's mouth, pointing off toward the space below.

"Something changed," he said quietly. "Watch."

"I'm sure they saw me," Jef said. "Which is reason enough for me to get going. Both of us. Like I said, we don't know what's going on there, but I'm sure that it's something we don't want any part in."

The trail of dust swirled above these others. And it *was* dust. There had been a moment when Lathan had wondered if it might be shadow. Having seen the shadow earlier had left him wondering if maybe there would be others. It was rare, but what if these strange soldiers had a way of using it?

"I think that's sandor," Jef said.

He and Jef knew of different elementals, even though they had barely seen a fraction of the named elementals. Lathan's father had always been good at ensuring that Lathan knew how to identify different elementals. He had felt that it was important for Lathan's education. And he had made sure that Jef was included.

"Why would sandor come through here? Maybe to the west, but we don't have that elemental." It was an earth and wind elemental, and it was one that Lathan's father had described, though he'd never seen it. There weren't many combined elementals like that anywhere, though hyza was said to be a mix of fire and earth.

"Like I said, we don't want to be here. I don't know what they're doing here, but... oh."

Lathan looked up and noticed the swirling of the dust coming toward them.

If it was nothing more than a dust cloud, a binding stone wouldn't work.

But if it was more, then he should be ready. That was what his father had always taught him.

Lathan reached into his pocket for the binding stone that they'd used on hyza.

He rolled to his back, looking up. He didn't want to release any of the hyza energy, but he needed to be prepared. It could let out a surge of flame. If this was something of wind, the heat would generally chase it away.

"What are you doing?" Jef whispered.

Lathan looked up. The sky still held the haze above him. It seemed to be taking on more of a shape than it had before, as if the cloud were getting darker —and solidifying. That wasn't what he knew of sandor, though he didn't really know what sandor could do.

"Staying ready," he said.

Jef crawled closer. "If you're going to do anything, use the—"

Heat flared suddenly.

That wasn't from the binding stone that he held.

The cloud started to shift, now swirling differently than it had before. It moved, heading away from them and toward the source of the heat—which seemed to be behind the two of them. There was something familiar about that heat...

Lathan flipped back over and saw a faint reddish shape in the distance.

Hyza?

The elemental had run off, but now there was *another* one? They had known there were more elementals these days than usual, but this was incredibly uncommon. Finding one in a day was rare, or at least it had been until recently.

"Are you doing that?" Jef asked.

"I'm not releasing anything, if that's what you're afraid of."

Jef looked over, his gaze going to the binding stone in Lathan's hand, then frowned. "Maybe you're releasing it and don't know it?"

Lathan pushed on his friend and forced him to turn.

Jef looked toward the distant sign of the elemental. His eyes widened slightly. "Is that—"

"Hyza. Don't know if it's the same one or not."

That would be odd. Seeing one of the fire elementals was rare, but seeing the same one twice would be incredibly unlikely—especially after he'd just shot the elemental with his crossbow.

The crossbow.

He fumbled for it, slipping it off the hook at his waist while grabbing for another binding stone-tipped bolt. If things went well, they could have *two* hyza binding stones. And if that wasn't hyza, it had to be a fire elemental of some kind. Which would be reason enough for him to try and trap that power so that they could hold it.

As he crawled forward, the fiery elemental bloomed with an explosion of heat. Fire surged, bright as the sun, forcing Lathan to turn away from it. When he looked back, the sandor—or whatever elemental that had been —now swirled toward the fiery elemental.

Then it began to circle.

It was almost as if the sandor elemental made a pattern around hyza. It caused the hyza to slowly fade, the heat no longer surging the way that it had at first, slowly easing back and becoming fainter and fainter.

The heat started to dissipate while the other elemental—and now Lathan was certain it was some elemental—focused on it. And the soldiers converged. They moved steadily toward hyza, surrounding it.

"Are they using the other elemental *against* that hyza?" Lathan asked.

"I've never seen anything like that before."

Neither had Lathan. There were plenty of people who hunted elementals, but this was something different altogether. They had spread out, ringing around a small grassy hillside where the hyza stood, and they moved as a unit, heading toward it. As they did, the sandor started to close in, moving closer and closer as well.

The hyza tried to use fire.

Lathan could see the flash of flame. He could feel some of the heat—and some of it came surging through the binding stone he held.

He looked down at it. The stone had started to glow

slightly. It was a pale white, and not so hot that he couldn't hold the stone, but still hotter than was comfortable to carry.

"Fiery Skies," Jef breathed.

Lathan looked up.

The soldiers had hyza surrounded.

Now it was fighting. There was a thrashing sort of energy coming off hyza as it struggled to get free. Lathan could practically feel the panic. The swirling dark cloud continued to loop around the hyza, then—with a point of one of the soldier's hands—the sandor swooped down and solidified.

The hyza roared.

It was a painful sound to hear, a mixture of steam and a wolf's howl.

Then it faded.

Lathan stayed low, not wanting them to see them but wanting to know what they were doing. He and Jef were collectors but this was something other than collecting. What they did was borrow just a little of the power from the elemental. What he witnessed was a way of holding —and seemingly controlling—the elemental.

He poked his head high enough to watch, noticed that they wrapped something around the hyza's snout then around the legs, before backing away.

From the distance, he caught a glimpse of a flat gray. *Binding stones.*

But it was nothing like any binding stone that he'd seen. For one, they were larger. And they seemed to hold not only the elemental, but the light around the hyza as well. There was a surge, a flash of heat and light, then the hyza seemed to disappear.

One of the soldiers marched toward it, took the stones, and slipped them into a large pouch, before moving away. The cloud of sandor moved with it, though it floated more slowly, as if the battle with hyza had taken something out of it.

The men moved away, back toward the road, and disappeared over a ridge, but not before one of the soldiers—the one that had looped the binding stone around the hyza, he thought—looked back toward him. Almost directly at Lathan. The man's eyes twitched slightly.

Lathan prepared to run. If needed, he'd release the trapped hyza—and the shadow, he decided—to escape. But the man turned back and disappeared.

After a moment, Lathan got to his feet, watching.

"What did we just see?" Jef said.

Lathan shook his head. "I don't know."

"That looked like—"

"A different kind of collecting than we do," he said.

Not just collecting. Hunting.

And they'd captured the hyza.

But where had it gone?

CHAPTER 3

The town of Gorawl nestled into a hillside valley, with the nearby Nolin Hill providing much of the shelter from the steady breeze that gusted through this part of the world. Some of the breeze came from the steady drifting of wind elementals that floated over Gorawl, as if they wanted to test and see what the hunters living in the village were up to. There had been attempts over the years to try and capture those elementals and see if there would be a way of holding them in place, but none had been successful.

Lathan and Jef had been quiet during the walk toward the town. Neither of them knew what to make of the soldiers, though they had speculations about what they were doing out there and why they had been pursuing elementals.

"It's probably just because of how frequent the elementals have been moving," Jef offered as they were getting closer to town.

"It seems like a strange reason to send soldiers out. Especially since there are plenty of people, even within the Saval, that would be perfectly capable."

The Saval was where most within the kingdom went to train and learn, including about elementals and the connections to them. There was a time when Lathan had wanted to go to the Saval, but that had been early in his life. Now the only thing that he appreciated about the Saval was there interest in purchasing the elementals that he had captured. Most who studied their trained to work with the power the elementals were connected to, specializing in utilizing that connection and helping hone the power within it. Some were craftsman, creating armor or weapons, and others were more practical, finding ways to create furnaces or plumbing or other ways to add conveniences.

Lathan cared about none of that. All he cared about was chasing and capturing elementals.

"I don't know. And maybe... What does *she* think she's doing?" Jef muttered.

Lathan tore his focus off the binding stone and turned to see who Jef grumbled about before noticing Marin standing near the rocky ledge at the edge of town, looking down over the water. A pair of stout bridges, both of them infused with the power of different earth elementals, stretched across the valley that separated them from Marin.

"The same as she often does," Lathan said, before shrugging. Marin's idiosyncrasies didn't bother him the same way that they seemed to bother Jef. They'd known her their entire lives, back when they were all foolish enough to run through that stream valley below, thinking that they might find something of the elementals. That was before Jef and Lathan had discovered their knack for hunting elementals. Well, really it was Lathan's knack, but Jef often went with him to provide a measure of support.

"Talking to them," Jef said, shaking his head as they neared the bridge. "She thinks they're going to answer her."

"What makes you think they won't?"

"Not you, too."

Lathan grinned. He enjoyed tormenting Jef, especially when it came to Marin. Despite his grumbling, Lathan had seen the way his friend looked at her. "*I* don't talk to the elementals, so I can't say whether they're answering her. What makes you think they aren't?"

He sniffed as he started toward the bridge, where he paused and looked down. Lathan joined him. The narrow stream ran through the valley far below. It was a wonder that it managed to cut through the rock the way that it had. When Lathan had said something about that to his father, he'd been reminded that the stream, and water, didn't need to work quickly. Time gave it the advantage over rock. That, and its ability to move, whereas rock had to stand still.

"'Oh, Jef'," Jef started, raising his voice to mimic the way Marin would speak, "'all you have to do is let yourself listen to them. They're out there, you know. And if you would only open yourself to them, you wouldn't have to hunt them the way you do'." He shook his head, resting his hand on one of the stone pillars supporting the bridge on this side. "Talk to them. I doubt she's even seen an elemental, let alone tried to talk to one that was flashing with heat and fire as you tried to avoid getting blasted by it."

Lathan grinned. "I've talked to them."

"Wait... what?"

"Mostly just to tell them not to move. It's easier to hit them that way."

Jef had been watching him, a question in his eyes, but at the comment, he snorted.

Marin looked up and saw them. She raised a hand, waving to them. Despite the overcast sky, her golden hair seemed to catch whatever sunlight was there, reflecting it in such a way that made her practically seem to glow. If Lathan didn't know her the way that he did, he would have suspected that she had a stored elemental power, but Marin didn't trap any power. She tried to free the trapped power that others captured, though never any of his.

"Now we've got to go over to her," Jef muttered.

"I think you wanted us to do that anyway."

Jef started across the bridge without looking back at him. Lathan followed. At the center of the bridge, he paused so that he could look down. The stream glistened from this vantage. Down below, he knew that it burbled as it raced past buried rock. Marin might think she could talk to some of the elementals from above, but Lathan knew better. There might be the occasional water elemental that passed by Gorawl, but that was uncommon. Even the wind that gusted through here didn't carry that much of the wind elemental influence.

A flicker of foam in the stream caught his attention. That was unusual. The stream was normally quiet, at least from here. Seeing that made him wonder if maybe she *had* seen something. Leave it to Marin to have success in talking to one of the elementals.

"Are you coming?" Jef asked after reaching the far side of the bridge.

Lathan stared for a few moments before looking up. The froth he'd thought that he'd seen didn't return. Maybe there wasn't anything there at all. Just a reflection of the overcast sky overhead.

He hurried across the rest of the bridge. When he took time to really look at the bridge, he always found himself marveling at it. Made entirely out of stone, it would have taken a considerable amount of stored earth elemental power to hold the stone in place while constructing the bridge. And for the founders of the town to have made *two* bridges...

That was excess. And it suggested that there had once been *more* of the earth elementals—probably *all* elementals—than what they had now. He couldn't even imagine what it must have been like to have that kind of power at one point. There wouldn't have been much of a market for someone like him, were that the case.

"You found one of the hyza?" Marin was saying as he approached.

Lathan looked over to Jef, who stood slightly too close to Marin. He offered a half shrug.

"We chased it to the rock, but then it disappeared."

"Please tell me that you didn't hurt it," she said, turning her attention to Lathan. He noticed the irritation in Jef's face as she did.

"There's nothing that we do to the elementals that hurts them," Lathan said. They'd had this conversation before, and he knew how she felt, but she also knew how *he* felt. "All I'm doing is trying to—"

"Strip a part of them away. What if I did this?" She grabbed his arm with a quick twist of her fingers, pinching him harder than he would have expected. Lathan jerked away, and she left a bright red mark. "Or something like that," she said softly.

"Were you trying to pull part of *me* away?" he asked.

She shrugged. "You should know what it feels like. I know you think it doesn't hurt them, but what you're taking from them is a part of the elemental."

"That they can replace by their connection to the elements."

That was his understanding of it, at least. Lathan didn't fully know how the elementals accessed the power that they did, only that they were somehow connected to the power of the elements. The binding stones allowed him to strip away some of that power, but not so much that it would lead to any harm.

"You don't know that." She looked past him, her attention on the stream down below. "What if the way that you use your stones tears some part of them away so that they can't ever regain it? It would be like you losing a finger!"

Jef looked over to Lathan. "I doubt he'd mind that much. This *is* Lathan, after all. He doesn't really care if he has all ten. You do still have them, don't you?"

Lathan held his hand up, wiggling his fingers. "It's not like that anyway. If anything, it's more like having a strip of flesh peeled away. That regrows."

"You're horrible," Marin said.

"I'm not saying that's what it is," Lathan said. "Just that you're wrong about it being a permanent change. We know it's not."

There had been attempts to test that over the years. The easiest way to prove it had been capturing an elemental, binding a bit of their power, and then waiting to see if that power were restored. Each time it had proven to be. That was why Lathan didn't think it was the same problem that Marin did to borrow some of that power from the elemental. And it *was* borrowing it. Nothing he took was gone from them for good.

"Well, you don't know whether it's a permanent change or not since you can't—or won't—talk to them. If you'd take the time to try to speak to them, you'd understand that there's more to them than you know."

Jef started to smirk when Lathan shook his head slightly. There was no point in getting into an argument with her, especially not about this. This was the kind of thing that would not end well for them.

"What are you doing out here?" Lathan asked, wanting to change the subject with her. "Don't tell me you found a water elemental here." That would be incredibly unusual, especially so close to town.

"Oh, you can't really speak to water from up here. You can try," Marin said, turning back toward the rocky valley and leaning over the ledge, peering down and toward the water far below, "but water doesn't like to shout. The wind does. Sometimes fire. Always earth." She smiled as she said it, as if she were sharing some inside joke with them that only she understood. "Water likes it when you get down with it. There's something about sitting with water and letting it work over you that you just don't get with some of the other elementals."

"Wind doesn't always shout," Jef said. When Lathan looked to him, he shrugged. "Sometimes it's like today. Just a little breeze. Nothing more than that. There's no shouting. A whisper, if anything."

She tipped her head back and breathed in slowly. She really did look ridiculous with the way she was standing, but then she straightened and nodded carefully. "That's right. Ara likes to whisper. I think it's easier. Some of the elementals have an easier time than others with that. They don't really understand us, you see."

Lathan looked over to Jef, who was shaking his head, but Lathan turned back to her. "You didn't tell us what you were doing out here."

"Looking for signs of their passing."

"The elementals? You won't see anything up here." Not usually, but there *had* been that strange surge of turbulent water. That might have been something.

"Not them. What the wind told me is coming. If you

listen, you can hear it talking to you." She tipped her head to the side, and made as if she were listening.

Jef opened his mouth to say something, but Lathan raised a hand to keep him from doing anything that he'd regret. Arguing with her would be something that Jef would most definitely regret, especially when it came to arguing over what the elementals might—or most likely *not*—have said to her.

Lathan tried to listen. The wind pulled on his hair, fluttering his jacket, but there wasn't anything in the wind that he could hear. Not at first. But as he stood there, he began to feel it whistling past his ears. There was *almost* the sense that there was something to it, as if the wind *were* trying to give him a rhythm of sound that meant something.

"Stupid," he muttered to himself. Jef started to grin, but thankfully Marin didn't appear to hear him. He didn't want her to think he was calling *her* stupid. It was his foolishness to think that there might be something to what she was saying. It was just the wind. Nothing more than that. "What's the wind saying to you?"

Lathan decided that it might be better to try and placate her rather than attempting to argue with her while she was out here and acting strange. With Marin, that would often be for the best.

"Like I said, you have to listen. I can hear it talking. There's something in the wind that's trying to tell me what's coming. And I think that you'd be able to hear it too if you would only let yourself. Especially you, Lathan."

Jef looked over to him, and mouthed, "Especially you?"

Lathan shrugged. He didn't know what she was going on about, but at this point, he wasn't going to try to push it either. There was no point in trying to argue with her to figure out what she meant.

"We'll leave you to listen to the wind, then. Enjoy."

As he started to head away, she reached over and grabbed him by the wrist, pulling him close to her. "I know you can hear it."

Lathan pulled his hand away from her. There had been a strange tingling when she'd touched him, though maybe it was just that he was surprised by what she had done.

"I don't hear anything."

Almost as if to challenge that comment, the wind whipped around him again.

Marin straightened, and she grinned at him, a victorious expression that seemed to try to tell him that he *did* in fact hear what he claimed not to. Lathan backed away from her, rubbing his wrist where she'd grabbed him.

"Come back out here if you want to listen again," she said, then she turned back toward the rock overlook and stared down toward the water. After a moment, she dropped to her hands and knees and leaned forward, looking at the water. Her mouth moved, but Lathan didn't hear her saying anything.

"We should get back. We need to see what we can sell hyza for, anyway."

"That's the only one?"

He raised a hand to cut Jef off before he said anything about the shadow. He didn't need to get into another discussion with Marin about what he had uncovered, as that would only keep them with her longer than he intended. Jef glanced past him and toward Marin before nodding.

When they had gotten some distance between them, Jef looked back. The evenly spaced stones that formed the road led toward the bridge, and Marin stood about twenty paces to the side, still bent over and leaning so that she could presumably look down toward the stream below.

"Do you think she can really hear anything?" Jef asked. "I mean, the wind *did* seem to gust right as she was talking about what she was able to hear. What if she *can* speak to the elementals?"

"What do you think they'd say?"

"I don't know. Maybe they'd say, 'Lathan—don't shoot your crossbow at me because I don't like how you take all the prizes and the glory. Let Jef have a chance'. Or something like that."

"I share with you."

Jef nodded and tapped his booted foot on the stone, pausing as he did to tip his head as if he were listening to the stone when he did it. When nothing came, he looked up and grinned at him. "You'd better. I could have hit hyza."

"Not the shadow."

"And I'm not convinced you did anything there."

"Then we'd better find out."

"You don't mean—"

"I do."

"He's not going to be happy to see us."

"He never is."

There weren't many people who were willing to talk to Lathan about elementals, especially as he and Jef had pursued a more nontraditional path to learning about them. Only one instructor at the Saval had ever been interested in working with them with any consistency.

But how much was Lathan willing to reveal?

CHAPTER 4

"Where are you going?" Jef asked.

Lathan turned back to his friend, pausing for a moment as he looked over to him, and then touched the binding stone in his pocket. It was strange to have a binding stone touched by shadow, especially after having spent so much of his childhood chasing after signs of shadow. Lathan had to believe this would be what his father would've wanted, and it was the kind of thing that he wished that he had a chance to share with his father.

Without him, it felt somewhat hollow.

"I can meet you back here," he said.

"Meet me? You going to leave me? We just saw several different elementals, and now you want to just abandon me? No. I'm going to stay with you until I get my cut. Unless you're really planning on keeping it all?"

He started to laugh softly. He felt more than a little

giddy at this point. "I'm not taking your cut. You don't have to worry that I would even think about that."

"Oh, I know that you're not going to take it, but if you plan on going to see your mother, I think that I can be a part of it."

And why not? This was Jef, after all, somebody who had studied with Lathan, who had known Lathan's father, and who understood everything that he had gone through, everything that he had sacrificed, in order for him to reach that elemental.

"Come along."

They passed through the outer section of the village and a series of small stone buildings. These were some of the oldest that were here, built in a time before the kingdom had spread this far. The structures were simple, quaint, and nearly indestructible. Those who lived in the homes did so thinking that there was the power of an earth elemental within the building itself that kept them so well protected, though Lathan was not entirely sure if that was even true. Or possible. Unless they were binding-stone buildings, able to trap the power of the elemental, it seemed impossible to believe that they would have anything more to them.

"Can I see it?" Jef asked, leaning close. His voice had dropped to a whisper, and he shoved up against Lathan. It was one thing talking about trapped elemental power in a place like their village, especially given how they were not a part of the Saval and didn't have a traditional education, and it was another to speak about a shadow elemental. That was nearly impossible to believe.

"You can look at it," he said, grinning at his friend, pulling the binding stone from his pocket. It was just a binding stone, after all, and didn't look altogether unique, even though as he held onto it, Lathan was acutely aware of the energy that seemed to hum from deep within the stone. He wasn't at all sure whether that came from the energy of the binding stone, something that was possible, as binding stones had their own unique power to trap an elemental, or whether it came from the shadow elemental instead. If it was that, then he thought that it would be even more impressive.

The real challenge would be in finding someone who could help them understand the elemental power that might be trapped within the binding stone, and to see if there might be anything that could be done with that. Lathan wasn't exactly sure if he could. He wasn't exactly sure if he wanted to do anything with it.

"What do you think we can do with it?"

Lathan wasn't even upset that his friend automatically assumed that it would be both. Jef had always hunted with him, and he wanted to let his friend take part in their success. And it was success. It might be a different form than what they had anticipated before, but it was definitely a victory.

"I've been trying to remember all the things my father told me about shadow elementals," Lathan started, keeping his voice pitched low. Now that they were dealing with shadows, he wanted to make sure that he didn't draw any sort of attention. Shadows were rare, and talking about them, and about their power, was a way of revealing to others what they had done, something that he didn't want to do. "He didn't really talk all that much about what it might do. I was wondering why and figured that it was probably tied to the fact that he never expected to find anything."

"Because no one has," Jef said. "I can't imagine what some of the instructors would say if you told them about it." He regarded Lathan for a moment. "I can't tell whether you intend to tell anyone about it."

Lathan shrugged. "I haven't decided, honestly."

"That's what I figured. You have that look about you, you know? It's one that tells me that this one might just be for you. Even if it might be valuable, you don't care."

"Hyza is plenty valuable," he said, taking the shadow elemental binding stone, slipping it back into his pocket, and pulling out the other binding stone. This one had started to take on a bit of warmth so that he could feel some of the elemental trapped within it, even if he didn't understand what that might do. Once they sold the collected power, it would be out of their hands. He would be given the binding stone back, and he could use it to draw upon another elemental. That was how they worked. There were some who could theoretically release elemental energy from binding stones without needing to go through all of the steps that he and Jef needed to do, but that was beyond his understanding. "Think about how many would be thrilled to have seen an elemental like that?"

"Like what we saw chasing it," Jef said.

Lathan nodded slightly. "Just like that."

They passed another series of small stone buildings, and then he paused a moment before turning along the street leading toward his home. It was late enough in the day that he suspected his mother would be home, and he wanted to share with her the success that he had, thinking that she would want to revel in the fact that he had collected the shadow elemental. She would know everything that he'd gone through, and she would understand all that they had done to get to that point.

Of course, she would feel the same way that Lathan did and wish that his father could be around to have shared in it.

"Why don't you go and talk to her on your own. I'm going to check out a few things, and then I can meet you back outside of your home when I'm done," Jef said.

"You don't have to meet me outside of it. She's perfectly content for you to come in."

Jef winked, and started to laugh. "Oh, I know that she is, I'm just saying that I want the two of you to have a chance to talk. She's going to want to celebrate with you. As she should. But you need to make sure you give me credit. I was a part of it."

"My mother is going to know that you were a part of everything that I've done. But shadow is something that I need to talk to her about myself." The only person who would understand that was Jef.

"You and your family, all of this shadow business." He shook his head. "You know, were it not for you, I probably never would've heard about a shadow elemental to begin with. It's rare enough to even think about chasing down a spirit elemental, but here you are more interested in shadow. You know how many people would be far more intrigued to go after spirit?"

"I'm not saying that I would turn down the opportunity to go after a spirit elemental. I doubt we'll ever see one."

"Sort of like we were never going to see shadow?"

"I always thought we would."

"It might be better if we go after something like a draasin. At least with that, there is a prize to chase. Can you imagine if we told someone that we caught a draasin?"

"I'm not so sure that anyone could catch a draasin. It's more likely that the draasin would catch you. And probably rip you apart. The last thing you'd feel would be the burning flames of the elemental as you were shredded." He held his arms out, mimicking what he imagined the draasin would look like flying over the land, though he didn't know how to mimic breathing fire.

Jef stuck his tongue out at him, shooting him a look. "You make it sound much worse than it needs to."

Jef waved at him, and then marched off along the street. Lathan trailed his hand over the binding stone, feeling the strangeness of it, and knowing that it now connected him to shadow, something that seemed impossible to believe.

He couldn't feel the shadow. It wasn't the same as when he trapped earth, which gave off a trembling, powerful sort of energy from it, or water, which felt wet and sometimes sticky, or even air, which left the binding stone lighter than it had been before. Hyza was hot, as often the fire elementals were hot, though not unpleasantly so. It was almost as if the binding stone mitigated some of the element power, but not all of it. With shadow, there was a sense of power within it, and the sense that he had connected to something, though he wasn't entirely sure what it was. He squeezed his hand around the stone, feeling that power, and wishing that he had some way of understanding it.

More than that, he wished that he could share it with his father. His father would've loved that. He would've loved to have had a chance to know what it was like to catch shadow.

Not just catch. Chase it. He wouldn't even have cared if they hadn't caught it. It would've been the hunt, the search, the possibility that they might have found something from it, that would have been far more intriguing to his father than anything else.

He picked his way through the village, ignoring several of the binding-stone structures that trapped energy within them. Most of them were for fire elementals, as that created a tracing of light in the evening and overnight, and gave off heat. There were veins of earth that were worked throughout the villages well, defensive lines that lingered, though they were old. Most of those were before the kingdom had been here, like many things that Lathan found in this part of the world. Old binding stones, things that had history that Lathan had never taken the time to learn about, because he had rarely attended the Saval despite his mother's desire for him to remain a part of it.

He found himself touching the shadow elemental binding stone more often than he probably should. He wasn't going to find any answers just touching it. But he couldn't shake the feeling that he wanted to try. It seemed to him that there was some aspect within that binding stone that reverberated within him, as if he should be able to feel something more with it.

He reached his home. He didn't spend as much time here as he once had, partly because he and Jef were so often busy chasing down elementals.

He hesitated, hand on the door, and closed his eyes for a moment. It was difficult not having his father around any longer. Some times were harder than others, though. He was the one who had the interest in elementals and had pushed Lathan into learning about them, and to this day, Lathan wasn't even sure that he knew even a portion of what his father had known.

"You would have caught it more easily than I did," he whispered.

His father had lived his entire life collecting, having had no formal training other than what life brought him, and he had supplied much of the elemental energy for the entire village. Far more than those within the Saval ever did.

The door came open as he was standing there, and his mother frowned. Her graying hair was pulled back into a severe bun while sweat stained her brow. "Lathan?

What are you doing here? And why are you just standing there?"

He looked past her. "Are you going somewhere?"

"Only to the market. I was going to gather a few supplies for my work."

"I could go with you."

Her lips pressed together in a tight frown. "Are you trying to coddle your mother, Lathan? I'm doing quite well, you know."

His father had been gone for the better part of two years, and in that time, Lathan had probably had a harder time than his mother had. She had accepted that there were risks inherent in what his father had done, and it was because of those risks, and those dangers, that he had gotten caught up in something worse. An elemental that had put him into danger.

"I'm not trying to coddle you at all. Can't a son care about his mother?"

"Oh, you can care about me, but you check in on me too often. You're a young man. You should be off chasing women, finding fortune and fame, and whatever young men like to do."

"I'm not chasing any women."

"Unfortunately," his mother said.

"I *have* chased women. It's just that I keep busy."

She scowled at him. She pulled the door closed, and then crossed her arms over her chest. "You're too busy with your little venture. If you would've stuck with the Saval training, you wouldn't be so busy."

"Father wanted me to do this."

Her brow darkened. She took a deep breath, letting it out, and some of the tension in her eyes began to ease. Not completely. Lathan wasn't exactly sure that the tension would ever completely fade. Since his father's accident, she always had it. "I just want you to be careful. I know you want to make him proud. I know that you probably think like he did that you have only to find a way to capture that one prize and you will never have to work again, but I also know everything that he went through in doing that."

"I know as well," Lathan said.

She regarded him for a moment and then motioned for him to follow. "I know that you do," she muttered, shaking her head. "And I know that you will be careful, but your father was careful too. And sometimes being careful wasn't enough. With the kind of power you're dealing with, it's not always easy to ensure your own safety. Sometimes you need to do things that put you in danger. These are wild creatures you're dealing with, you know. And you can't control something that's wild like that. You might be able to use those stones and find some of the connection that you're looking for, but there's always the risk that you will lose control. It's the same warning I gave to him, so don't look at me like I'm treating you like a child. You are still my little boy."

"I'm not saying that you were treating me like anything," Lathan said.

"Now," his mother said, pausing at an intersection. "Do you care to tell me why you came looking for me?"

The market was just up ahead, and the sounds of it

were drifting toward him. It was mostly voices. The town wasn't large, which meant the market itself wasn't very large. Still, they were one of the largest settlements at this edge of the kingdom. From here, it was several days to the next largest town, and a difficult journey at that. Voices drifted toward them, shouts and raised voices and even an occasional song. The market could be strange like that. Through it all was a faint trembling. Lathan was always aware of that. It came from the veins of earth that worked underneath the city, giving a constant stirring of energy, along with the connection to earth, that swept underneath everything.

"I came because..." He hesitated. Did he really want to tell his mother now? She had already made a point of commenting on the dangers of the elementals, of which he knew there were many, and he didn't necessarily want to make her think that he was in any danger. Still, this was his mother. Wouldn't she celebrate shadow with him?

His father would have.

He took her arm in his, guiding her off the side of the road, letting Packer and Gartha, an older couple who owned a bakery not far from here, move past. They nodded at Lathan and his mother, before moving onward. Flour covered Gartha, creating a dusting across her skirt. Packer wasn't much better, though he was usually the one manning the oven and not the one doing the baking, from Lathan's experience.

He dropped his voice to little more than a whisper. "I found it."

His mother looked up, and slowly realization dawned on her face. "You found shadow?" She said it so quietly that he could scarcely hear it. It was as if she were afraid of asking, as if she were afraid of hearing the truth. Or perhaps it was just that she felt the same way that Lathan did and that he shouldn't be the one to have found it on his own.

"I did. Jef and I did. We caught some of it." He pulled out the binding stone and showed it to his mother. "I'm not exactly sure that there is anything here that can be useful, but I did it." He grinned and couldn't help but feel as if he were a child showing off to his mother. And in this case, perhaps he was. "He would've loved it, Mother. It moved so quickly, but it was there. We chased it. We *caught* it."

Lathan still couldn't believe his luck, struggling to believe that he had managed to capture it, but he had.

"And now what?"

"What?" Lathan took the binding stone back from his mother, slipping it into his pocket. "I caught the shadow elemental. What we've been looking for all this time."

She looked up at him. She wasn't a tall woman. She always seemed larger and more substantial, but that was simply because of the stern air that she often carried about her. "So you finally accomplished what you've been trying to do all this time. You caught an elemental you've been chasing. Now what?" She tipped her head up, looking at him, holding his gaze. "Will you keep chasing after the shadows, or now that you've seen one and managed to catch some," she added, pointing to his pocket, "will you be content?" She waited, and when Lathan didn't say anything, she nodded slowly. "As I thought. You and your father were not so different. Of course, I've always known that. You've chased him around since you were old enough to walk, and he brought you with him on his collections when you were old enough not to get hurt. At least, he claimed you were old enough not to get hurt." There was a hard edge in her words that Lathan was accustomed to hearing. It was probably well earned, though. He had gotten hurt on one of the early collections, and Lathan remembered all too well how his mother had directed her anger at his father. "He never stopped looking, you know."

"What do you mean?"

"I mean that once he saw the shadow, he never gave up the search to find it again. You know your father, Lathan. He thought he could find it, connect to it, and understand. In his mind, it was the key to much more than just collecting a few elementals."

That hadn't been Lathan's experience with his father. Oh, his father had certainly been eager to collect shadow, but it wasn't about power for him. It was about the hunt. Ever since his father had been young, when he had first glimpsed shadow, he had wanted to try to catch it. It was the same for Lathan. Having had a chance to see shadow, he had wanted to try to find it again.

"I just wanted you to know that I did it." He tried to hide the disappointment in his words. He had hoped that his mother would be far more excited about it then she seemed to be. "After all the time that he spent searching for shadow, I thought you would have appreciated it." He didn't hide his disappointment all that well. "Do you need any help with anything before I go?"

His mother regarded him for a moment, her gray eyes softening. "I don't say it to hurt you, Lathan. I say it because I love you. I just don't want you to get caught up in the same things that he did, always chasing the impossible." She hesitated a moment. "But no. I don't need your help. I would, however, enjoy some company while I eat later. That is, if you're not too busy."

"Of course. I will stop by later," he said.

She nodded and kissed him on the cheek, before making her way toward the market. Lathan stood there, tracing his finger along the shadow elemental binding stone, and had a hard time shaking the question. She wasn't wrong. Now that he had collected it, what else was he going to do?

"There you are," Jef said.

Lathan turned. He pushed away those thoughts, forced a smile, and waved a hand toward the distant Saval building. "Why don't we go and see what we can get for hyza?"

CHAPTER 5

The market was quiet today. It was midweek, a time when the market was active normally, and there was something about it that was even more somber than usual. They had trudged through the edge of town, reaching the occasionally bustling market along the border, before the two of them had paused. Lathan had kept running his fingers along the binding stone that he thought held the shadow, though he wasn't sure if there was anything in that which would work for him. Jef had gotten increasingly excited the further into town they went, practically dancing. "Do we really need to go through the market?" Jef asked.

"Not really," Lathan said, "I just figured that I would see what's here. Besides, it's helpful to get an idea about what's moving these days."

"Nothing we sell is moving here." He shook his head. "At least not for as much as they will pay at the Saval."

Lathan knew that, and it did nothing to change the fact that he was here anyway.

His father had been the one to teach him to go to the Saval to trade. He always approved of Henash, the old elemental collector and instructor at the Saval who Lathan had come to know reasonably well over the years. That was who he was going to now. Henash treated fairly, as well, which was another benefit of doing business with someone who he trusted.

"Oh, Fiery Skies," Jef muttered.

Lathan looked up, and he frowned.

"Not Wexler," Jef said.

Wexler was about their age, but a traditional student. And by traditional, that meant that he spent his days studying at the Saval and only intended to leave town when he graduated. He believed that everything he did was in service to the king.

"Just avoid him," Lathan said.

"I've tried to avoid him, the same way that you have tried to avoid him. The problem is that he gets into his uptight ass that he needs to harass us any time he sees us." Jef straightened, and he forced a smile. "Why, hello, Wexler."

Wexler had crossed through the market on his way over to them. He was dressed almost regally, with a vibrant blue jacket and formfitting cream pants, and he even had a sword sheathed at his side, as if he were playing a soldier. Lathan resisted the urge to laugh at him.

"Boys," he said, managing to make it sound both as a greeting and a slight. "How has your hunting gone?"

"Quite well, in fact," Jef said. "We were just going up to your little school to sell what we collected."

Wexler pressed his lips together into something of a frown. "Probably for less than what you usually sell, though," he said.

"And why is that?" Jef asked.

"Because everyone is having success these days. Even students are going out and collecting."

He flashed something of a smile, but Lathan didn't return it.

Maybe Henash wouldn't be quite so accommodating.

"It's always a delight to see you," Jef said.

"I feel the same way, boys."

He moved through the market, disappearing.

"I can't stand him," Jef muttered.

"You just don't like him because he is able to afford the Saval."

"Like you wouldn't go," Jef said.

There was a time when Lathan thought that he might've wanted to go to school, but that had been long ago, and before he had spent all of his days with his father, where he had come to feel as if he found his true purpose.

"It doesn't matter. Let's go get Henash."

They moved through the market as they made their way toward the Saval, where they would find Henash. Many of the booths were the usual. Tomman and his table that was taller than it needed to be stacked with ceramics he continued to source occupied one corner of the market. Lathan had wondered where he managed to get the ceramics, but then he'd seen that he had a contact with Kos Warint, one of the merchants that stopped in town every month. Kos collected the ceramics and sold them to Tomman, who then sold them in the market. Most were simple, which was fine for a place like Gorawl, though there were some that had more decoration to them. A couple of local farmers selling their produce were next to Tomman, before the market turned, and there was another of what Lathan considered a useful stand.

Paras had her stand in another corner, farther from Tomman, and her blankets generally sold well, though many were worn. The fabrics had faded, but they were of a decent quality. Next to her was Liama Olar, an apothecary who preferred to trade than to sell, mixing whatever medicines a person might need at her overly complicated cart.

Liama had a reputation with her apothecary work, though it was one that she'd cultivated to make it seem like she used elements in the mixing of her medicines. Lathan thought that it was so she could charge more for what she sold, but that didn't seem to be the case. Given that she worked with many of the binding stones, it *was* possible that she tried to use them while she was mixing her compounds, though he'd never heard of anyone actually getting anything from the elementals like that.

"What is Wexler doing now?"

Lathan looked over, and he saw him meeting an

older man with graying hair near a small square set aside from the rest of the marketplace. Lathan had never met the man, but he recognized him. There was quite a procession when Tolinar had arrived, sent by the king to lead the Saval.

"Who knows," he said. "Probably finding some new way to ingratiate himself into the king's good service. What does it matter? We need to get over to the Saval and get rid of the hyza stone."

"Just that one?"

"You know that we aren't going to sell the other."

"You mean you aren't going to sell it."

Lathan shrugged. "Fine. You know that I'm not going to sell the other one."

"Even though it could sell for quite a bit."

"We don't know that."

"Lathan—"

"I'm not going to sell it. My father wouldn't have wanted me to."

It was a testament to his friendship with Jef, and to the relationship that Jef had also had with Lathan's father, that he didn't argue.

Instead, he just shook his head. "Let's get moving. I don't want to look at Wexler any more than I need to, anyway. And I don't want to be here when he's done talking with Tolinar, because he's probably just going to be all smug and pompous."

"So really no different than normal?"

Jef snorted. "Pretty much."

They hadn't gone very far before they saw a familiar

figure—and the same person they were heading to go see. Henash clutched a basket at his side and had a leather satchel slung over one shoulder. He had a long blade of grass clutched between his teeth, and he eyed Jef as if waiting for him to do something foolish.

"What you got?" Henash finally asked.

"What makes you think we've got anything?" Lathan asked.

"Seeing as how the two of you are looking around the way you do? And I'm guessing you're coming to see me at the Saval."

Lathan shrugged. "Maybe."

"Well? You found me. So get on with it. I've got to chat with Tolinar a bit more soon enough, so need to keep moving."

Lathan instinctively reached for his pocket, though wished that he hadn't. He didn't need for Henash to know that he had something of value. The older man's yellow eyes drifted toward Lathan's pocket, squinting for a moment as if he could see into it, then looking up.

"You going to tell an old man what you found or are you going to make me guess? Not much activity out in the hills these days, so I wouldn't expect that you found much of value, but then..." He pursed his lips together, tapping a finger to them. "Maybe you haven't stayed in the hills. Wouldn't put it past you to try and go a few places that you shouldn't."

"What makes you think we shouldn't do anything?" Lathan asked. "We've been hunting elementals for years."

"Right. And I've been at it for decades. A man begins to know limits the longer he's at a thing." He tipped his head to the side and his nose wrinkled slightly. "Not that the two of you know anything about limits. Or about being men." He started to smile, then took a seat at his table. "What did you find? Hyza?"

Jef gaped at him. "How did you know?"

Lathan would have been more impressed had Henash known about the shadow, but it was still somewhat impressive that he knew they had seen the hyza.

"Ah, there are certain signs when they're in the area. I used to be like you. Used to go running after everything like that, thinking that I needed the big score. Same as you boys."

Lathan bristled at being called a boy, though he knew he shouldn't. Compared to Henash, everyone was younger . And he wanted to know what signs the old hunter knew to follow. That could be useful. Lathan had learned different techniques following elementals but there were times when he wished that he could simply *know* where to go to find them. If there was something that Henash knew, then Lathan wanted to learn.

"What tipped you off?" Lathan asked.

When he looked up at Lathan, he smiled broadly. "Some things you can learn from the Saval still, Lathan. You have to learn to listen. You go running off when you see tracks, as if that's the only way to know what's moving through an area. Those of us who've been around a while know that it's more than the tracks. You have to learn to follow what the others are doing. Pay attention."

At first, Lathan thought he meant they needed to pay attention to the elementals, but then Henash held up one of the binding stones. He twisted it between his fingers, then squeezed.

A hint of wind stirred from it.

He was releasing some of the stored power in the stone.

That was a dangerous thing to do, especially close to a market where there were others around, but it was the fact that he was willing to do so just to prove a point that seemed the most surprising.

"Now. See the way the wind is blowing?"

Lathan leaned forward. Jef squinted, though he didn't move.

The wind stirred, but it wasn't with much power. When it came to feeling that wind, he wasn't sure there was anything of power there that he was supposed to detect. Only that he felt something.

Then he saw it.

Wind could be difficult. Most of the time, it was felt and not seen. That was what made it difficult to catch, though perhaps it shouldn't. You could follow the direction of the wind, let the pressure of it guide you. But in this case, it wasn't so much of what he felt as what he saw. The wind had seemed to take on a shape...

"You *captured* it?" Lathan asked, turning his attention to Henash.

Henash ignored him, still holding onto the stone.

"Oh don't start to get indignant on me. This isn't an elemental. Not sure that I'm skilled enough to be the one to hold one. Can't say I would try, either. They can be difficult to hold, and they can be angry if you attempt to do so. Just ask old Fenner about his experience with the loran back a decade ago." He laughed, as if it were some joke, though Lathan couldn't imagine capturing a loran at all. He'd scarcely hunted them.

They were strange, snakelike creatures that were bound to earth. Useful, but only to the right person and only if they managed to get close without loran opening a pit in the ground as you approached. The only time that he'd even tried to go after a creature like that had been when he'd seen it from afar. A targeted crossbow bolt made a difference, and as he shot, hoping the binding stone would stick, there was the possibility that all he'd do would be to anger the elemental and that would end with him running.

"Anyway, not holding the elemental. You store the essence the right way and you're getting a memory of what it touched, nothing more than that. You have to have seen it."

Now Lathan *did* reach into his pocket, feeling for the binding stone that he'd used on hyza. Had there been a memory? The stone had gone slightly warm, so in that regard, he supposed that he could see it in the same way, but it had never felt like he was capturing some memory of the elemental. Just tapping into the power that they had and trying to hold some of it.

"Let me see what you grabbed."

Henash held out his hand, and Lathan hesitated.

"Don't you worry that I'm going to release all your hard work. All I'm doing is letting some of the essence slip out. Not enough to release what you did. Just enough to see what you caught."

He glanced to Jef, who still stared at the stone that Henash had been holding. Lathan understood. If Henash could show what they'd captured, they could use it for shadow as well. There would be no need to question what they had found.

"You going to hold out on me?" There was a hint of danger in the way that he said it, though Lathan didn't think that Henash would ever do anything to him.

"Fine. Just don't release it."

He handed the binding stone over to Henash, who took it and turned it up toward the sun. Henash turned it from side to side, his gaze lingering on it for a long moment, then he rested it in his palm, tracing a pattern on the stone.

"Have to make sure I don't release too much, just like you said," Henash told them, as if it explained what he was doing by tracing his finger along the stone. "Can't be too careful, you know. These kinds of things can get a little touchy. Especially when you're dealing with... it *is* hyza." He glanced up at them before turning his attention back to the stone. "Fiery Skies, I didn't know if you were telling the truth. You wouldn't be the first to think to capture a bit of ashath and claim it's something more."

Ashath was a *very* weak elemental for fire. It did little

more than create a tracing of smoke, though there were some who claimed that, in enough of a concentrated fashion, even ashath could be useful for generating a little flame.

"Would you look at that." He had squeezed the binding stone, then winced. "Ah. Now I see what you did. Turned the stone into an arrowhead. Clever."

"Crossbow bolt," Lathan said, reaching out for it.

Henash didn't hand it back. Instead, he continued to squeeze the stone. As he did, there was a tracing of heat, then a faint reddish shape began to emerge from the stone. As it did, Henash held tightly to the stone, as if the stone would lose all control if he let go.

"There he is. Male. Small. Probably little more than a few years. Not bad for a little thing like that."

"How can you tell?" Jef asked.

Lathan shook his head, but he knew that Jef wasn't paying any attention. For all he knew, Jef thought that Henash was telling the truth. And maybe he was, at least as he saw it. Though the hyza *hadn't* been all that large. Lathan didn't know how someone could tell the gender of one of them—and to be honest, didn't know if there were genders for them. The only thing that he really knew was that hyza could be difficult to track the way that he'd managed to do it.

"There's a signature to it. You have to see the connection to the bond, of course. Then you can trace that to the elemental, which you should have been able to do anyway. Especially if you're going to tap into it this way.

Got to be a bit respectful if you're going to ask this from a creature like that."

"We didn't ask anything."

Henash squeezed the stone. For a moment, Lathan thought that he might try to release the elemental within it. If he did, Lathan didn't know what he would be able to do to stop him. Not much. With the binding stone in hand, it was possible that Henash would be able to release everything in the stone. Lathan wouldn't be able to do much other than complain. Or take Henash's stones.

Then he relaxed. He handed the stone back to Lathan. "You need to be careful if you're not going to ask. They prefer it if you ask permission. Most of the time they tell you that it's not a problem."

"Not you, too," Jef groaned.

"What about me?"

"Nothing."

Henash glowered at them. "Just because there are some of us who think that it makes sense to ask a creature before you go poking it and taking a part of it doesn't mean that's wrong. You could learn a thing from a girl like that." He looked toward the edge of the market, and Lathan followed. Marin had come to the market and now looked over to them, a deep frown on her face. "Can't say that I know what she hears, but there's no doubting that you can listen and get them to talk to you. There was a time when that was considered normal, you know. And that's the kind of thing you could learn more about if you spent more time in a formal education."

Lathan had heard the stories. Most who hunted the elementals had heard the stories. They spoke of a different time, when the elementals had been more common, but more than that, they spoke of a time when the elementals spoke to men. No one really knew what had changed, only that they'd started to avoid men.

Probably because we started using binding stones.

That was the only way to take some of the power of the elemental, though. Without the stone, how would anyone be able to tap into the power of the elements?

"You look like you've got something else on you," Henash said.

The comment forced Lathan to look over to him. "I do?"

"Well, you've got a look about you that makes it seem like you found something more. What is it? I haven't heard much from the elementals about others. Heard the hyza passing through, of course, but not about anything else. What are you holding out on me?"

Lathan made a point of avoiding looking to Jef. He'd just give it away, and that was something that he most definitely didn't want to do, certainly not with someone like Henash who would definitely want to test whether he actually *had* managed to catch the shadow.

And maybe for now he would keep that to himself.

"We saw something else," Lathan began.

Jef gave him a hard stare, but Lathan ignored it. They didn't understand what had happened, so it was best to ask someone who might have more experience.

"As we were coming back, we saw soldiers. And not

wearing Iradaln colors," he added quickly. "These were soldiers who seemed to use sandor to capture a hyza elemental."

Henash stiffened. "Where was this?"

"Outside the city. Not too far."

Henash's eyes narrowed as they shared what they had found, and he grew increasingly agitated.

"Come on," he said. "Much as I'd like to be an expert in all things, this seems like the kind of thing that we need to talk about with someone who knows a bit more than me. Not that I want to admit that to Tolinar when I tell him."

"And here I thought you liked to fashion yourself as the most knowledgeable person in town," Lathan said.

"Most of the time, I am. But in this case, I think there are certain things that I'm going to need help with. And if my suspicions are correct, this one might be more dangerous than we know."

CHAPTER 6

Wind whistled around them as they approached the bridge, looking for Henash, though not seeing any sign of him. He'd gone hurrying off into town, making some comment about needing to get help while telling the two of them that they should head back out to the bridges.

"Are you sure that we should even be here?" Jef asked.

Lathan nodded toward the bridges. Marin was there, again leaning forward and seemingly whispering to the stream down below. "We saw what we saw."

"Right. And do either of us really know what we saw? Fiery Skies, Lathan, all I saw was a group of soldiers, some swirling dirt—and it's been dry, you know—and maybe something else, but even in that, I'm not entirely sure."

Lathan stopped and frowned. "You can't be serious.

You're trying to ignore what we saw? There was a hyza—maybe the *same* hyza—and they captured it."

More than captured it, though, and that was what had bothered him. It might be what had bothered Henash, though it could be difficult to know with him. It wasn't like he and Jef spent that much time with Henash.

As they approached the bridge, Marin looked up and smiled.

"She's going to think we came to see her," Jef grumbled.

"You can tell her that you did."

"You know what's going to happen then. She's going to get all attached and never leave me alone. It's my curse. Women love me."

"I'm sure it's a real struggle for you," Lathan said, patting him on the shoulder as he headed past Jef.

"Are you going back out?" Marin asked. She looked up, quickly flicking her gaze toward the sky, frowning as if she had seen something there. When she looked back to them, her brow had creased. "Something is coming."

Jef looked over to Lathan.

"That's why we came back out," Lathan said. "We weren't sure what to make of it before, but Henash thinks there's something—"

"I most definitely do," a voice said behind them.

Lathan spun. He hadn't even heard Henash approach. He wasn't alone. Behind him were a dozen men and women, though Lathan only recognized a few of them. Velay sat on the women's council, advising the baron. Her deep brown eyes seemed mostly irritated that she'd been called out here with Henash. A pair of women stood behind her, one a pretty and younger girl that Lathan had seen throughout town but didn't know her name, and another stout, slightly older woman who seemed as unimpressed as Velay. A tall, distinguished man stood off to the side of Velay, making a point of not looking in her direction. Marcus Holach, head of the merchant guild, was one of the most powerful men in Gorawl, and he was joined by five others who shifted their weight as they followed, several of them looking toward Lathan and Jef before ignoring them and turning back to Henash.

What had Henash done here?

When he had suggested that he was going to get others who were more knowledgeable than him, Lathan hadn't realized that he was going to pull leaders out. Then again, somebody like Henash with his standing at the Saval would have an easier time getting others outside of town.

"What is this about, Henash?" Velay said. She managed to make it sound both irritated and curious at the same time. "You said we needed to come out here to discuss terms, and that—"

"We need to wait," Henash said.

Marcus practically growled. "Wait?" He started to turn but then caught himself. "You knew *he* was coming?"

"I sent word," Henash said.

He turned out to be the baron.

Lathan had seen the baron. Most in Gorawl had an

opportunity to see him, though few spent much time with him. Lathan and Jef tried to sell their collections to the baron's household first, as they were the ones with the most income to spend on such things, though they were rarely successful.

"What's this about?" Lathan asked Henash as the others all turned to face the oncoming baron. He was an older gray-haired and decidedly *round* man, and he had seven men following him, four of them armed with swords and crossbows. The other three were dressed in the colors of Iradaln, servants to the baron.

Henash looked over. "It's about what you saw."

"So you summoned the *baron* out here?"

Henash turned. "What do you know about your binding stones?"

Lathan glanced to Jef, who shrugged. He reached into his pouch and pulled one out, turning it in his hand from side to side. "The same as most, I figure."

"Not most. I don't know too many people who shape their stones."

Lathan ran his finger along the edge of the stone that he'd pulled out. The stone was slightly sharpened, with an edge to it that he'd placed there so that he could try to trap something dangerous. Mostly fire, as that tended to be the most valuable, though catching any of the elementals added a measure of value.

"Most people don't know what you can do with a stone when you place an edge on it," he said. "It's something my father taught me." He'd been young when his father had first taught him to shape one of the stones.

The stones themselves were difficult enough to obtain—almost as difficult as tracking down the elementals. You had to know not only where to look, but how.

"That's a part of it," Henash said. "And you're not wrong. Too many don't get the truth of the stones. Including you." He snatched the binding stone out of Lathan's hand and pointed it at him, as if he intended to jab Lathan with the sharpened end of it. "What happens when you use the binding stone on an elemental?"

"I trap some of their connection to the element."

"And you tie the elemental to the stone."

The words seemed to hang in the air.

"You're telling me that I'm binding the elemental? That it was the same hyza that we saw?"

"That's what I'm telling you. You link it. Some elementals don't really mind. They just drift off until that power is returned to them. Others stick around. When you bind something like hyza, something that is dangerous on its own, you have a different issue, don't you? You get to have an elemental that might come at you."

Jef whistled softly and looked over to Lathan. "Maybe it's good those soldiers captured that hyza. Better than it coming at us."

From the way Henash looked at him, Lathan knew that wasn't the point that Henash had been trying to make. Lathan wasn't sure what point he wanted to make, only that he needed to know the elemental was dangerous.

"I'm here now, Henash. Do you care to tell me why

you made a point of having me summoned out here?" The baron stood in the center of the group, dressed in the deep navy of Iradaln. Soldiers had positioned themselves on either side of him, as if he were in danger from Velay or Marcus.

"Tell him what you saw," Henash said, elbowing Lathan.

The old man's elbows were sharp, and Lathan winced but made a point of keeping from reacting too much. There was an opportunity here, though he wasn't exactly sure how he could take advantage of it.

"I *think* Henash called you out here because we came across a hyza elemental," Lathan began. He kept his focus on the baron, ignoring the way that the others turned to look at him. He didn't want to lose his nerve. "Jef and I are collectors. You've bought some of our collections before," he added hurriedly. "And we caught sight of hyza tracks and followed it out near Blackstone. I managed to collect a sample before the hyza escaped and—"

"You called me out here for an *elemental?*" the baron asked, turning away from Lathan and focusing his irritation on Henash. "I understand these creatures are rare, but I have more important things to be doing. Don't think that because I've bought from you in the past that I'm going to remain loyal to your services." He glanced toward Lathan. "Besides, if he managed to snare hyza —"

"That's not why I called you here," Henash said. "And it wasn't me that called you. Blame Tolinar."

Jef's breath caught—and probably for the same reason that Lathan's had.

Henash would cut off the baron?

Tolinar stood off to the side of the others, remaining quiet. Lathan was just happy that he hadn't brought Wexler with him.

"Then why *did* you bother me? The king—"

"Will want to hear of this too," Tolinar said softly, his voice carrying a bit of an accent to it that Lathan couldn't quite place.

The baron turned his attention to Lathan expectantly. Lathan knew that he needed to respond, but wasn't sure that he'd be able to do—or say—anything that would appease the baron.

"Well," he began, even more aware of the audience they had, now including Marin—who had sidled over and stood behind Henash, watching, "we had started to head back when we came across a dust cloud. We thought nothing of it, but decided to take a look. We saw soldiers, but not Iradaln. I didn't recognize them, but they surrounded another hyza"—he was *not* going to give Henash the satisfaction of alluding to how it might be the same one—"and used a series of binding stones on it. The hyza... well, it just disappeared."

And he knew how foolish that would sound. A disappearing elemental. There were some elementals that could certainly disappear quickly, but they were things like ara—who could float away—or udilm—who could retreat into the sea. Not hyza. That was a fire elemental, and everyone knew they didn't just disappear.

"Where was this?" the baron asked. His voice had dropped to a whisper and his face had paled.

"An hour or so to the north."

The baron watched him for a moment before pulling his gaze away and turning to Tolinar. The head of the Saval nodded, as if he agreed with the baron's unspoken fears. When the baron turned, he had managed to compose himself again. "We will gather soldiers—armored—and these men will lead us."

Lathan blinked.

"You know what this is?" Henash asked.

"Unfortunately," the baron said. "Dangerous. They should not be found here, but we have been on alert for the possibility, especially given the rumors of elemental migration."

They were more than rumors, but he wasn't going to challenge the baron on that. And the idea that they would be leading soldiers — including armored soldiers, who had weapons and mail infused with earth elementals to protect them — suggested a much greater concern.

The baron turned, motioning to Marcus and Velay, who followed. "We must make preparations for the possibility that we need to evacuate."

"Evacuate?" Marcus said, his voice incredulous. "We don't know if this boy saw anything."

"He's not wrong," Velay said, looking over toward Lathan. "It's possible they didn't see what they—"

"Did you hear the description?" the baron said. There was a sharp rebuke in his tone. Velay glowered at him, but Marcus took a step back. "There's no denying what he saw, nor is there any denying what must be done. I will get word off to the king."

The others around him all nodded.

"What *is* this?" Jef asked.

Marcus shot him a look, but Jef ignored it.

Lathan was glad Jef had asked the question as it was the same one that he had. Whatever was going on was serious enough that it got the attention of the baron. But what *was* it?

"It is fortunate that you told someone," the baron said.

"But what is it?" Jef asked, sounding exasperated.

"It can be only one thing. Derithan," Tolinar said simply.

The Derithan.

Lathan had heard of them. Anyone who lived in Iradaln would have heard of them.

In some stories, they were little more than vicious fighters who invaded and destroyed. In other stories, they sought to rule. In others, they killed with impunity, using the elements in ways that had long been lost. Throughout all the stories Lathan had heard, the Derithan used leashed elementals to attack—which must have been what they'd seen.

And now they were coming to Gorawl.

CHAPTER 7

They hadn't gone far before Marin caught up with them.

She seemed agitated, though with Marin, it could be difficult to tell as she was often agitated. Marin held something in one hand—a book, Lathan realized—and kept her other hand atop a pouch.

"Do you think it's really the Derithan?" she asked.

Lathan thought she was asking Henash, who stood near one of the bridges leading across the valley, but she had focused on Lathan.

He shrugged. "I don't have any idea. I haven't any experience with them."

"But you've heard the stories. Everyone has. And you saw—"

"I didn't know that we'd seen the Derithan," he said, looking to Jef, who had turned so that he could stare in the direction of town. He'd fallen quiet, which was never a good thing when it came to Jef.

"What, exactly, did you see?"

Lathan met her gaze. There was an intensity in her eyes the way there often was, especially when she was dealing with the elementals. She knew something, he suspected. The question was whether it would matter to him.

The Derithan.

That mattered.

Besides, he'd *seen* what they had done to the hyza. They had used binding stones to capture it. More than that, they had used sandor to attack it.

"If you were listening, you would've heard what we saw."

"Better question is what you *felt*," Henash said, finally turning back to him from where he'd been looking down and staring at the water. It was almost as if he'd figured out some answer. "I told you about the stones. You tie yourself to the elemental when you use them. That's what you would've done with that hyza."

"We don't know if it's the same one," Jef said.

It seemed as if he'd finally managed to shake himself from his stupor. He'd pulled a binding stone of his own out of his pocket—one that they'd used on a small swirl of ara they'd come across a few weeks back—and gripped it as if he intended to release it. Lathan knew he wouldn't, as Jef enjoyed catching elementals but didn't care to experience them in any other way.

"You bound the hyza. It followed you. The same way that ara is following you," he said, waving a hand above his head, as if trying to swat at a fly—or a particularly difficult-to-see elemental of wind. "The same hyza. Which is why it matters what you felt. You find something in that stone of yours that would trigger anything?"

Lathan held onto the stone. "I wouldn't have known, I guess." He held it up, but Henash didn't bother taking it from him. "When you released a little of hyza while testing the stone, did you feel anything?"

"That's not how the binding works."

"Then why would you have expected him to have felt anything?" Jef asked.

Henash looked as if he wanted to argue, but bit back whatever he'd been about to say. "It's too bad that you didn't detect anything. If you had, I think you might know whether anything can be done to save that hyza. As it stands, they might already have used it for whatever they plan."

He turned back to the bridge, standing next to one of the pillars, which left Jef and Marin with Lathan. Neither of them said anything.

Lathan looked at the binding stone. There wasn't anything particularly unique about it that he could tell. It was a binding stone, of which he'd acquired quite a few. Once collected, they would typically take the stones to someone who had *another* stone—or something like it —and transfer it so that the binding stone could be reused.

Jef said something to Marin, but Lathan ignored it as he stepped closer to Henash.

"The binding stones don't hold elementals to them." When Henash didn't look over to him, Lathan pushed on. "They hold a little power. That's how we can transfer it."

"Some do," Henash said. He was staring down below, and Lathan looked to see if he could tell what Henash was looking at, but couldn't. Maybe just the water, but if that were the case, why would he do that here—and the same way that it seemed that Marin had been studying the water below? "When you use a weak binding, all you're doing is taking some of the element power out, storing it in the stone, which can then be transferred. That's why there are reservoirs of power." He patted the stone of the bridge. "The right binding allows that connection to the element to build over time. Layered. But some stones—and some people—bind more tightly than others." He looked up to him. "You carve a stone, and you add intent to it. That makes the stone more effective, and links you to the elemental in a way that you wouldn't have been otherwise. It's your *type* of stone that matters. You have another that's a weaker bond..."

Which might be the shadow stone, Lathan decided. If he'd bonded the shadow—and he didn't know whether he had—he hadn't shaped the stone, so wouldn't have added any intention to it.

"My father never taught me that," he said.

"Most don't talk about it. Fiery Skies, most don't know about it, if I'm telling the truth. Collectors like to think they gather power of the elements, pinching off a bit from each elemental. In most cases, that's what happens. In some... well, the binding is too effective." He shrugged, then looked past him, and over toward Gorawl. "Seems like it's time for us to go."

Lathan followed the direction of his gaze and saw a dozen soldiers marching toward them. Each of them wore dark gray leather—though different than the Derithan that he'd seen. Shoulders and wrists were marked with slender pieces of gray stone. Binding stones. There were others on the thighs and boots.

"What about their bindings?" Lathan asked.

"Layered power," he said.

Henash crossed his arms over his chest as the nearest of the armored soldiers approached. "They tell you what you're up against?"

The lead soldier—a raven-haired man named Dorn that Lathan had some experience with—nodded. "The baron claims we've got Derithan outside of the city." His tone suggested that *he* didn't believe it. "We're to assess and neutralize."

Dorn raised his hand and motioned. The other soldiers lined up behind him, waiting.

"Well. Far be it from me to keep you from *assessing* and *neutralizing*." Henash snorted. "Lead on, Lathan. Show this brave man where to go."

Dorn regarded Lathan as if they'd never met. They hadn't had *that* many interactions, but Gorawl wasn't such a large city that Lathan wouldn't run into a man like this from time to time. "You saw them?"

Lathan drew himself up. "I did."

"Then it's not Derithan." He turned to the other men behind him. "Ready to depart."

"Why do you say that?" Lathan asked, barely bothering to hide his irritation.

When Dorn turned back, he didn't even look in Lathan's direction. "If it were the Derithan, you'd be dead."

They started across the bridge.

The soldiers' boots sounded overly loud on the stone. *Armored.* The boots probably echoed against the stone, reacting to the binding. There were plenty of uses of bindings throughout Gorawl and the kingdom, but using a binding specifically on something like the armor was a different use than most.

Henash glowered at them. "They'd better be ready," he muttered, shaking his head, "because I'm not going to be able to save them when they run headlong toward death."

He followed the soldiers, though his feet were nearly silent.

When Lathan started forward, Jef caught up to him. "I'm not so sure about this."

Lathan shrugged. "Can't say that I am, either." Marin had followed. "I don't know if you should come. It's going to be dangerous."

"I hear that," she said.

"Derithan," Jef told her. "You know what that means, right? Elementals attacking. Fighting. Destruction. All the kinds of things that you don't really want anything to do with."

She tilted her head back, lips pressed in a frown. "All

things that I *need* to be a part of." She stepped past Lathan and followed Henash across the bridge.

"Well, this will be interesting," Jef said. "Between Henash looking like he wants to strangle the soldiers, Dorn looking like he wants to go back and drink, and Marin who plans to make sure they don't do anything that hurts the elementals, I think this is going to be *quite* the interesting adventure."

"It's no adventure. We're just going to guide them out toward where we saw the hyza. Then we can get back to town."

"And afterward? You heard the baron. They're making plans to evacuate, Lathan. If this *is* Derithan, what do *you* plan to do?"

Lathan didn't have a plan.

"See where the wind takes us, I guess."

"Great. That means you plan on following more of the elementals." He started to laugh. "I suppose I shouldn't expect anything different with you, though. You've always followed them—and the wind."

They made it across the bridge, and once on the far side, Lathan had a strange sense of unease. He didn't know what he felt, though questioned whether it came from something of the Derithan, but doubted that he'd be so attuned to it that he'd feel anything.

Marin looked up at the sky, tipping her head to one side, almost as if she could hear something there. Lathan didn't see anything other than the clouds. There was no sign of dust—certainly nothing to suggest that sandor was there, though he did feel something.

"What do you see?" Lathan asked her.

"You don't really want to know."

"I'm asking, aren't I?"

Jef started to smirk, but Lathan ignored it.

"I've heard whispers from one of the ara elementals," she said. "I don't chase them the way that you do—it's not necessary to hunt them to have a conversation with them—but they will sometimes whisper. When you listen like I told you to do, you can hear their voices." She paused, and tipped her head toward the sky.

As she did, Lathan couldn't help but feel as if she were playing with him somehow. He'd known Marin most of his life, and knew that she had quirks. Most who spent any time around her understood that about her. But it wasn't anything like this.

"You've talked about that before, but I never believed you."

Marin shrugged, as if unconcerned about whether he did or didn't believe her. And it was possible—probably, really—that she didn't care. Marin rarely cared much what others thought about her. "Should I believe that you're able to use your crossbow to hunt elementals?"

"That's not what—"

"Oh, I know you aren't hunting them. At least, you claim you're not hunting them, but you still use that crossbow of yours to try and tear some of their power from them. There are better ways, Lathan."

They reached a small ridgeline. In the distance, Blackstone seemed to absorb the sunlight, reminding him of the shadow stone. After what he'd heard today, he couldn't help but question if the binding stone would allow him some way of drawing the shadows to them. And if it did, would they be able to use it?

Lathan doubted that he'd have anything with the stone that he could easily use, but there might be a technique that he could try—even if it meant simply releasing the elemental and nothing else.

The soldiers had descended the steady embankment, though Dorn had lingered, waiting for Henash, who had paused and looked toward Lathan.

"You mentioned Blackstone," Henash said.

Lathan hurried forward. "That's where we first found the hyza." He pointed. "It wasn't far from here. We tracked it nearly to Blackstone. We'd wanted to get to the hyza before it disappeared on us."

Dorn flicked his gaze toward him. "Why would the stone have mattered?"

"Tracking elementals can be tricky under the best of circumstances," Henash said. "Some of the elementals can disguise their passing. Hyza isn't usually one of them. The creatures are a mixture of—"

A shout rang out from one of the soldiers.

Then the men began to shriek.

Lathan reached for a binding stone, fearing a wild elemental, though an attack on a group their size would be unusual. These days, with the elemental movement, there was much that was unusual.

"What is it?" Jef said, sliding up next to him, holding onto a binding stone himself. His was small and round, and he gripped it tightly in his hand. He rarely carved the stones the same way that Lathan did.

"Earth," Henash said.

When he did, Lathan *felt* it.

It was a steady rumbling. It built, but it came from someplace that was deep below him, leaving his entire body feeling the thudding that came. It was a steady sound, and he knew that were he to stay here for too long, he'd feel the shifting of that power—right until it exploded.

"How many stones do you have?" Henash asked.

He was calm—far calmer than the soldiers, and they were armored. Two had fallen, and it seemed as if the ground itself worked to swallow them. If this was an earth elemental, and Lathan couldn't tell which one, only that he agreed with Henash that it *was* earth, then it might very well swallow them. The others had backed away, weapons at the ready, though there weren't many —or any—weapons that would work against something like a hidden earth elemental.

"I have enough to hold a few elementals."

Henash cocked his head to the side, then he tapped his foot on the ground a few times, tipping his head down so that he could try to listen. "Can't say with any certainty how many there are. But you had best be prepared for the possibility that it'll be more than one. With earth—"

He never had a chance to finish.

A burst of dirt exploded near Dorn, tossing him to his

feet. He rolled, seemingly unharmed—the armor protecting him—before bouncing up to his feet. Dorn carried a short sword that caught the pale light.

A binding stone sword?

Lathan couldn't think about that any more.

This was something that he had experience with.

Most of the time when chasing elementals, there was a risk of the elemental attacking. Lathan and Jef were skilled enough, and had enough experience, to avoid the attack, but they also had some close calls over the years.

To use the stone, he needed to have a clear line of sight. He could feel the elemental, but he couldn't see anything. Until he could see it...

Grabbing for his crossbow, he took one of his binding stone tipped bolts and readied it. The crossbow should have enough force to penetrate all but the hardiest of earth elementals. And he didn't necessarily need to take any of their power, just scare them off.

"Not like that," Henash said. He stood on the edge of the hole formed by the elemental, holding onto a stone that he set down on the ground. He shifted a few steps, then placed another. Then another. "We place these like this, and then you get the elemental to settle."

"We're not trying to settle the damn thing," Dorn said.

He moved forward with his blade, his elemental enhanced armor giving him a much greater measure of protection than what Lathan had. Still, Lathan couldn't help but feel as if he didn't take these elementals as seriously as he should.

"You need to settle the elemental if you don't want it to snap and rip you apart. Even your armor isn't going to keep you safe if you've got a wild elemental thinking that it needs to defend its place."

He sounded so at ease.

Of course, Henash was the elemental master at the Saval, so he would have a measure of comfort that others did not.

"You can provide a little guidance here," Henash said, looking to Lathan. "I think you might be able to offer us a measure of protection, but be careful not to bind the elemental to yourself. We don't know which one this is, and an earth elemental can be a handful if you're not ready for it."

"What are you talking about?" Dorn snapped.

Henash ignored him, keeping his focus on Lathan. "I would suggest you—"

The ground surged.

But this time it didn't explode the way that it had before. It began to bow upward, but when the elemental reached where he thought the binding stones to be, it began to flex upward, as if it were going to push against some barrier that the binding stones had created.

"What are you doing?" Dorn asked.

"I told you what I'm doing. I need you to pay attention and be ready."

He was talking to Lathan again, and yet Lathan didn't know what he might be asking him to do. Use the binding stones, but not so much that he bonded to the elemental? How was he supposed to control that?

He didn't even know what he did when using the stones.

The elemental surged again, pushing upward against the barrier that had been formed. Lathan still couldn't see what the elemental looked like as it strained to get free. When Dorn jabbed with his sword, Henash spun, thrusting his open palm—or not *quite* open as there was a stone clutched in it—toward him. A burst of wind gusted outward and threw Dorn back.

"Quickly now," Henash said. "Anything that you might use to draw some off the elemental, but nothing that you've crafted that will draw too much off. Does that make sense to you?"

Lathan thought that it did, though he wasn't sure what he was going to need to do.

He tested the different stones that he had. Some of them were ones that he *had* carved, though not all. When he got to one that he hadn't carved, he pressed toward the earth elemental.

A rumbling echoed.

It came from deep beneath him. The elemental strained against the stones Henash had surrounding it, but then it retreated. The stone Lathan held felt slightly cooler, a sign that something had changed for it.

And he couldn't help but feel that Henash was right about the stone. This one—much like the stone he'd used on the shadow elemental—didn't change quite as much for him as the one that he'd used on hyza.

The ground trembled, then fell still.

Henash quickly gathered his stones.

Dorn stormed over to him, sword still in hand. "What do you think you're doing?"

"I think I'm keeping you alive," Henash said, still bent over as he gathered one of the stones. "I know it might not feel like that, but if you stabbed that, you would have been torn in half."

"So it's fine that *he* just used a stone on the same elemental?"

Lathan pocketed the now bound stone.

"He knew what he was doing. Unlike you."

Dorn glowered at him. "I've been trained to handle things like that."

"Not like that."

"What was it?" Jef asked.

Lathan saw the other soldiers had gotten freed from the ground and were now gathered in a small circle, though they all still had their weapons at the ready. The ground was calm and quiet now. They'd managed to stop the attack this time, but if the elemental—and he didn't even know *what* elemental that had been—came again, would they be so lucky?

"That was terad. Haven't seen one around here in a while," Henash said.

"Terad doesn't move through here," Lathan said.

His father had taught him all the local elementals. That was how he'd been effective at hunting them and collecting from them. In all the time that he'd learned of the elementals, he didn't remember anything about terad.

He *had* heard of it, though.

It was a powerful earth elemental. Some elementals were more powerful than others. Some of that was natural, based on the size of the elemental, whereas some of that was tied to the land itself, according to his father. There were some elementals that were more powerful in some places than in others. Lathan didn't know the reason behind that, but he'd seen how some elementals that he'd learned weren't all that powerful had proven to be more than what he would have believed.

"Not normally," Henash agreed. "Which means something has changed. Probably the same thing that we're looking into." He nodded to Dorn. "Which means we should keep moving. If we're tracking the passing of this hyza, there's a possibility that we don't have that much time before we will lose it altogether. Now, I'm sure you don't want that. We need this elemental for us to find what has happened with the—"

"We'll follow *him* this time," Dorn said, nodding to Lathan. "And you keep silent."

Henash smiled.

Lathan couldn't help but wonder if that was what he'd wanted all along.

Dorn turned to Lathan. "Well?"

The Blackstone was in the distance, but that wasn't where they needed to go. "We found the hyza here, but we didn't see the others. It's *that* way," he said, pointing. "But I don't know if we're going to find anything there."

"Whatever is out there, we're going to be ready," Dorn said.

The ground rumbled again, though it was distant and faint.

Lathan couldn't help but feel as if they wouldn't be ready.

CHAPTER 8

The sky had turned dark.

They hadn't found any further sign of elementals, though from the way that Henash looked—a distinct lack of surprise—he seemed as if that had been his expectation. The soldiers were arrayed out and around them, though they hadn't needed any additional protection.

"What do you think he knows?" Lathan asked, dropping his voice to a whisper and looking over to Jef.

"Dorn—"

"Henash. He knows something. Or seems to have expected much of this." Lathan had spent some time trying to determine whether he'd known that they might come across the earth elemental, though didn't *think* so. Why would he have let them get targeted like that if he knew something was coming? "I wish he'd tell us what he knows."

"Probably no more than you. He felt the elemental back there the same as us."

"Maybe," Lathan said.

Marin looked just as unbothered as Henash, though hers was a different attitude. It was as if she were looking for something around her to talk to. Maybe an elemental, but Lathan couldn't believe that she actually expected to talk to one of the elementals.

Dorn had been regarding Henash with a different expression ever since Henash had released the elemental power from a binding stone on him. Lathan wouldn't deny that he'd been impressed seeing that. There was a measure of control in how he had done that. It had been almost easy, though he couldn't imagine how anything that he'd done would actually be easy. Maybe there were things he could still learn from a more traditional approach. Not that he would ever admit that to his mother.

"What are we going to do when we get there and there's no sign of the elementals?" Jef asked.

"There's not going to be anything," Marin said. "If there was something there before, it would have been gone by now. I think Henash wants to see if there's any residual from the attack."

"Can you follow the Derithan based on what you detect as a residual?" Jef asked.

He looked at her as if she were keeping something from him, though Lathan didn't know the answer either.

"It depends. If the influence is significant enough, there's going to be a residual that remains, but I don't

know that I can say with any certainty what we'll find."
She nodded toward Henash. "I think he might know, but
he won't say until we get there."

It was later in the day when they reached the space
where they had encountered the Derithan. What was
strange for Lathan was that he could feel a slight vibration in the air, as if there really was some lingering
aspect of what had happened here, even though it would
have been long enough ago that they wouldn't be able to
detect anything more from it.

Henash went straight toward the spot where the
hyza had been captured—even though Lathan hadn't
told him anything. Lathan neared him, staying close to
him, watching him for a moment.

"How did you know this was where it was?" Lathan
asked, keeping his voice low.

The other soldiers, including Dorn, were circling
around the area, sweeping out as they made certain that
there wasn't anything more to be concerned about.
Lathan appreciated that, especially as he could still feel
what he could only call a vibration, though the vibration
seemed to come from everywhere around him. It was a
constant sensation, lingering in the air that he breathed,
along with up his arms and along his sides.

"Is it?" Henash asked, though he didn't look up
at him.

"You knew that it was. How? Marin said that you
might be able to trace something. Is that what you did?"

Henash held out a small item of stone that he'd

slipped onto his finger. It was a binding stone, though the way it was carved was different than most that Lathan had seen or used before. "You aren't the only one to bind the elementals, Lathan," Henash said, his voice low and his gaze lingering on Dorn. "You saw me use this before. I wouldn't have unleashed it quite as potently were I not convinced that it's necessary, but..." He crouched down, then he looked up, breathing in slowly. "Can you feel it?"

"Is the vibration I feel from you? What are you doing?"

Henash nodded slowly. "Vibration. That might be a reasonable way to describe it. Perhaps a bit different than I would have called it, but a vibration fits." He let out a long, slow breath, then he flicked his gaze around him and got to his feet. "The hyza came through here. What you're feeling isn't the binding stone that I've used. It's the effect of the binding stones that the Derithan used. Powerful objects. That much I suspect you can tell, but it's more than just the power that's in them. There's something else to them."

He started making a slow circuit before stopping, then heading to the north.

"Here's where the trail picks up," Henash said, calling out to Dorn.

"You'd have me believe that you can detect that so quickly?" Dorn asked. He was standing with two other soldiers. One of them had been injured during the elemental attack, though he seemed as if he were trying to hide that fact. The other was an older, leaner man who had a thin beard and shadowed eyes. "I doubt there is anything even here."

"Of course you do," Henash said. "You weren't convinced there was anything out here in the first place. You would have wanted to come out and wear the armor, though even in that—"

Dorn unsheathed his sword and pointed it at Henash. "We lead out here."

Henash grumbled and shook his head, looking back to the ground. "Then lead," he muttered, but he kept it quiet enough that Lathan didn't think Dorn would have heard unless the wind swirled and carried the sound over to him. Instead, Henash motioned to him. "Follow your vibration."

"What will it show?"

"I'm not sure. I don't feel the vibration, but there's something else here that I *do* detect, only I'm not entirely sure that it's going to lead us where we want." He whistled, and Marin came strolling over, Jef following after.

He leaned close to Lathan. "I'm getting the feeling that they don't like each other all that much," he said, nodding to Henash, then to Dorn. "Didn't think anyone really had strong feelings about the old man."

"He has enough standing at the Saval to make him dangerous," Marin said, "which gives him the baron's ear."

Lathan looked over to where Henash now crouched, waiting on Marin to join him. When she did, he looked up, stood, then the two of them began to whisper softly to each other.

"Are you coming?" Henash asked.

"Guess we'll have to ask him later. Think he'll tell us anything?" Jef asked.

Lathan didn't know.

Dorn followed Henash, though he was doing it in a way that served to make it look as if he was most definitely *not* following. It was almost as if Dorn were trying his best to listen to what Henash and Marin were saying but careful not to get so close that they knew he listened. A hint of wind swirled, and for a moment, Lathan thought that he noticed something in the wind, a little bit of a translucent figure.

Elemental.

He followed it, tracing it back to Dorn.

Then laughed softly. "Well. Looks like Dorn is trying to use an elemental against Henash. Wonder how long before—"

The wind suddenly whipped, though it carried from Henash and then over to Dorn, who was forced back a few steps.

"Guess he noticed," Lathan said.

Lathan caught up to Henash. "Now you're just using bonded elementals against each other? Why waste that power when we don't know what we're going to need to do when it comes to the Derithan?"

"Because I need to make sure that he doesn't think that he's in charge here," Henash said, raising his voice. "Oh, he's in charge of his soldiers, which is fine enough, but that's the extent of it. Now were he to conscript the two of you—or the Light knows, even me—we might have a different issue at hand, but I have a hard time thinking that he'd want to make a commitment like that with a pair of untrained men." Henash turned his attention away from Dorn and then back to Lathan. "Care to follow this vibration that you've been feeling? Seems to me that it would be a good time."

Lathan wanted to ask more questions—especially about what it might mean for them to be conscripted into service. Men volunteered to serve the king's army, though they were paid well. They weren't forced. At least, they hadn't been for many years. But he also could still feel the vibration, and the more that he felt it, the more he thought that it made sense for him to follow it and see if it might help lead them somewhere.

Letting out a soft laugh, he looked over to Jef, who was watching him. There was a question in his eyes, and Lathan thought that he knew the reason behind it. Jef wanted to know what it was that Lathan could feel—if anything.

The strange tension that he'd been feeling lingered, persisting along his arms, but there was a steadiness to it that drove him. If he followed that, he couldn't help but wonder if he might be able to use that to follow the Derithan—or at least the binding stone used on the hyza.

"Hold your own stone," Henash said, leaning toward him and dropping his voice. "Keep it close to you. You should be able to use that to follow the sense of what they did. When you do, then you should be able to use that to try to track toward where they went. Should, though that's not to say it will work."

Lathan focused on the stone he gripped tightly in his hand. He *could* feel something from it, though the sense of vibration within the stone hadn't persisted as it had when he'd first started noticing it. Now there was a different sense to the stone, almost a steady burning that began in his palm and radiated through him. Some of that burning had to be from the stone, but the rest of it might be something altogether different.

Dorn stayed nearby, which distracted Lathan. His sword remained unsheathed, but at least he wasn't swinging it around and pointing the blade at anyone the way that he had before. Lathan wouldn't react well were he to do that. The other soldiers were nearby, and they seemed to have been arranged behind Dorn, readied for the possibility that their commander might attack.

"This is getting out of hand," Jef whispered, staying close to him. Ever since they'd stopped, Jef had been on edge. Lathan could see it in the way he stood, hands at his sides, the darkness in his eyes seeming even more pronounced than it normally was. "What are they doing here?"

Henash spun, grabbed Lathan's outstretched hands, and pulled him forward. "Keep moving," he said.

Lathan didn't have a choice but to do what Henash wanted from him. He was tempted to pull away, but if he were to do that, he wasn't sure that he'd be able to get far enough from Henash to keep him from doing whatever he tried to do to him anyway. There was a strange heat in his hands as well, one that seemed to react with the stone and left him thinking that maybe Henash had some other way of using his stones.

"Keep searching," he said. "We need to find them before these fools go off on their own." He flicked his gaze back toward Dorn. "They like to think they know what they're doing, but they're just going to end up on the wrong end of an attack. Elemental or otherwise."

Henash continued to hold on to his hands, squeezing them.

"What do you detect now?" he whispered.

"Just you holding on to me," Lathan said. "Would you let go?"

"None of this would be necessary if you would have learned what you needed when you were first learning how to carve the stones, but you were taught to hold the elemental power, and nothing else. That means we've got some catching up to do, and now isn't really the time for it, but we've got no choice."

His grip started to work against Lathan's wrists, rubbing more tightly, and with a different pressure. The stone heated even more, but it wasn't only heat that Lathan detected now. It was the vibration that had shifted, starting to work through his fingers and up into his hands. There was something uncontrolled about it. From the way that Henash looked at him, he suspected that he knew exactly what he did to him.

"Feel it," Henash said. "Feel for the guidance. That elemental isn't gone. Just held by them. You can stay connected to it, and you can use that connection. So *use* it."

Lathan wasn't sure what he needed to do so that he could use the stone, but thought that if it would somehow connect him to the elemental, then he needed to try it. He squeezed the stone, trying to feel for any sort of power within it, but didn't detect anything other than the steady vibration that he'd been feeling already.

"What am I supposed to do?" he asked, whispering softly. He didn't know if he needed to distrust Dorn the way that Henash did, but he'd exercise appropriate caution. That seemed to make good sense to him.

"I showed you that there are ways of releasing that bonded energy. All you have to do is maintain your connection to it, then you can find a way to let some of it out. It needs to be done slowly. Nothing more than a wisp of power. Then we can follow it."

Lathan looked down at the stone. If it worked...

Then he might have an easier time with trying to draw on something more. There were times when having the ability to draw upon the stored power of the binding stone might be useful. He'd never learned to control it the way that it seemed that Henash had. All he'd ever learned to do was to release the stored power into another binding stone so that others could use it.

The stone was warm. Henash had been doing something with his hand—and the stone—to cause it to heat that way, though he didn't know what that was. There was a hint of power in it, though that power seemed to be stored deeply in the stone.

Henash had rubbed his wrists, which had helped him release some of that power.

What if he tried something similar?

Not with his wrist, but what if he tried to rub the stone in a way that would unleash some of the power? He used his thumb, sweeping it along the flat edge of the stone. Lathan had sharpened this one, so he needed to be careful that he didn't run his finger onto the sharp edge of the stone, but that wasn't much of a danger if he worked quickly and carefully.

As he did, he began to feel something.

It was similar to the vibration.

It worked along his fingers, up his palm, then out into the stone. There was a heat that came with it, but it was a different sort of heat than what he'd felt before. This heat seemed to be tied to what was stored in the stone.

"That's it," Henash said. "Just like that."

Jef still leaned close. He looked at the stone, watching Lathan. "It looks like you're giving it a massage. You know, I have this spot on my back—"

Marin grabbed him and pushed him away from Lathan.

"Hey," Jef said. "Don't keep me from his magic thumbs. If he's going to rub something, it might as well work out this knot."

"Quiet," Henash hissed. "It's working. Just keep at it. Now we'll see what the wind can tell us."

Henash held out another stone, and there came a soft fluttering of the wind, though it was faint. As it stirred, it began to build, finally releasing the wind and taking some of the heat that Lathan had managed to release with it.

When it did, Henash hurried off.

Lathan noticed a faint swirling of smoke that had come from the stone. It was subtle, but it was definitely there. The wind—whatever elemental that Henash had released—caught the smoke and carried it, though Lathan didn't know how it did that or where it was guiding it.

"Look at that," Jef said.

"You don't care about that," Lathan said.

"Ah, not really, and I don't really care about you rubbing my back." He glanced behind him. "I just needed to be obnoxious so Dorn didn't get too close. He was pushing up on the two of you. Figured that I could try to upset him so that he'd back away. Seems like it worked."

Lathan chuckled. "Like you have to work at being obnoxious."

Dorn shoved past them, hurrying toward Henash. He didn't look toward the smoke, though it was still drifting slowly from the end of the binding stone. Some of it, at least. Not all. Most of it trailed out in the air, catching the wind, drifting steadily away. That was what Henash had followed.

"He could have given us a little space," Jef muttered. "Maybe I'll push on him the same way..." He trailed off as Dorn looked back and glowered at them a moment before turning away. "Or maybe not," Jef finished more carefully.

Lathan looked to the air around them, watching the wind, the swirling of smoke, and wondered what might happen if—or when—they reached the Derithan. Would they be able to do anything, or would the Derithan attack?

CHAPTER 9

The trail went quiet near dark.

The daylight had been fading for a while, leaving Lathan wondering what they might find. The rolling grasslands had shifted into something denser, and there was a hint of a forest in the distance. He didn't want to chase the Derithan into the trees in the darkness, though he wasn't sure that he had much of a choice in what they ended up doing. Henash had continued to follow something, though Lathan was no longer certain that it was the smoke from the binding stone.

The stone itself still had a hint of heat to it, though it wasn't as significant as what it had been before. Every so often, Lathan would run his thumb along the stone, testing whether there was anything that he might be able to release from the stone, before letting off.

The first few times that he'd done it, Henash had looked back at him, shaking his head as if he wanted to warn him off from doing anything that might reveal their presence. Then Henash had turned and tipped his head, nodding to Lathan, who took it as a sign that Henash needed for him to release more of the binding stone power. It happened enough that Lathan started to wonder if there was a limit to how much power would remain in the stone when they were done, if any.

So much for my prize.

They still hadn't seen the Derithan. There hadn't been any sign of other elementals, for that matter. Lathan kept thinking that they might find another wild elemental that might attack and started to think that maybe he'd be able to used release power on the elemental, but no attack came.

"How far do you think they're going to push us?" Jef asked.

He sounded tired. The two of them had traveled extensively together, so Lathan knew when his friend was exhausted—which he sounded now. So was Lathan, though. He'd love to have a warm bed. Or any bed.

"Hopefully not much more than this now," he said. "I stopped knowing what we were following a while ago." He held up the binding stone. Though he could still feel a hint of heat coming off the stone, he wasn't exactly sure that there was a trail they could track. Maybe Henash could follow it, though he didn't know if even he were able to do that.

"That would explain why Dorn and the others are getting so agitated. It looks like they want to snap at him."

"I'm starting to wonder if it would do any good," Lathan said.

The wind had swirled from time to time, enough that Lathan suspected—though didn't know—if Henash were responsible for controlling it. He suspected he did, the same way that he suspected the way he'd blasted Dorn in the first place had been tied to his control of the wind. Lathan wanted to know how he'd done it. That would be a useful skill. Certainly more useful than just releasing the bonded elemental and trailing after it.

They reached the tree line, and everyone stopped. Jef stayed close to Marin, which brought a bit of a smile to Lathan's face, while Lathan made his way toward Henash, who was standing at the edge of the trees, staring toward the forest. He had a piece of a binding stone in hand, though Lathan couldn't tell if he were trying to release any of the power in the stone or if he were simply holding it.

"What's your plan?" Lathan asked.

"To keep safe," Henash said. "They're are likely to keep pushing, probably because they are hoping to find some sort of rare elemental. With the recent migration, it would make a certain sort of sense."

"Will the elementals be different when we go into the trees?" Lathan asked.

His thumb worked along the edge of the binding stone, feeling the edge, though he was careful not to carve through his finger. He had to be cautious with the stone, not wanting to draw blood. There wasn't much warmth coming from the stone, though, so he didn't think he had much to worry about with power still stored within it.

"Earth is going to be different, mostly. Some wind. There won't be the danger of fire elementals, though it's possible that we'll still run into something like hyza." He stared, his jaw working as he chewed on it. "But that's where they went. I'm sure of it."

"Can you tell?"

Henash turned to him briefly. "You released enough of that elemental to follow. I'm surprised that *you* can't tell."

Lathan held up the stone. "I've been releasing some of it from time to time, but I can't really feel anything more in what I'm doing. I don't know how much of it is anything that I've actually released and how much of it is... just nothing, I guess."

Henash flicked his gaze to the gathered soldiers. "They'd like us to chase down the Derithan, but that means they'd go barreling into danger without paying much attention to how dangerous that might be. They've heard stories, I'm sure, but seeing them is a different thing altogether." His voice had trailed off slightly toward the end, though there was still a measure of irritation within it, even though he'd fallen somewhat quiet. "We can rest here and regroup in the morning."

Henash turned away, leaving Lathan to watch him as Henash approached the edge of the forest, though he didn't enter. From what Lathan could tell, Henash gripped a stone in one hand—maybe in both hands—and stared, saying nothing.

"What's he doing?" Jef asked as Lathan made his way over to him. Marin had separated from him, and she looked at the sky, probably trying to talk to the elementals the way that she seemed convinced that she could. "He looks like he's going into the forest. Or maybe that he doesn't want to go into the forest?" Jef screwed up his face as he stared at Henash. "Fiery Skies, he's an odd one, isn't he?"

Lathan wanted to agree, but increasingly he started to feel like Henash was the one they needed to listen to. He seemed to know what they were dealing with even more than the soldiers. More than Lathan did. And he'd known what to do with the elemental. That mattered to him, though maybe it shouldn't be as significant.

"We're staying here tonight."

"That's what I figured. We're not as ready for anything out here as we would be were the two of us chasing elementals. We should have brought better supplies."

"I don't think the baron—or the soldiers—expected that we'd be out here all night. The feeling I get is that they thought that we'd be here for a few hours, either find evidence that the Derithan weren't here, or maybe that they'd passed, and head back. The elemental—and Henash—changed that."

"That's just Dorn—"

"The wind is talking to me," Marin said, stepping in between the two of them. "It's warning me."

Jef gave Lathan an amused smile. "I'm sure it is. What's the wind saying to you?"

"Be ready."

"Yeah? Be ready for what?" Jef asked.

Lathan looked up. He didn't know whether she had any ability to speak to the wind, doubting that were possible, but he also knew better than to challenge someone on something like that, especially given what they'd been seeing on this journey. "Which elemental?"

"Ara," she said. "I mostly speak to ara, though there are times when I convince wisahn to talk. They're shy, though, you probably know."

Wisahn would be more useful. It was known as a powerful elemental, though it was rare. Not shy. When they'd dealt with wisahn, it had been a challenge for them to withstand it. He and Jef had managed to use binding stones on it, though that hadn't been as easy as some elementals, and certainly not as easy as with ara.

"There's a wisahn here?" Jef said, crouching slightly as if the elemental would swoop in and lift him. "I haven't felt it—"

"I said *ara*," Marin said, as patient as if she were speaking to a child. A very slow child, at that. "Not wisahn. We haven't passed by any wisahn since Henash summoned it to carry the trail." She turned toward him, shaking her head. "I wonder if he knows what's coming?"

She headed over to Henash at the tree line.

"You don't believe she's actually talking to elementals, do you?" Jef asked.

"I think *she* believes it," Lathan said, "though I don't know if she's actually communicating with them or not.

Ara comes through these plains often enough, so it's entirely possible that she's aware of it."

"Aware of it isn't the same as *speaking* to it."

A gust of wind rattled the treetops before falling still.

"Maybe she *is* talking to it," Lathan said.

When he'd seen Henash using his bonded elemental to knock Dorn back, he hadn't known which one it was, but wisahn made sense. It was a powerful elemental of wind, and that would have been enough to knock someone like Dorn back a few steps, even with his armor. Then there had been the powerful wind that had carried away the trail of heat that he'd released from his hyza binding stone. That might have been the same, though it seemed like it should be something different.

"We should prepare our defenses," Henash said, turning to the soldiers though he looked toward Lathan. "There is something coming."

As if to punctuate his words, the wind began to build and swirl again, now swaying the tops of the trees, bending them toward the ground. Some dust started to swirl...

Not dust.

"Sandor!" Lathan shouted. The soldiers turned to him, but Lathan hurried over to Henash. "It's sandor. That's what the Derithan used against the hyza. If they're bringing it against us, we need to use whatever wind you have to defend us."

"That might be a part of it," Henash agreed.

As during the earlier attack, he sounded so much calmer than what Lathan felt. With the wind picking up, the dust that he noticed in the air, the sandor elemental would be there soon.

"How many stones do you have on you?" Henash asked.

"Uncarved, I probably have—"

"I think in this case, we need any you've carved."

"You said that the carved stones would bind the elemental to me."

Henash nodded, still looking up and toward the sky. The wind was whipping around them with a violence that made it feel as if there were a storm coming, though they'd not seen any sign of a storm. There was nothing other than the heavy wind—and the dust.

"I know what I said. I think your connection to the binding stones might be more effective than something that will only lead to a partial capture. What we're looking for is a way to have some measure of control."

He reached into his pouch, pulling something out. It was a binding stone, but one that was shaped into a long, slender rod with a pointed tip. An earth spike, as his father had called them. They were useful for a very specific kind of elemental, though none that were typically found around here.

"Do you have anything like this?"

Lathan sorted through his own pouch before shaking his head. "No spikes like that. I never found them useful here."

"Unfortunate. Had you a more traditional type of training—"

"Do we have the time for that now?" Lathan asked.

Henash just shrugged.

Lathan didn't have a spike, but there were a few other earth elemental items that he had. Henash wasn't wrong. There were times when specific carvings made a difference to the type of elemental that they captured. That was part of what made him as effective as he often was. He could use a carving that was tailored to a kind of elemental that would be useful, though there were also times when he just used nonspecific carvings.

When he had gathered the earth elemental binding stones, Henash looked at them, studying them as if he were going to challenge him on what he'd withdrawn. He nodded slowly to himself, though, touching one of the items, then moving on to the others.

"These might work. You'll need to change the shape slightly." The wind picked up, whistling now. "And I'm afraid that you won't have much time."

With the words, Lathan had the sudden feeling that the wind had been holding off sandor. Could that be what was going on? Were they trying to buy time? Lathan didn't know if he could carve the stones quickly enough, but adding a spike to the end would shift them somewhat and make them more like a true earth spike.

"Encircle us," Henash said.

Lathan stepped off to the side, grabbed the stones, and started carving. Jef came behind him, leaning over his shoulder.

"Are you changing your stones now?"

"Henash wants earth spikes. I don't know if it'll make a difference, but he seems to think the stone will matter."

"If it's sandor..."

"I know."

Sandor wasn't only earth, though it was *mostly* earth. There was wind worked in, which was probably why Henash was trying to use the wind now, using it to push on sandor and send it away from them. It wasn't a use of bonded elemental power that Lathan had seen used before, but then he'd never known how to release the bonded elemental power from his stone and use it, either.

Lathan worked his knife along the edge of the stone, carving a point to it. It took a steady hand and a careful maneuvering to ensure he didn't chip off the stone from the end. It wouldn't do for him to shatter the stone tip, though as he worked on it, he could feel the stone starting to shift beneath his hand.

One done, he handed it to Jef. "Place this where Henash wants."

"It's your stone."

"He's guiding this." The wind continued to swirl. Now Lathan could *feel* something in it that was rough and irritating. Before long, the sandor elemental would reach them, and if it did, Lathan wasn't sure that whatever Henash had done to protect them would be enough. The armored soldiers might be protected, but he and Jef —and Marin and Henash—wouldn't be.

Jef took the stone and headed away.

Lathan set to working on other pieces of stone.

It was slow progress.

He had to make more spikes, but he wasn't sure that

he'd be able to do it fast enough for this to work. He didn't know if he could work as quickly as Henash wanted.

When he'd finished carving all the stones he had, he joined Henash in the center of the small clearing, looking toward the trees. Henash still gripped something in his hand that Lathan couldn't quite see, though he could feel the energy of it, almost as if the power that was trapped in the stone poured out as he held it.

"What now?" he asked.

"Now we wait. If this works..."

The wind started to swirl.

Lathan wasn't sure if the swirling of the wind was tied to sandor or if it came from the wind elemental that he was holding. It seemed to reach a point around them, but never quite penetrated all the way.

The binding stones were holding.

Jef leaned over. "Is this working, or am I imagining things here?"

Lathan shrugged. "I *think* it's working, but I don't know if it's going to be enough to hold back what's coming."

Neither of them really knew what it was that was coming, though if it *was* sandor, they had seen it attack before. It could hold them—maybe even corral them— and then...

Lathan turned his attention to the binding stones that now ringed them.

Hold them.

What had they done?

"This isn't right," he said, starting toward one of the stones. "Remember when sandor attacked the hyza?" Jef joined him, nodding. "The elemental didn't do anything other than hold them in place." He looked up, still feeling the wind gusting, though there wasn't any trail of dust within it any longer. "What if we've just done that to ourselves?"

CHAPTER 10

The binding stone spike protruded from the ground, though there was a hint of what seemed like power that came from it. Lathan stayed an arm's length from it, not wanting to get too close, but knowing that there might be something he'd need to reach. There was a feeling of the wind, and a feeling of the power that swirled around them, but nothing more than that.

"What are you doing? You spent all that time trying to make those things, and now you're going to—"

"Nothing," Lathan said.

He straightened and looked around.

The wind had shifted. There was no other way to describe it. The wind didn't blow with the same intensity that it had before, now fading somewhat. That couldn't be good.

It was dark enough that he couldn't see much out and around them, but he had a sense that there was a wind blowing nearby. That was the only thing that he could feel, though he didn't know if that was what was out there. Maybe that *was* sandor.

"Henash," he said, turning.

When he did, he saw Dorn with his blade unsheathed, pointing what looked like a binding stone sword toward the ground. Two other soldiers flanked him, though they were getting close to Henash, as if they were going to attack.

"What did you do?" Dorn was asking.

"You might want to take a step back," Henash said.

As before, he somehow managed to sound as if he were completely at ease, as if there was no problem for him having three soldiers approaching.

More than three.

Some of the others had started to work their way around.

"What's going on here?" Jef whispered.

"I think a pissing match," Lathan answered. "Maybe they're trying to figure out who serves the king—or the baron—better."

"I don't know what you've done, but you aren't going to trap us here."

Henash snorted. "Then you haven't been paying attention. I'm not the one who's done anything here, am I?"

Henash turned toward Lathan.

Fiery Skies...

Lathan squeezed the hyza binding stone, feeling the heat within it. For some reason it was reassuring to hold onto the stone, even though he couldn't release any more of the power that was trapped in it.

But he had *another* binding stone.

No.

He wasn't going to release the shadow elemental as he didn't even know what the elemental might do to them—if anything. It was possible the elemental wouldn't be able to help the way that the other elementals did.

Dorn barely glanced toward Lathan, though. "You'd have me believe that it's *him* who's holding us here?"

"Well, I'd actually suggest that it's your armor that's holding you in place, but I doubt that you'd be interested in hearing that, so you can blame me. Or Lathan. Or the Light. I don't care."

Jef snorted.

Lathan elbowed him.

Marin had taken up a position behind Henash, and from the way she stood in place, it was almost as if she were there to try to help Henash. She claimed to speak to the elementals, but he'd never seen her using elemental power in binding stones before.

"Relax, Dorn. This will be over soon."

Almost as if he were answered, the wind picked up, swirling again.

Henash looked up. He held a small, circular binding stone into the air. There was a shape carved into the stone, though from the distance, he couldn't see what was carved on it.

The wind whipped at them.

Then he felt something else.

Not just the wind, but a grating sense that blew toward him.

But it wasn't toward *him*. It was toward the binding stones—the spikes—that were plunged into the ground. Despite their presence, Lathan could feel something beginning to burn, as if it were ripping at his flesh.

"You might want to activate those spikes," Henash said, nodding to Lathan. "I'm afraid that it's about to get a little worse here."

"Don't move," Dorn said.

Henash flicked his hand toward Dorn.

Dorn was ready. He whipped his sword up. The wind that swirled out of the stone that Henash was holding was drawn into the sword where it simply faded.

That was a different use of power than Lathan had seen before.

Dorn stormed toward him. "I thought you would try that again. Don't think that we're not trained to deal with men like you."

"Like me?" Henash said. He took a step back, dropping one of the stones. Wind poured from it, though it didn't push anyone back. Rather, it just swirled. "Lathan?"

Lathan stirred himself.

He wasn't sure what he needed to do to activate the binding stone spikes, but with the burning that continued to whip around them, he thought that he was going to have to try something.

"Don't let him—"

The wind raged.

It was like a torrent.

This was different than the wind that Lathan had felt before.

This was sudden. Violent. And it threw everyone to the ground.

More than that, it seemed to keep the pain at bay. The burning that had been building began to fade, the wind pushing back what Lathan suspected was sandor.

He staggered to his feet, crawling toward the spikes.

One of the soldiers was near him, and Lathan ignored him, trying to reach the nearest of the spikes. How was he supposed to activate it? He didn't know what Henash wanted from him, but with the wind coming like this, he thought he would have to try something.

"You have to feel the elemental within it," Marin said.

How had she gotten there?

She was crouched near one of the spikes, and she leaned toward it, sniffing at the ground as if she'd be able to detect something from the smell of the spike. Lathan took a deep breath, wondering if maybe there was something to the way that she was doing it, but didn't smell anything other than the damp earth and a hint of the meadow nearby.

"Feel it?" he asked, feeling foolish.

He didn't want to have to trust her to know what they needed to do, but then she seemed confident, and she *did* claim the ability to speak to elementals

"Just touch your spike. You have to tell it what you want it to hold."

"I want it to hold sandor so it doesn't peel the flesh off of us."

Marin looked up. She was close to him. He met her deep brown eyes as she smiled at him. "Oh, it would probably do much more than that, though I suspect you know that. Or maybe you saw it when you came across the elemental before? Either way, you *don't* want to get caught by this elemental."

Lathan pulled back but wasn't sure if he should stay where he was. If sandor were to rip through them, shouldn't he want to be near a stone that could hold it? He didn't know if the spike would make a difference, but it seemed to him that Henash did.

Behind him, he could hear the scuffle between Henash and Dorn. Lathan couldn't see what was happening, but would have expected the soldiers to make quick work of Henash, though he seemed to hear more of the soldiers shouting than he did Henash. Wind whistled, though it didn't seem to make it past the barrier of the spikes, as if the spikes were holding on to the energy around the clearing.

Lathan reached for the first earth spike, resting his hand on it. He didn't feel anything other than foolish while holding it. There would have to be something in the spike though he didn't know how to trap the elemental in it.

"There," she said.

She rested her hand on top of his. Her skin was warm

and soft. He felt a strange tingling that passed between them, though thought that it came from whatever was happening in the air around them. The power of the earth spike, he suspected.

"What do I do now?"

"Just call to the elemental. I suspect they're already bound by the Derithan, which is why he wanted you to use the spike. It concentrates the calling, you know. You should be able to disperse some of that power out and into the ground around you, but it's going to take you to talk to the elemental. Don't worry, I'll guide you through it."

Lathan could only imagine what Jef would say about her guiding him through talking to the elemental. But if it worked...

"What I'd suggest you do is ignore everything that's happening around us. You can feel the energy, but you need to let the power that you can use begin to—"

Wind slammed into them.

Lathan tried to steady himself, but he was tossed forward, slamming into the ground. His hand reached for the earth spike, and pain shot through his palm as he slapped the spike.

Then he felt a steady build of a strange pressure that he hadn't known before.

Was that the wind—or was that him somehow activating the elemental?

"You should back away," Marin said.

"What is it?"

"I don't know, but I can feel that something changed. Maybe it wasn't you, but there *is* something here."

Lathan began to slide back.

Marin pulled on his arm.

They backed toward the soldiers. Dorn was pointing his sword at Henash, who was still standing calmly, as if waiting for him to retreat.

"Something is going to happen," Lathan said. "I can feel—"

The air exploded.

His breath popped from his lungs, and though Lathan tried to fight it, he couldn't ignore the power that slammed into him. He gasped, struggling to catch his breath, but couldn't get enough air.

He wasn't the only one who struggled.

All around him, the other soldiers seemed to have the same difficulty.

Not Henash. He stood as calm as before. As did Marin.

"Lathan?" Jef hissed. He tried to suck a breath, but his eyes bulged as he struggled.

Lathan couldn't do anything to help his friend, but he felt as if he needed to try something. He couldn't breathe, much like it appeared that Jef couldn't breathe. It felt like the wind in his lungs was drawn out. Pain seared through him.

Had sandor continued to attack them despite whatever strange barrier he'd managed to get into place? How would they overcome this?

Henash raised his hand. With a swirl around his head, the wind intensified again, lashing at them.

Lathan could breathe.

He sucked in a long breath and looked at the others with him.

The only one who seemed unbothered by what had happened was Henash.

And Marin.

She stood behind him, and it looked as if she were talking to someone, though Henash was turned in the opposite direction, so he didn't think that was who she spoke to.

"We need to leave this place," Henash said. He looked to Lathan. "They switched from earth to wind. Another gust like that and none of us will survive it."

Lathan wasn't sure that was true. It seemed to him that Henash was able to tolerate whatever they were doing.

"Where?"

They wouldn't reach town very quickly. And unless Henash had other hidden elementals that they could use, they weren't going to have the necessary power to overwhelm anything else.

"The forest. We should have enough space to get through there, though it's going to be difficult. There will be other elementals we can work with. I suspect that we can—"

The wind whipped again, and it threatened to pull the air from his lungs. Henash raised his hand over his head, swirling it again, and it seemed as if he were drawing something with it as he did. The wind started to ease, but not completely.

"Not much time now," Henash muttered. He turned to Marin. "Guide them to the trees. Get them safely there, and I will follow. I'll need Lathan to help in whatever way he still has bound to him."

"I've used most of hyza," Lathan said. Or thought that he'd used it, though he didn't know if he had. It was possible that there was still some residual power in that binding stone, though it didn't react to him the way that it once had.

"Perhaps most, but I'm hoping that you haven't used all of it. I suspect we're going to need it." He rounded on Dorn. "Gather your men and retreat to the trees. That is, unless you think you can challenge the elementals here. I count three, though I could be off. It's possible that they are using some that I'm not familiar with."

From his tone, Lathan sensed that was unlikely.

Lathan had felt sandor, and there was whatever wind they were using to make it so that they couldn't breathe, but what else were they using? More than that, was there any way that they'd be able to counter it?

Not with hyza. That was mostly fire, though there were some who believed it was bound somewhat to earth as well. If that were the case, the elemental *might* be able to counter the wind. Fire wouldn't.

There was something that Lathan hadn't revealed, though he didn't know if the shadow elemental would make any difference. Lathan didn't know enough about the strength of that elemental to know if it would matter.

Henash might know something about that elemental, but that was if he were willing to reveal it—and now wasn't exactly the best time to do so.

Wind whipped again, followed by a trembling.

There was the third elemental that Henash had suspected. Earth.

"Move," he said to Marin.

Jef followed Marin as they headed toward the trees. Lathan went with her, but Henash grabbed his arm, pulling him back.

"I might need your help here. The spikes should hold sandor and whatever they've got tunneling toward us, but I don't think they're going to hold onto the ranth or the vilas." He stared at the sky, still clutching his binding stone. "I might need you to help capture them."

"I don't know what either of them are," Lathan said.

He'd never heard of either of them. How was he supposed to help if he didn't know anything about either of those elementals?

"It's no different than what you've done with others. You have to use your stones, focus on what you want them to do, and try to hold some of that power trapped in them. I'd ask Marin, but she doesn't like the idea of trapping the elementals. She's too sensitive about it, but in this case I think it's a necessary thing for us to do."

Lathan didn't have many binding stones remaining.

With the way the wind had picked up, he didn't think that he'd have a chance to collect more, though this *was* the kind of place where he thought that he'd have a chance of success in collecting them. With the earth spikes in place, he thought he might be able to find places where the binding stones would hold more effectively.

"We should just go with the others," he suggested. "Get into the trees with them, and we can—"

Lathan couldn't finish.

There came a loud crack, followed by an increased trembling of the ground.

The spikes had failed.

Henash sighed. It was the first real reaction he'd mustered. "I thought that would hold longer. It seems they've got more powerful elementals tied to them than I expected."

"I told you about hyza."

"There are more powerful than hyza and sandor, Lathan."

He sounded as if he were giving a lesson to one of his students, rather than dealing with the suddenness of violence from the elementals that were coming at them. Lathan grabbed for his remaining stones, pulled the crossbow from his shoulder, and readied for the attack.

When it came, he wasn't completely ready.

The ground heaved.

Henash managed to do *something*, and the earth settled again.

Lathan needed to find a way to use the crossbow against the elementals, but he didn't know what to target. The earth elemental that attacked them had broken through the earth spikes, so whatever was there would be powerful. Wind wouldn't work. They needed a different kind of binding stone to use on the wind. That left the sandor, though Lathan thought that if anything were going to have worked, it would have been the binding stones on sandor—and had the feeling that Henash had expected that would have worked too.

The earth heaved again.

Lathan was tossed off his feet.

He scrambled up, knowing that if he were to get caught by an earth elemental, there wouldn't be any escape. Henash still stood in the center of the clearing, sweeping his gaze around him at the others that had disappeared into the forest.

"They're coming," Henash said.

"Elementals?"

Henash looked over, and his gaze was dark and tormented. "Derithan."

CHAPTER 11

"I'm going to buy you as much time as I can. I don't promise that it'll be enough, but get to the trees. Once there, find the others. There is strength in numbers—and in the armored soldiers."

"If you were going to have us rely on the armored soldiers, shouldn't we have kept them here with us from the very beginning?" Lathan looked toward the trees, but he didn't see a way to reach them safely. The wind was whipping around them, making it difficult for them to reach. He could feel the energy coming off of the elementals, and it was near enough that he thought the elementals blowing in their direction would overwhelm them.

"They wouldn't have been able to do anything against this. I hadn't known they were bringing so much to bear out here. When you'd mentioned the Derithan, I had not thought they would bring so much power with them. I fear what it means."

He raised his hand again, motioning to the sky,

waving the binding stone that carried with it the power of the wind.

"They're after something," he went on.

"The hyza."

Henash shook his head. "It's more than that hyza. If that were all it was, they wouldn't have brought so much against us here. I'm not sure what it is, but I suspect they're after something here..." He looked over to Lathan. "You said that you saw them target the hyza, and then they came here." His brow furrowed. "Could that be it? Are they following your stone?"

"We were using the stone to follow them, I thought."

The wind continued to gust. He swung the crossbow from side to side as he struggled to find a place and thing to aim at, though the elementals that were out there were raging around them. He wasn't exactly sure how they were going to get away from them.

"We were, but I wonder if they were following something else." Henash looked over to him. "I don't suppose you know if there was anything else that you saw while you were out with Jef earlier? Did you see anything that would explain what they would be after?"

Henash stood just as calmly as before, though this time it was Lathan who started to feel uncomfortable.

There *had* been something else, and it was something that he hadn't shared with Henash, but perhaps it was time that he do so. Then they'd know if there was anything in his find that would make a difference with the Derithan.

"Shadow," he said, his voice dropping. "There was a

shadow elemental. We weren't sure if it was there or not, but after the hyza disappeared, we saw a shifting of darkness across the ground and went after it. Well, I went after it." He pulled the binding stone from his pocket and held it up. He couldn't feel anything in the stone, and didn't know if there was any sort of residual bound power within it. The only thing that he *did* know was that there was a sense of energy in *him*.

"You came across a shadow elemental out here?" Henash had dropped his hands to his sides, and the wind that had been raging seemed to ease, though the ground would still tremble at times. He didn't know what caused it, which elemental might be there, but he could feel the steady trembling that persisted around him. The wind had shifted, and even that seemed to have eased somewhat. Had Henash done something to change that? "They shouldn't reach here."

"My father used to tell me about shadow elementals," he said. Now wasn't the best time to have a conversation like this, but he felt as if he wanted Henash to know how he had recognized the elemental. It had been difficult, though he hadn't been entirely sure about what he'd seen. "When we caught sight of that shadow, I thought to bind it. I didn't know if it would even work. I've heard they're difficult to bind."

"Incredibly difficult. I can't remember the last time that I heard about someone successfully binding shadow." He held out the hand without the wind binding stone toward Lathan, and started to reach for the stone before drawing back. "That must be what they're after. Perhaps not the stone—but a way to track the shadow." He looked up. "Now it's even more imperative that we get out of here."

He took a deep breath, and it seemed as if some part of Henash changed. Raising his hands, he pressed them upward. Wind shifted when he did. When he took a step, it seemed as if the ground started to calm, the tremoring of the elemental beginning to ease and fade from them. Henash brought his hands down in a sharp crack, and the air sizzled.

How many different binding stones did he have on him?

Why would he release so much power at one time?

The more that the air around them crackled, the more that Lathan felt as if he were guided away from where he was standing. There was a sense of strange power that continued to push on him, and Henash had to be the one responsible for it. Lathan didn't know what the older man was doing, only that it seemed to be connected to the binding stones.

With another blast of air mixed with a trembling of the ground, Henash motioned toward the trees. "Run!"

Lathan hesitated.

When he did, he caught sight of a single figure in the distance. They were dressed all in black and had a long slender blade outstretched. There was something about the blade that drew Lathan's focus, though he wasn't sure why that would be. It was almost as if the blade were a binding stone.

That much stone would be difficult to collect—and control.

"Do you see that?" he asked Henash.

"I can feel it. If you're seeing one of the Derithan, then you need to move. We both do. If they've already come, then we're in more trouble than I realized." His voice dropped to a whisper, and Lathan didn't think Henash spoke to him with what he said next. "I thought we had more time."

Henash spun and his hands strained out from him. The binding stones that he clutched in either hand seemed filled with some strange power, though Lathan wasn't sure why he could feel that so well.

The trees.

That was where Henash wanted him to go. Reach the trees, get to the others, and then they could try to stay ahead of the Derithan.

With the wind battering at him, he ran.

The distance wasn't great. Under other circumstances—that being a lack of elementals attacking him, along with the Derithan leaving him alone—Lathan would have been able to reach the trees in little more than a few moments. Not even that.

But it was more than the wind that picked up, trying to pull him back. It was the way that the ground trembled, the stones slipping beneath his feet. The earth—and the earth elementals that were here—were angry. Then there was the heat that built in the air.

Another elemental.

The heat hadn't been a problem for him before. There

had been heat, but nothing like what he now felt pressing upon him. This was nearly overwhelming, a steady and rising heat that lifted from the ground, as if the earth and the fire elementals were working together.

And they might be.

Such a thing wasn't completely uncommon, though he wouldn't have expected to have seen that here. Lathan had only the hyza elemental, and as he used it, he couldn't help but wonder if it might not be enough for what he needed to do. He had pressed out through the stone long enough that there wasn't that much power still there. It was possible that he didn't have enough left in it for himself.

The ground rippled.

Stone slipped to either side, and Lathan did the only thing that he thought might be effective here. He raised his crossbow and fired directly into the ground.

He didn't know if there was anything there that would make a difference, or if the crossbow would do anything. The bolt had a binding stone tip on it, but that might not be enough against what they had to face.

The ground calmed.

It was only for a moment, but in that moment, he managed to race forward a little further. Lathan hurried into the trees, reaching the edge of it, before spinning.

The crossbow bolt that he'd fired was not that far from him. It jutted from the ground, and all around it, everything was quiet. If that bolt *had* bonded to the earth elemental, then he wanted to have an opportunity to use that.

How could he get there before the Derithan reached them?

Henash still stood where he had been before, holding his binding stones, elemental power raging around him, which left Lathan wondering what he was doing—and how.

Who was Henash, really?

That would be a question for another time, but he couldn't shake the curiosity that he felt seeing him standing in the middle of the attack, holding the stones and commanding the elementals like an elemental warrior out of the stories he'd heard when he was a child.

The Derithan moved closer to them.

He was a shadow, nothing more...

Shadow.

Had Lathan made a mistake and bonded to some part of the Derithan?

They were powerful, he knew, and none really were able to say what the Derithan did with their power, or how they managed to control it, only that they were able to control more of the elementals—and in ways that others could not. What if they were connected to the shadows?

That might explain why they'd seen the shadow elemental near the hyza in the first place. Then Lathan had made a mistake in trying to bind a stone to it.

And he'd drawn the Derithan.

A lull in the attack gave him a chance.

He raced toward the crossbow bolt.

When he reached it, he scooped it off the ground and tucked the bolt into his pouch. The ground started to tremble again, as if the earth elemental had suddenly detected him and tried to target him, but Lathan managed to slip back toward the trees. Strangely, once he was at the border of the forest, the attack eased so that he didn't feel as much of the power pushing against him.

Henash hadn't moved.

Maybe he *couldn't* move.

"Henash?" he called, raising his voice to get above the sound of the wind.

"Go," Henash called back to him. "I can hold them, but..."

He had started to turn toward Lathan, but a layer of dust whipped around him, battering at him. Was that sandor or another elemental? How many different elementals did the Derithan have access to during their attacks?

The ground trembled again.

From where he stood, he could see how it rippled, the earth seeming to heave and rise up so that it worked to capture Henash.

The Derithan was making his way ever closer. Not much longer and he'd reach Henash. There wasn't much that Lathan thought he could do. The hyza elemental binding stone had been partly, if not completely, spent. The only thing that he had was the earth elemental crossbow bolt.

Why wouldn't that work?

He could fire it at the Derithan.

Lathan didn't think that it would hurt someone with as much power as he suspected the Derithan had, but then it wasn't about hurting him. It was about trying to get him to release Henash. And the benefit of a binding stone crossbow bolt was that it would fly through most elemental power. What it didn't, it would strike and then start to absorb some of that power.

That was what he could use. What he had to use.

Readying the crossbow, he took aim.

The distance was farther than he preferred but he thought that he could reach the Derithan from here. It would take a good aim, but he could do it.

Henash looked toward him.

Lathan fired without thinking much of it.

The crossbow bolt streaked across the space between he and the Derithan. His aim had been good. Lathan hadn't counted on the Derithan plucking the crossbow bolt out of the air.

He turned it to look at it.

Then the earth that Lathan had stored in the bolt erupted.

It was like an explosion.

That was something that Lathan hadn't experienced before. Most of the time when capturing elemental power in the binding stones, he was able to pass that power over to another binding stone, and from there, he could transfer it and free his stone so that he could use it again. In this case, having fired the crossbow, he hadn't known what would happen—and certainly hadn't expected that the stone would seem to know that he wanted to unleash the power that was trapped inside.

The Derithan was thrown back.

Henash staggered forward a step.

The ground that had been rumbling around him ceased. The wind whipping calmed. And even the heat in the air seemed to lessen, if only a little.

Henash started toward him.

"Go," Henash urged.

"I fired at him to free you, now don't make me regret wasting that binding stone."

Henash took a step, then something shifted. The air seemed to change, as if it had gotten thicker. He slowed, but Henash strained through it, raising his hand, and pressing outward with what looked to be another binding stone. As he did, the air eased, and he moved forward, making his way over to Lathan at the edge of the trees.

"That was not what I expected," Henash said.

"Really? What did you expect?"

"They wouldn't be that open unless there was something that they truly wanted."

Lathan pushed on Henash, sending him into the cover of the forest. They wouldn't have much time before the Derithan came after them. Lathan didn't know if the trees would shield them, but it seemed to him that the forest seemed to reject the power that had been pushing against them, as if the forest itself knew that there was something dangerous out there and coming at them. Lathan doubted that he could put that kind of intentionality on the forest, but what other explanation would there be?

"Move," Henash said, shoving on him. "We can get ahead of them."

"If it's the shadow, I doubt they'd send that much at us," Lathan said. "I think they use the shadow. To hunt. And they don't like that I bonded to one of their shadow elementals. I think they would destroy me—and us—rather than letting me have access to that."

Henash jogged past a tall pine, resting his hand on the trunk. "You might be right, but we don't' know. The Derithan have been a mystery for a long time. We don't know what they're able to do, only the destruction that follows. Now, we need to keep moving into the forest and see if we can find the others."

The ground trembled.

"They're trying to get through," Lathan said.

"I doubt they'll find it that easy for them to make it into the forest. Oh, they may try, but there's a difference between the elementals that they have managed to capture and some of the old elementals in the world."

He laughed, as if he were making some joke that Lathan should understand.

They hurried forward, and Lathan followed the path that Henash seemed to recognize. He pulled the shadow binding stone out of his pocket, twisting it in his hand for a moment, before slipping it back into his pocket. If that were what they were after, wouldn't it be for the best if he just gave it to them?

When he said as much to Henash, he shook his head.

"They know that you have the shadow, but perhaps all they care about is the hyza. Either way, they know. And now they know you've attacked them. They will push until they no longer have to push because they believe that you will pose too much of a threat to them otherwise. We must keep moving. That is how you're going to stay safe."

The ground trembled again. The wind whistled through the tops of the trees. And when rain began to fall, Lathan couldn't help but feel that it was an elemental attack on them.

All because he'd stored an elemental in a binding stone?

Or was there another reason, one that even Henash didn't know?

CHAPTER 12

By the time they reached the others, Lathan had started to worry that they had gotten caught by the Derithan. They'd been walking for the last hour, and Henash hadn't shared anything more with him, though he would periodically stop and press one of his binding stones into the ground or hold it up to the sky, then bring it back down so that he could cup it in his hand. He did that several times before finally stopping and looking over to Lathan.

"They've eased off. For now. I don't know how much longer it will be that way. I suspect the Derithan have started to search for an alternative way to reach us."

"They wouldn't just follow us here?" Lathan looked around at the trees, trying—and failing—to come up with a reason that the Derithan wouldn't have followed them here. There was nothing about the forest that seemed to be intimidating. There might be a different sort of elemental power here, though if that were the case, it was the kind of power that Lathan had not yet found—or felt. When he focused on the pine trees the way that Henash did, he didn't uncover anything odd. Certainly nothing to suggest the kind of power that Henash seemed to use with the binding stones.

"They might, but that would be a dangerous thing to do. There are powers here they wouldn't be able to control. The Derithan prefer to control the elementals."

They had reached a narrow stream which flowed through this part of the forest. The water was clear, though it burbled softly, and a green film would occasionally drift past. Lathan suspected that was a kind of elemental, but it wasn't one that he was all that familiar with. There were many in these lands that he'd interacted with during his hunts, but others that he'd only read about. Given his lack of access to some of the records within the kingdom, Lathan was at a disadvantage with the elementals, especially compared to some.

"And with the elemental movement, that becomes even more of a challenge," Lathan said.

"I suspect it is more than just that. I'm not entirely sure what it is, but we need to be ready for the possibility that they will continue to move on us." Henash paused at the stream, and he dipped his hand into the water, tracing a pattern as he did. "What do you feel when you come here?"

"I don't think it's time for you to give me a lesson on the elementals. My father has done enough in that regard."

"Oh, I'm sure that he did. Or he intended to. Your

father prepared you much better than most ever have the chance to be. Have you considered the reason why?"

Lathan crouched next to the stream, dipping his hand into the water and taking a drink. "I come from a long line of people who have collected elemental power."

That was one of the first memories of his father, in fact. He'd shared with Lathan how they were collectors, and then had proceeded to show him a variety of different elementals that they would have collected. His father had kept records in a journal, detailing different kinds of elementals. That was where most of Lathan's knowledge of the elementals came from. It was an informal education, nothing like what was taught by those like Henash.

"You certainly do. And I am not asking about that. What I'm getting at is what did your father teach you about the elementals in particular? There's a reason you believe—and know—that the binding stones will work. It's the same reason that you believe the stones don't actually hurt the elementals the way that some believe."

Lathan snorted. That was difficult to deal with. Marin believed that using the binding stones would steal some part of the elemental but she wasn't alone in thinking that way. It had been Lathan's experience that there were plenty of people that were like her.

"They're connected to a greater power," Lathan went on, thinking about the way that his father had described it. "Even though there are hundreds of different kinds of elementals of each element, they are each connected to the same source of power. Earth. Wind. Fire. Water." Those were the primary elements, though there were others. Spirit, though Lathan had never seen an elemental for spirit. Shadow didn't really have a place, though everyone knew that shadow existed. There were a few others like that. "When we bind them, we connect through the elemental to that greater power."

Henash got to his feet, wiping his hands on his jacket, and twisted one of the binding stones that he gripped in his hands as he turned to the rest of the forest. "Far too many people believe that an elemental can be destroyed by connecting to it, but instead, the binding stone allows access to something deeper." Henash regarded Lathan for a moment. "Your father's under-standing of the elementals continues to surprise me."

Henash regarded him for a long moment, and Lathan could see the question in his eyes. They started off again and hadn't gone very far before the wind whistled in the treetops once more, shaking some of the massive pine trees, leaving needles cascading down around them. The ground was soft and spongy, made worse for the rain that poured down through the canopy. Each time that Lathan took a step, his boot stuck, as if earth were trying to hold him. So far, it failed.

They walked a circuitous path through the forest. Each time he questioned Henash about the direction they were taking, the other man waved his hand, dismissing his concern, before he guided them on. He still paused from time to time, lifting his head to smell at the air, but for the most part, he used binding stones that he gripped tightly, as if he were prepared for the possibility that they might be attacked by an elemental. The longer that he used them in that way, the more Lathan began to question if that was how he intended to use them, or if perhaps he had a different purpose behind them. Maybe Henash poured power out from them.

They saw no further evidence of the Derithan.

It was late, long since growing dark, little more than a sliver of moon picking up through the canopy, when Henash started to slow, motioning for him to pause. They reached a small clearing with a series of rocks in a strange formation, almost as if they had been set in that way. Henash approached the rock slowly, and held his hand out, another binding stone held there. The moonlight seem to drape the clearing in silver light, leaving the stones glowing softly. As Lathan approached, he realized why.

"Binding stones?" He looked over to Henash. "All of those are binding stones?"

Henash moved carefully forward, and he stopped at the nearest of the binding stones, pausing and resting his hand upon it. He traced his hand in a circular pattern before finally patting it softly, as if he were talking to the stone itself.

"I thought your father taught you how to harvest binding stones," Henash said.

"He did, but we never found them in places like this."

Most of the time, when Lathan came across binding stones of any quantity, he had to dig it out. It was imperfect and slow work, but it was the only way that he knew how to do it.

Henash rapped his knuckles on one of the stones, and there came a surprising crack, and a piece of stone sheared free. He held it up to the light, twisting it in his hand, before turning and offering it to Lathan. "To resupply you."

"How did you do that?"

Henash held up his hand, and Lathan realized he was clutching a binding stone. "I wish I could say I was just strong enough and managed to break through it, but unfortunately, that isn't the case." He started to laugh. "Earth can crack earth, at least with the right blow. These stones are unique, as you know. They aren't exactly earth. They aren't exactly fire. Or wind. Or water. They are a bit of each, which is how binding stones hold the elemental power." He brought his hand up again, and then slammed it down toward the binding stone once more. Much like the first time, there came a loud crack that carried through the forest, and another chunk of binding stone sheared free, dropping near him.

Henash tucked this one into his own pouch.

"There's so much here. Is this where you sent Marin and the others?"

"Not here. I don't know if she would have even recognized this. I suppose if she was listening well enough, the wind might've guided her, or perhaps the stream, but then again, I wonder if she had known if she would've gone a different direction. She doesn't care much for these."

He brought his hand up again, and slammed it down. The crack that came from him was quieter, less violent. It rumbled steadily and then began to fade.

As it did, another chunk of the binding stone peeled free. It wasn't as large as the others. It was slightly rounded, with some of the sides of the stone carrying irregularities to them that normally were not present. When Lathan harvested binding stone, he used knives and shovels to dig into it and gather it from the earth. Henash's method was not exactly effective, but it wasn't ineffective, either. And having access to the binding stones lying out like this, they didn't need to dig anything.

Lathan made his way into the small clearing and looked at the binding stones. Henash wasn't wrong; it *was* quite the prize, and it was one that he never would have imagined finding—and so close to Gorawl. Not that it was close, but close enough that he could reach it and resupply.

In the moonlight, the stones seemed to glow in a way that made them look like they took on power of the moon and radiated it outward. The effect was amazing. Lathan crouched in front of one of the stones, tracing his hand along the surface of it. The stone felt slightly warm, which left him wondering if the stone had already bonded to something else.

"Are they active?" he asked, glancing toward Henash.

"The activity of a binding stone—especially one like this—is fluid. As you've seen with the stones that you use, some of the stones are active continuously, and some need for you to discharge the elemental from them for it to be effective. And there is something to how the elemental is bound that makes a difference, much like there's something in the way that you carve the stones that makes a difference."

Lathan reached the edge of the clearing, and he looked out into the growing darkness. He was tired—but at the same time, he wasn't as tired as he knew that he should be. The day's events had left him on edge, and made it so that he felt like he *needed* to be alert.

"Where did they go?" he asked, turning briefly so that he could see Henash.

He still carved away at the binding stone, working to peel layers of the stone away. How much would he strip off before he was content with what he could take?

"They won't have gone far. Marin will be easy enough for us to follow, anyway. Either her, or your friend." Henash straightened. He'd gathered nearly a dozen strips of stone that he'd sheered away from the binding stone. "They are connected to the elementals, and we can use that connection to follow them."

Henash dusted his hands on his pants, taking the stones and slipping them into his pouch. Most fit, but there were a few of the stones that were long enough that they jutted out. Lathan had plenty of experience with binding stones, and it told him that stones of that size would be able to hold a more powerful elemental. At least, it would contain a greater amount of the elemental connection to the element, though after having seen the way that Henash had used his elemental power, Lathan was left to wonder if it really even mattered.

"We shouldn't leave them," Lathan said. "We don't know how long they have before the Derithan—"

"The Derithan won't be able to reach them as quickly as you fear. They will be protected. For a time. That's the advantage of the forest." He tapped his hand on one of the stones.

When he did, Lathan turned his attention to the others scattered around the clearing. Was Henash saying what it seemed like he was?

"How many of these are scattered around the forest?" Lathan asked. He'd never seen anything like it before. When he'd harvested binding stones in the past, there had been no elemental power inside of them already. They were inert, and needed for someone—him, preferably—to find the power that would be held within them. "Is that why you think that they can't reach us?"

"There are others," Henash admitted. "In this place and in others like it. These are places of power, and old as well. When you find the power within them, you can learn to follow them. They can provide refuge."

"Which is why you wanted us to come here." Lathan snorted, laughing to himself. "Why not just tell us to come to the forest for that reason?"

That wasn't the only reason, Lathan suspected. And it wasn't until he'd revealed that he thought he had captured a shadow elemental—at least some of shadow's power—that Henash had started to reveal anything to him.

"What was this place?" Lathan turned. It was a clearing in the forest. Nothing more than that. The stones were scattered in no particular pattern that he could tell, but when it came to trapping elementals—and that was what he suspected the intent of the stones here was—there didn't necessarily need to be a pattern.

"Long ago, a place of refuge for those who needed it." His voice trailed off and Henash closed his eyes. "It's said that you can feel the elemental power in a place like this." He breathed in deeply.

"If you knew this was here, why not just come and transfer some of this to the binding stones?" It would be easier than collecting.

"There is no need. And I'm not the only one who understands the utility of places like this."

Lathan regarded him for a long moment. "The king?"

That seemed surprising, but then the king was rumored to understand the elementals as well—or better—than anyone. The armored soldiers that patrolled around Gorawl were nothing compared to the power that the king controlled.

"He's one. Would the king not need to know about such things?"

Lathan closed his eyes again, feeling for the energy. Maybe Henash was right. There was a certain peace in being here, a certain energy that lingered in the air. When he really thought about what he detected, he was acutely aware of that energy, even if he couldn't really do anything about it.

Reaching the edge of the forest, he inhaled deeply.

Maybe it was his imagination, but it seemed to him that the air hung with a different odor on this part of the forest than it did in the clearing. Maybe that was the effect of the binding stones, but he wondered if perhaps there was a different reason that he didn't understand.

"I suppose that he would," Lathan finally said, and he turned so that he could look all around him. "Why not let others know of them?"

"Defenses," Henash said. "These places offer a measure of protection to the kingdom that can't be found in other ways. By having these here, and having the ability to defend the kingdom using them, he keeps us safe. Or can if we were to be under attack."

"And you're just taking some of his binding stones?" Lathan asked with a smile.

"I'm taking what's needed—for *our* safety." He joined Lathan at the trees. "We should keep moving. The others will be waiting for us, only I doubt they know it yet."

Henash started off, whistling softly as he headed forward and through the trees. Lathan looked around the clearing again, wondering if he might find a place like this again, before following him. It was a place of bound elemental power. He could feel it. There was something comforting knowing that a place like that even existed.

He caught up to Henash as he paused near a pair of pine trees that rose in front of them. The pines grew close together, as if they marked some entrance to a path. When Lathan started forward, Henash raised his hand, halting him.

"Not yet."

"What are you waiting for?"

"To make sure we are permitted to pass."

Lathan looked over to him, thinking that he was making some kind of a joke, but he looked completely serious. His brow had furrowed into a tight line, and there was an intensity in his eyes. "How will we know when we are permitted?"

"You listen."

"You're starting to sound like Marin."

"You make fun, but she has learned to listen in ways that many others have not. They feel that there's nothing for them to listen to, but those of us who can feel the elementals can hear them as well."

Lathan had the distinct sense that Henash included him in those who could feel the elementals. He wasn't sure how he felt about that. He certainly didn't think that he could hear them, but he didn't deny that there were times when he could feel them. It seemed to be more prominent when he was tracking the elementals away from the city, as if time removed from the city gave him a way of feeling things that he wouldn't have otherwise.

A faint stirring of wind whispered through the trees, and Henash lowered his hand.

"Now we may go."

He stepped between the pines, rather than going around them.

Lathan looked up. That wind could have been natural, but the way that it had suddenly started to gust like that left Lathan wondering if perhaps it were tied to an elemental. And perhaps it was an elemental that he couldn't fully detect.

Following Henash, there was a strange stirring that washed over him, as if he had stepped into a cold bath. Then it passed, but not before he noticed the wind whipping around him for just a moment.

Henash waited for him.

The trees were not spaced as closely together out here. They seemed almost as if they permitted passing, as if a path had opened. Lathan realized how ridiculous it was for him to think like that, but he could see the path shifting, and he couldn't help believe that it was possible that it had opened.

When he looked back to the pine trees, they were still situated close together. Maybe they *did* serve as some sort of a sentry blocking him from getting through. What would have happened had he not waited the way that Henash had suggested?

"Elementals?" Lathan asked.

"Of a sort. Trees themselves are not—or, at least, are rarely—an elemental, but they live alongside them, and they feel much of the same power of the earth as the elementals. They connect to water. They feel the wind. They are not elementals, but they live among them in ways that we don't always understand."

Lathan looked up at the trees with a different intent than he had before. He'd never considered the fact that trees would be in contact with so many different elementals, but it made a certain sort of sense. "What do the trees tell you, then?"

Henash rested his hand on one of the pine trees. "They tell me that we had better keep moving." He looked behind him, back in the direction that they'd come. "The Derithan remain a danger to us. And we need to keep moving to ensure that we can stay ahead of them."

They hadn't gone very far when Lathan noticed that the wind started to swirl overhead again. At first, he thought that it was something in the forest, as if whatever elementals were here had started to react to what they had done, but then he noticed that the swirling of the wind had a pattern to it.

"Elementals," he whispered.

Henash stopped. The forest had parted slightly, and started to slope upward. They'd been climbing for the better part of several hours since entering the forest, and Lathan hadn't seen anything that would tell him where the others had gone, though Henash seemed to know where he was going.

"Can you see them?" Henash asked.

He'd pulled one of the slender lengths of binding stone that he'd peeled from the other stones in the clearing, and now he was holding it, pointing it upward as if it were a sword that he could use against the night.

"I can't see them. I can feel something," Lathan said.

And he realized that was what it was. There *was* something that he felt, though he didn't know what other than the distinct sense of elemental energy that he'd started to feel aware of.

"Then I think we had better run."

They hurried.

But weren't fast enough.

The ground trembled. The wind gusted. And a haze of heat built around him.

The Derithan had caught up to them.

CHAPTER 13

Henash handed Lathan one of the pieces of binding stone that he'd gathered and nodded solemnly. His eyes darted around, taking in the trees and seeming to pause when he looked to the sky, as if there was something in the shaking of the trees that would help him know what they needed to do. "Hold this. We can use it the way the Derithan use theirs. If it comes to it, you should be able to release some of the stored elemental power in that."

Lathan squeezed the binding stone, all too aware of how it felt almost like it was some sort of a sword. He hefted it the same way he would a sword, something that he'd only done a few times in his life. Lathan had never wanted to be a soldier, unlike so many boys who grew up around him. So many wanted to train with weapons, to serve the king, but Lathan had been content collecting the elementals. It had always felt like something that he was meant to do.

Henash started jogging through the forest, moving quickly and demanding that Lathan keep pace. He did, but each step he took seemed to drag him deeper into the ground, as if the earth were slowly trying to hold onto him. He didn't know if that were the case or if it was nothing more than his imagination, but that was what he could feel.

"They're doing something to me," he muttered.

Henash slowed enough that Lathan could catch up to him, then waved a hand toward him. It was empty other than one of his binding stones, one that was small and seemed to fit easily into the palm of his hand, as if he had carved it in such a way that it fit perfectly. Perhaps it did. Lathan didn't know if he'd done anything like that or not, but why wouldn't he carve them out the same way that Lathan carved out the binding stones for his crossbows? That was an unusual use of binding stones as well, though it worked for him.

"You must push past it. This is going to get worse before it gets better."

"That's reassuring."

"It's not meant to be reassuring. It's meant to be the truth."

Henash motioned again, pointing to the ground. It rippled again, similar to how it had rippled when he'd been trying to outrun the earth elemental when the Derithan had attacked near the edge of the forest.

Lathan managed to get his feet free, and he hurried forward.

Each step became easier. Henash lagged, holding

onto his stone, sweeping it in front of him, and then he froze.

"Henash?"

"Damn them," Henash muttered.

He fumbled for one of the sections of the binding stone that he'd peeled free from the boulders in the clearing, tipping it ever so slightly so that the stone radiated with a hint of energy. Lathan could feel that energy, along with the vibration it carried with it, as the stone wobbled for a moment before going still.

Then Henash staggered free.

The Derithan must be close if they were able to influence him in such a way. Lathan hadn't seen them, but if there was something there that he could feel...

The air hummed.

"Move!"

They raced forward. Henash waved the stone behind them, and it seemed almost as if the trees responded to what he did, bending ever so slightly toward the ground, as if they were trying to get out of the way.

Lathan held onto the binding stone. Even holding it the way that he did, he could feel some of the energy of it. The stone seemed to hold that power, latching onto it, keeping it within the stone. Would he be able to release it the same way that he'd released the power from his own binding stones?

The stone trembled as he held onto it. It seemed to Lathan that the stone knew something was happening—and wanted to be a part of it. That had to be imagined, as he couldn't believe there was any intention to the stone itself, as if it were sentient.

The ground cracked.

A tree near him split, and a branch came tumbling down.

Lathan braced for impact. The branch was enormous. When he held the long, slender binding stone up as if to deflect, the stone seemed to *push* outward, as if there was some part of the stone that pushed back the massive branch falling toward him.

Henash grabbed him and shoved him forward.

Lathan barely managed to stay on his feet.

He staggered forward, and when the crack came again, he threw his hand behind him without even thinking. The air thundered with the sound of another explosion. It took Lathan a moment to realize that it had come from him.

When he looked at the binding stone, Henash pulled on him.

"Not now."

"Was that me?"

"Not you. The stone. Told you there was some sort of power trapped in it. That's what we need to borrow."

"Am I borrowing it or am I releasing trapped power?"

"Does it even matter? All that matters is that we're getting through the forest."

They hurried forward, but Lathan wondered if that was all that mattered. If the Derithan had already caught up to them, then they couldn't lead them toward the others. They needed to lead them *away*.

"Keep up."

Henash tossed something—one of the long, slender binding stones—behind him. It plunged into a tree, far deeper than Lathan would have thought possible.

The tree didn't collapse.

With that kind of power pushed into the tree, he would have expected that it might have. Instead, the tree trembled, then seemed to swell.

Had Lathan not seen it himself, he wasn't sure that he would have been able to really understand what just happened. Elemental power took over the tree and filled it.

Then another tree started to swell. And another.

They formed a line behind them.

Each of the trees had started to change. The tall pines had morphed into something different. Stone seemed to radiate from the trees, as if the trees had been pulled by the power that was there. He tried to understand what he'd just seen, but as before, Henash pulled on him.

"The trees—"

"I know what just happened. You'll have to trust me a bit here. We need to get some distance between us and them, then we'll be able to keep them from following altogether. It's not going to be pretty, but as long as it's effective, pretty doesn't matter."

They raced onward.

The ground that had been trembling began to ease.

The wind didn't whip the way that it had, either.

The forest started to thin. The Derithan didn't catch

them, so he started to think that they might be able to stay ahead of them.

Henash stopped near another line of trees. It was almost a perfect line, as if they had been planted just that way. "Move forward."

"Why? What are you going to do?"

"You'll have to wait. I think this is a place where the cleavage lines should permit this, but I'm not entirely sure. I've been trying to listen, but I'm not as good as others with earth."

Lathan stepped forward, and then Henash took another of the pieces of binding stone that he'd gathered from the clearing and jammed it into the ground. Rather than holding it in place, he shoved it down. The ground began to tremble.

A crack started to form.

"There," he said and jumped across the crack and pushed Lathan forward. "You need to keep moving before this spreads too far."

Lathan backed away but he kept his gaze fixed on the ground in front of him. The earth had split, though the binding stone that he'd used seemed to stay in place, as if it were transfixed by something.

"What's happening?"

"The binding stone is asking the earth to create enough of a separation that they won't be able to get to us. It'll delay them, but I doubt that it's going to be effective for long. As you've seen, they have powerful elementals they can use, and it's possible that it won't take them long to find an earth elemental that can bridge this. The only hope that we have is that I'm borrowing from the elementals that are here naturally so there's a bit more potency in that."

The gap continued to spread and grow deeper. Soon a massive ravine stretched in front of them. Lathan wouldn't be able to reach the other side, and when he approached, he could see the bottom far below.

It would be enough. It had to be.

Henash pulled him away from the gap and they headed deeper into the forest, away from the soft glowing. When they reached the trees that were on the opposite side of the new ravine, the wind whistled around them before falling still. It seemed to him that the wind approved, but why would he think that?

They moved on, no longer hurrying the way that they had before. Lathan kept pausing to listen, thinking that they might run into more of the Derithan, but there was no sign of them. Nothing to make him think that they could even chase them.

The sky had started to lighten when he felt a trembling of the ground.

It lasted a while before finally fading.

"Did they cross?" Lathan asked.

Henash frowned, tilting his head to the side as if listening, then shook his head. "I don't think so. Like I said, the earth is strong here. Now, we should hurry. I think I see the others, but we need to get to them before the Derithan figure out another way around."

They picked their way forward, moving toward what Henash had seen. Lathan followed, though he hadn't noticed the same thing as Henash. Every so often, he noticed another faint trembling, and he started to think that whatever was there had truly been thwarted. The chasm that had been formed by Henash using the bonded elementals must have worked the way he intended.

The landscape changed the farther that they went. The trees continued to thin, and there was less of the dry grass and more of a plush meadow that stretched around them. He held onto the binding stone in one hand, hesitating to let it go after having been chased for as long as they had.

Then they found a small path.

Henash took the path, weaving along it as they gradually descended down what looked like a narrow ravine. The rock tumbled as he stepped, slipping beneath his feet, but he caught himself and managed to keep from spilling down to the valley below. That was where Henash led them.

After descending for a while, Lathan started to notice shapes.

They were faint. He couldn't see much other than dark figures that looked to be slipping along the ground, but as they stepped further down the path leading toward the valley floor, he started to think that maybe they *had* finally found the others.

The wind had shifted.

At first, he thought that it was his imagination, but the more that he paid attention to the wind—listening, in a way—the more that he could feel the wind as it gusted and could feel some part of it pushing on him. The wind seemed to start from someplace high overhead, and as it swept toward him, he found it working through him in a way that seemed as if the wind wanted to pull the breath from his lungs.

"Elementals," he said.

Henash looked up. "They've been following us for a while now. They won't harm us."

Lathan had been taught the same thing by his father, though it was more of a cautious approach, one where he was to believe that the elementals could harm them but not that they wanted to.

The wind continued to whip toward him as if it wanted to tear his breath out of his chest. There were stories of angry elementals that had harmed collectors when they'd gotten too close to them without having adequate preparation. There were ways to ensure that the elementals didn't attack, but it involved having a binding stone around you in such a way that would keep the elemental from risking such an attack. He had a binding stone—the feeling of the wind whipping around him was the reason that he'd clung to the binding stone as long as he did, wanting to ensure that he was protected if the elemental were to attack.

They stepped forward, and he noticed a slight stirring along the ground.

Lathan looked up. The shadow might be a bird or another flighted elemental. There were plenty of powerful elementals that could fly, though he would have expected to have seen one before now if they were out there and coming for them. The gray sky was empty.

Which meant shadow.

"Henash," he said, starting carefully. He knew better than to startle a shadow elemental as he didn't know if there was anything he needed to be careful about. Now he had the binding stone angled downward, pointing at the ground so that he could dismiss the elemental were it to come for them. "I don't want to startle you, but I *think* there's a shadow elemental just off the path."

"I see it," Henash said, his voice tight and strained. "Keep moving. If it starts to come toward us, I want you to use the binding stone on it."

"I'm not sure that earth is going to scare away shadow." There was a hierarchy when it came to elementals. Lathan wasn't exactly sure where shadow fit in, but thought that it would be somewhere above earth, especially with what he'd seen of shadow in the past.

"I'm not talking about using the earth-bound stone. Use your shadow stone. I don't know if it'll come to that, but you should be prepared for the possibility that it will."

Lathan reached into his pocket, grabbing for the other binding stone. He hadn't considered that might be necessary but maybe he was right. If they needed to use something against the shadow, they should use a similar elemental. That might be enough to push it back.

Might.

The shadow swirled closer.

It still hadn't come onto the path, though the further

that they walked, the more it started to get nearer to the path, making him think that the elemental was trying to decide whether it would move toward them. If it did, Lathan had to be ready.

The binding stone for shadow was cool. He squeezed it, and the shadows swirled toward him again. A slight energy in the stone crackled out and around Lathan.

"It's working," he said.

Henash nodded. "I thought that it might. I wasn't sure. It really depends upon what type of shadow you've bonded."

"I didn't realize there were that many different types of shadow."

"There are different types of earth, wind, fire—"

That didn't make complete sense to Lathan, as shadow was shadow, but within each other type of elemental, there were variant forms the elementals could take.

After another few steps, a rock slipped beneath Lathan's boot.

Henash tried to catch himself before tumbling down the rock, but the rock carried him. Lathan struggled to keep on his feet. The ground trembled. Earth worked against him. That was the only explanation that he had for why it would move so quickly and so hard against him.

He went to the ground and rolled.

Lathan reached for the binding stone, pushing it out from him so that he could use it to hold the earth. When he did, the ground exploded.

He was tossed into the air and went rolling to the side. Lathan tucked his head down, then felt a surge of wind.

It carried him *up*.

He flailed.

Lathan had been around angry elementals before. It was difficult to work as a collector and not have any experience with an angry elemental. Some—well, most of them—didn't care much for the way that collectors would stalk them and try to draw elemental power off them.

This was something else.

The wind carried him, pulling him upward, and though he had the binding stone, it wasn't going to let him back down. Lathan tried to swirl the binding stone in the air, thinking that he might be able to use that to catch some of the elemental power and keep the elemental from sending him even higher, but that didn't work.

"Henash!"

His voice was cut off by the wind.

Lathan flew.

There wasn't any other way to describe it. Though he flailed against the wind pulling on him, he was soaring through the sky, heading away from Henash and the others. The binding stone wasn't going to work to help hold him in place, despite how much he tried to work with it.

Another gust of wind caught him.

This time, Lathan went up the slope that they'd been

climbing.

As he did, he understood what was happening. The Derithan had to be using the wind against him.

Why me?

Was it the shadow elemental that he'd bonded with the binding stone? Or maybe it was that the two of them had run from them and the Derithan didn't like losing. Whatever the reason, he felt as if he had to keep fighting.

A haze worked around him.

Sandor.

That was the elemental that had ahold of him now. As sandor whipped around him, he tumbled, bringing him ever higher into the sky. He tried to fight against it, but he couldn't.

Another pressure of wind.

This time it swirled near him, sending him back down the slope.

Now it felt as if there were two different kinds of wind that were battling to try and hold him. One of them pushed on him, trying to send him up the slope, and the other worked to send him down the slope.

Could Henash be trying to help him?

He had a control over the wind, though his control over the wind was something different than what Lathan had seen from the Derithan. They had considerable power and could use that to carry him the way that they had carried the hyza. Were he not careful, he'd be drawn to the Derithan and then...

Another surge of wind.

This one carried him even higher.

He rolled and looked down at the ground beneath him. The valley was far more rugged than he had realized. The stone cut downward, creating a massive wound that spread below him. It reminded him of what Henash had done when using the binding stone, only on a greater scale.

Then another gust caught him.

He was thrown even higher.

Lathan couldn't scream, though he was terrified.

He feared suddenly falling. The wind didn't release him, but he worried about what would happen if it were to do so. There was the sense of competing elementals pushing on him, almost as if he were caught between them as they held him aloft.

Henash was down there. Lathan saw him standing with his hands upstretched. A hint of the pale gray of the binding stone caught his attention. It *was* Henash who was responsible for keeping him from sailing away. Lathan tried to direct his movement more, letting the wind keep pulling on him, thinking that he might be able to use that to direct himself back to Henash, but the wind whipped at him, and his arms flailed out to either side again.

The binding stone.

That was what the wind was after. It was trying to rip the binding stone from his grip. Lathan had to hold onto it tightly or he'd lose complete control. For now, he still could hold onto it, but if the wind elemental—or both or more, depending on how many were here—had their way, they'd tear the stone from his grip, and he'd drop it to the ground below.

He held tightly, but even as he did, the wind continued to tear at him.

When a shadow slipped around him, Lathan was too startled to do anything but squeeze the stone again, hoping that he might be able to hold onto it.

How would shadow be here?

That thought was followed by another surge of shadow, one that slipped outward—and then wrapped around him.

And then Lathan was falling.

CHAPTER 14

The wind no longer pulled at him the same way.

Lathan tried to kick at the shadow, but it didn't make a difference. The darkness had completely engulfed him, and now swallowed him, blotting out some of the light—though, not all of it. Lathan could make out the ground screaming toward him, moving faster and faster as he dropped toward it, watching as his death raced toward him.

This is it.

This was how he would die. From the elementals.

When he'd learned how to collect elementals, he had never considered that they would pose a danger to him. They were wild, but no more wild than some of the animals that were found around Gorawl. There were foxes and wolves and even feral cats that could be plenty nasty. All wild, and all dangerous in their own right. The elementals were not dissimilar to that. They were unknowable in so many ways, but they were also wild—and powerful.

The very first elemental that he'd hunted to collect had been with his father, like so many of the elementals. It was a small elemental of earth. Lathan's father had always enjoyed chasing the more mobile earth elementals, mostly because he thought there was something of a game to it. In the case of when they'd gone after the bulgan, a tiny elemental that looked like a rock with four legs and two tiny eyes that were no more than pits in what made up its head, the bulgan *had* treated it like a game.

"See the way it pokes its head up?" his father had whispered. "Something like a groundhog."

Lathan had been lying on a ridgeline, looking out toward a rocky field. He hadn't known what they would find, though his father had seemed more than excited about taking him out on this excursion. Nervous? Lathan didn't think that was likely. His father was never nervous. But when he'd been collecting the binding stones that he'd bring with them, he had been whispering to himself, speaking softly as if he were trying to convince the binding stones that they needed to listen to what he wanted of them.

"Are you sure it's not a ground hog?" They had plenty of them around here, and the small creatures could be playful. Lathan had once asked why animals weren't considered elementals, or even people, for that matter, and had been told that it was because they didn't attach to the bond—whatever that meant.

"Quite sure. You'll see."

They had lain in wait. There had been a faint breeze, a steady slipping of the current around them, though it was nothing to suggest a wind elemental. There were faint aspects of the breeze that would warn you if an elemental were present—and you wanted to be warned. The air was still, the smell of the dampness from the recent rain filling his nostrils, but soaking his pants where they knelt. Even then, Lathan had known not to move too quickly, nor to get up when his father believed there was something he wanted to show him.

For a long time, he saw nothing.

Lathan grew bored, but his father had trained him to be patient. "They aren't coming."

His father sniffed softly. "You need to find a calm within yourself. The elementals react to that. Find your calm, then they won't fear revealing themselves. It's when you're nervous—"

"You're nervous," Lathan said, looking over to his father.

His black hair was tucked beneath the hood of his cloak, as if he didn't want it to reveal that they were there. The cloak was a dappled gray, and would blend into the stone, though didn't do such a good job of that here. A small scar on his chin was distinctive, a mark from 'a mistake made long ago' that Lathan longed to hear about. "Not for the elementals, though. For you."

He turned back to watching.

Lathan had to find the calm within himself. That wasn't

the first time that his father had suggested that he needed to find a measure of calm. He tried, and though he knew how to steady his breathing, the calm—finding peace within himself and not allowing the nerves to show—was harder.

Boredom made it easier.

Then the rock in the distance started to move.

Lathan tensed, but his father pressed his hand on Lathan's. "Stay calm. Focus on your breathing. Remember you won't be hurt."

Him saying that Lathan wouldn't be hurt was enough to make him question if perhaps he *would* be hurt. *Find the calm.* That part was about breathing. Lathan had worked on breathing. It was useful for more than just chasing elementals. His father had taught him to find his breathing when using the bow—or the crossbow that Lathan preferred. It required a series of deep breaths that would trick his breathing into slowing, or so his father had always told him.

The next part was maintaining his focus.

Lathan was less certain that he could do that. The focus now was difficult as he could feel anxiety beginning to build within him—along with the excitement. He *wanted* to see the elemental, but if he were too eager, the elemental would react to that and disappear.

And it was *close*.

Lathan thought that he could pick up a rock near him and throw it, were he to want to, not that he would do that to an earth elemental. *We don't hurt the elementals. We borrow from them.*

"See?" his father whispered. "Stay calm, and they won't pay any attention to you."

"Until we use the binding stones on them," he said.

"Just watch," his father suggested.

The small stone creature turned slowly, then it dipped its head back down, blending into the rock. Had Lathan not seen it popping up, he wouldn't have known it was even there. Having seen it, he still didn't know how to find it again—until it popped up again. This time it kept its head up for longer, then started to turn.

Another popped up. Then another.

There were *three*?

Lathan felt his excitement starting to rise, but his father squeezed his arm again, a warning to relax. That required that he find a measure of calm that he wasn't exactly sure that he had. Instead, he started to focus on his breaths, thinking about what he would need to do so that he could calm himself again.

"There you go," his father said, now his voice little more than a faint whisper. "Watch."

The bulgar started to roll. *Not only that,* Lathan realized. They were *playing*.

He smiled. The stones slipped over each other, rock rolling around, sounding like a rockslide, as the bulgar chased each other around in a circle that got slowly wider. One of them paused at one point and lifted another small rock in its stone hands.

"That's—"

"It is," his father whispered.

A binding stone. His father must have placed them earlier, knowing that they would find the bulgar. As the bulgar turned the stone in place, it held it up, and the others each grabbed it. There was a flash of soft white, then they dropped it and scurried off, disappearing once more.

Lathan watched, expecting that they'd poke their heads up again, but they never did. They stayed down or had disappeared altogether.

"Now we collect," his father said.

He moved carefully, watching every step that he took, which forced Lathan to do the same. He didn't see anything on the ground in front of him, but with his father cautiously moving forward, Lathan figured that he should do the same.

When they reached the binding stone, his father crouched down, whispered something softly that Lathan couldn't hear, then picked up the stone. "They gave themselves to the stone," his father said. "They may not have known what they were doing, but they permitted the stone to take some of their connection."

"But you don't always collect like that."

He'd heard the stories of his father stalking dangerous elementals until he managed to catch them and use his binding stone on them. None of his stories had been like what he'd seen here. Nothing that suggested that he'd have the elementals give some of themselves to the binding stone. Elementals could be dangerous. That was what his father had always taught him. But these elementals didn't seem like that to him at all. They seemed to do just what his father had suggested and had willingly grabbed the binding stone.

"I don't always collect like that. The bulgar are small, so they need a different—and more delicate—touch than other elementals. Some are much larger, so you have to treat them differently."

"Because they're stronger?"

His father handed him the binding stone. "Size doesn't equate to strength with the elementals. Think of what you know of the wind. Ara isn't the largest of the wind elementals. Often one of the smaller ones. But that doesn't mean that ara isn't powerfully connected to the wind." He squeezed the binding stone for a moment. "That's no different with bulgar. They aren't weak. Just connected differently. When we borrow from them and when we ask them to give up a part of their connection to the element, we are asking for a specific part of them. That's what we need to remember." He slipped the stone into his pocket and swept his hand out and around him. "Some elementals will fight you no matter what you do. That's in their nature. They enjoy the fight, so you must enjoy it to collect from them. Others prefer the chase, and you must as well. Still others are clever, though you might not know it at the time. You have to be clever to borrow from them. Bulgar likes to play. So I knew that I needed to give them something to play with." He patted his pocket. "And now we have collected a connection to earth that we can sell. Easy as that."

He turned, picking his way across the stones, careful in certain places and for reasons that Lathan couldn't quite detect. When his father jumped, Lathan jumped. He didn't know why, but he wanted to be like his father, so he did as he asked.

They reached the ridgeline where they'd been crouching and studying the bulgar. His father knelt again, turning back.

Lathan did the same.

It didn't take long before more of the bulgar returned. They started slipping around, stone tumbling around them as they chased each other around the small stone clearing. They watched for a while, long enough that a question came to him.

"Why don't you collect more from them?" he whispered. Lathan wanted to be careful now. He didn't feel nervous the way that he had, but he didn't want to scare the elementals away. They were fun to watch.

"Oh, I'm certain that we could, but just because we *can* do something doesn't mean that we *should*. They're playing. I made a game of it before, and they held onto the binding stone long enough that we collected some of the earth aspect they connect to, but were we to do that to more of them, I'm not sure that's a game they'd play. It's better to leave them so that we can come back another time."

"Will they always be here?" Elementals were so rare that he'd thought that a strange possibility. If his father knew how to find them, then there wasn't a game to be played.

"Not always." He turned serious then. "There are some who feel differently than I do. They don't have any difficulty collecting and collecting—draining, essentially —from the elementals. It weakens them if you take too much, you know. A little doesn't hurt and they'll quickly recover, but take too much..."

He never finished explaining what would happen were they to take too much. Lathan wished that his father would tell him more, but it seemed as if that wasn't a part of the lesson that he wanted Lathan to learn this day.

They picked their way back toward their home, his father saying little more, but the lessons about the elementals and how to connect to them stuck with him. They stayed with him now even as he fell.

The air continued to whistle, and he had to find a way to understand the elemental, but to do it quickly so that he didn't land and die horribly. He didn't seem to be falling as fast as he thought that he should, though with the shadow around him, he didn't think that he'd be able to see much anyway.

Everything within him had gone tense. He knew that there was nothing that he could do about it but also knew that he had to find some way to relax, otherwise he'd end up tumbling painfully to a landing.

How could he find a way to calm himself?

That was what his father had wanted for him. Find a way to get calm, and from there, he could try to see what he could feel of the elemental. Each elemental had a different way of connecting to the world—which meant that he could find his way of connecting to the elemental, but only if he could find it fast. He had so little time.

Lathan breathed slowly.

What did it matter? Whatever he did wouldn't change the fact that the elementals had swirled around him. It wouldn't change that he wasn't in control of what they did to him. The only thing that fighting and struggling would do would be to force him to have less concentration and focus, which he needed now.

That realization helped him relax.

Not entirely, but once he started relaxing, he managed to relax even more. With each passing moment, he could feel his body unclenching. Then he could focus on what he detected around him. The chill from the elemental. The sound of the wind—though muted, it was there—whooshing in his ears. The smell... that was unexpected. Lathan hadn't paid much attention to the smell of elementals, but they all had one.

When he'd chased hyza, the elemental smelled of char and ash, the burned heat that came from fire. That was expected. The effect from the elemental was subtle, though it was one of the few things about hyza that was subtle. With earth, Lathan could smell the soft hint of forest fragrance, that of pine or rotting leaves, sometimes the sharp scent of decaying berries, even the smell of wet earth, though that was odd considering it mixed another element in with it. Wind could often carry the smells of wherever it came from, gusting with the blowing wind of its source, and breathing toward him when it readied to release its connection. And water wasn't just water, but sometimes smelled of wet dog or fish or had a mineral bite to it.

The shadow had a very different smell.

While the touch was cold, there was something to it that reminded Lathan of all of those elementals. It was as if the shadow had absorbed some part of each of them, held it, and used that. Lathan didn't understand the shadow elemental—they were rare enough that he'd never even expected to encounter one—but if they were somehow combined energies of other elements...

Why am I even thinking about that?

Because the fall lasted longer—far longer—than he had expected. And Lathan wanted to keep his mind on anything other than the possibility of his own demise. He felt as if he couldn't think of much else, though. Just the fall.

The wind had stopped moving around him.

The shadows seemed to cradle him, making it difficult to know with any certainty if it *had* stopped, but he thought that through the gusting of the wind, he could hear that something had changed.

Was he floating? How had the elemental held onto him? Perhaps it was only in his mind—or perhaps he was dead. Shadows were often tied to death, though that wasn't the way that it felt to him. He didn't feel as if he were any different than he'd been. In fact, he felt the same. Maybe better. He had relaxed enough that his mind had started to work, letting him get unstuck from the fear of the elemental and the chase and everything that had been happening around him. With the change, he could feel the power, but he could also feel that there was something that tried to hold him—but didn't try to harm him.

Lathan tried to move his arms, but they didn't work the way he thought they should. His arms were locked at his sides, and anytime that he tried moving, it seemed as if the darkness stretched out and grabbed him again, holding him in place.

The shadows didn't want him to reach outward.

There had to be a reason. Elementals had intent. They weren't mindless things. Some were smart, like a clever dog. In the stories, the elementals that had once talked to people had been more than just clever like that. They'd been intelligent. That hadn't been Lathan's experience, but then he'd never bothered to try to listen the same way that some did.

Marin would probably just tell him that he made a mistake in not listening to the elementals. Were his father still around, he would have said the same thing. It was about listening to what the elementals wanted, and giving that to them, even if it wasn't what he wanted.

What did the shadow want?

Other than to hold me.

Lathan didn't think there was anything he could give the elemental that it wanted. The shadow had tried to slip away from him when he'd used the binding stone on it. And now...

The shadow didn't try to run from him now.

It had slipped *around* him.

Was it trying to capture and hold him, or was there a different reason?

Understand them.

Those were his father's words, and they stayed in the back of his mind, lingering there as he tried to come up with what his father would have done. He wouldn't have gotten into this situation, though. He would have understood something about this kind of elemental before getting caught by it.

Lathan let his eyes fall closed.

He could feel the cold. Smell the hints of each of the other elements. That seemed significant. And he noticed a soft pressure on his skin, as if the shadow were trying to press around him. That was new—he was certain of it.

The shadow squeezed, but it wasn't just the way that the shadow squeezed, it was that it seemed to squeeze all around him and all at one time. That shadow pressed on him in a way that he could feel wrapping all around him, something like a blanket. A cold blanket.

When it started to squeeze even more, Lathan didn't worry.

The shadow had had been squeezing on him, pressing as if it were trying to squeeze through him, but not painfully. That was something that he'd been feeling since detecting the elemental around him, and he hadn't worried about it. Surprisingly, there was something comforting about it.

Slowly, though, the squeezing started to change.

It began to *hurt.*

Lathan tried not to react.

That was what his father had warned him about. Don't react. Don't do anything that the elemental would react to. Maybe he'd grown tenser because he'd been worried about what was happening and how he didn't seem to be falling anymore. Maybe it was that he had let some of his angst begin to spread outward. Whatever it was, he knew that he needed to find a way to relax again.

The squeezing shifted. Now it burned.

The burning was cold, reminding him of jumping in a just thawed lake at the end of winter. It made his breath catch, and when he tried to take another breath, it burned through him as well, as if the cold were trying to make it difficult for him to do anything. Lathan focused, thinking through everything that his father had ever told him about the elementals, but nothing fit with what he experienced now. His father had not given him much in terms of what to do when the elementals attacked.

The squeezing intensified.

The cold felt like it was *in* him. The pressure felt like it was in him.

The pain was enormous. Lathan couldn't think of anything other than the pain, the way that it left every part of him throbbing. It took his mind away from the fear of the Derithan attacking, the wind that had been trying to pull him away from Henash and the others. It took his mind away from everything other than the pain.

It was everywhere. Everything.

Darkness began to squeeze through him.

The shadow elemental was attacking him.

But it shouldn't even be an elemental. When he'd used the binding stone, he'd trapped some of the elemental energy within the stone, but he hadn't trapped an elemental. There were some who could, but Lathan didn't know how to do it. Even if he did, he would never have tried to do it, and certainly not against the shadow elemental.

The cold surged again.

Now it felt a part of his heart, pain surging with every pulsation through his veins. His lungs, burning cold with every breath. And his mind was so cold that all thoughts seemed to freeze, stopping inside of him.

Blackness overwhelmed him.

Lathan tried to fight, but he couldn't. The last thought that he had before he completely blacked out was that the elemental would do what the Derithan had wanted and destroy him. And then would move on to get the others.

CHAPTER 15

The cold eased.

Lathan thought it was his imagination at first. He'd lost track of how long the cold had been holding him, squeezing around him. He had started to think that would be all he'd know, but when he came around, the cold wasn't the same pressure that it had been before.

And the darkness around him had faded.

Not just faded. The darkness around him was gone. It had lifted.

Lathan blinked. He stood on a rocky ridgeline, stones slipping down from where he'd dropped. Had the wind lowered him, or had there been something else that had dropped him to the ground?

"What happened to you?"

Lathan turned, and the world spun around him, leaving him with streaks of darkness around the corners of his vision. It was a blur that passed, though seemed to linger longer than he had expected.

"Henash?"

A hand squeezed his arm. It felt warm and comforting, so much better than the cold that had started to press into his mind and so much better than how he'd felt with the wind threatening to toss him out and into the sky.

"I'm here. You got ripped upward and then floated there. I tried to do what I could to stop the wind, but that elemental power was more than I could control. I thought... well, I suppose it doesn't matter what I thought, only that I started to think the Derithan had grabbed you and were going to drag you back to them."

That was the same thought Lathan had. That the wind had released him—

Only the wind hadn't released him, had it?

The change had come from the shadow appearing.

That was the reason that he'd gotten free, though now he wasn't sure what had happened to free him from the shadow. Lathan looked upward, but as he stared at the sky, he didn't see any sign of the darkness that he had seen before. It was gone.

Lathan knew that he hadn't imagined that, though he didn't know why there would have been something that would have washed over him the way that it had. The shadow had squeezed him—and had squeezed through him.

"I don't even know what happened," he said, turning his attention back to Henash. "I could feel... I suppose it doesn't matter what I could feel, only that it was there, and it seemed to be all around me."

"How did you get out?"

Lathan glanced upward again. "To be honest, I have no idea. The only thing that I know was the wind seemed to release me. I don't know why, but I could feel that it was there, swirling around me, and then there was nothing."

Henash regarded him a moment, then patted him on the shoulder again. "Come on. I think we should keep moving before the Derithan decide to try another attack. If they think that last one was possibly successful, I wouldn't put it past them to try again."

Henash started down a narrow path, picking his way along the rock in a way that reminded Lathan of how his father had done the same with the bulgar when he'd taught Lathan how to play with them. Lathan didn't feel ready to follow him. He looked back in the direction that they'd come, studying the rock around him. He had come to a landing—and not hard enough to kill him the way that he'd thought it would be—not all that far from where he'd been before. Had Henash had a hand in that? Lathan wouldn't have put it past him to have tried to use the wind to keep him from crashing down.

He didn't see anything. The wind had fallen still again, leaving him thinking that maybe the wind hadn't been the problem in the first place. Maybe it had only been the shadow that had wanted to attack him. He *had* smelled the different scents that reminded him of the other elementals, so why wouldn't the elemental be able to draw on other aspects of the other elements?

Because it's shadow.

But what was shadow elemental? A shadow was a reflection, wasn't it? Light pushing off of an object and leaving a reflection of what had been there before. Why couldn't the shadow also have some way of using the other elements?

Lathan inhaled deeply and started down the side of the rock, picking his way carefully, stepping over the stone, and trying not to pay too much attention to the occasional chill that washed through him. He knew it was there, though he wanted to ignore it--even as it was increasingly difficult to do.

He caught up to Henash at the base of the trail. He waited for Lathan, and regarded him with a question that seemed to linger in his eyes.

"Did you keep me from falling?"

"Not me. The elementals sort of lowered you. I didn't get a good look. There was too much dust mixed with the wind for me to see anything clearly. Since you noticed sandor before, I suspect that's what it was."

Could that have been what it was? He didn't know if sandor had been a part of the wind attack. There had been competing winds, though even as he'd felt that, he hadn't known which one was which. Lathan had been too caught up in the nerves of what had been taking place to pay attention to that sort of thing.

"I guess so. I thought that I would have ended up there," he said, pointing behind him. The hillside rose in the distance, though it was quiet now. Lathan turned back to Henash. "When the wind first lifted me, I was carried toward that. I thought... I guess it doesn't matter that much what I thought."

As they continued along the path, a faint cold came through him, though he didn't know if it was from the memory of what had happened or because he still had a remnant of that cold from the shadow.

"I saw something," he said after they'd been going for a little while. In the distance, he thought that he could make out the shapes of the others that had been in their party, though now that even felt like an eternity ago. "When the wind caught me, I was up there, and shadow swallowed me."

Henash looked back at him. "It might have been sandor. From down here, it looked as if the elemental were thickening."

Lathan nodded slowly, but that wasn't what he thought he'd experienced. Maybe it had been sandor, but he wasn't sure. "This was not the same as sandor," he said. "I could feel the cold. I smelled other elements. It was shadow. And it started to squeeze me. I don't know what it was, but I thought that it was shadow."

They picked their way forward without Henash saying anything. A stone slipped beneath his boot, and he thought that maybe it was an earth elemental working against him, but then more began to slide around them. Not earth, but a normal rockslide.

"It's possible that you would have felt shadow, but

such a thing is rare. Incredibly rare. And for you to survive it..."

"I know it's rare, but I know what it felt like."

When he closed his eyes, Lathan could still feel it. That part seemed the most disconcerting, almost as if the cold remained there within him when he let himself find it drifting through him. He didn't want to think back to that cold, nor did he want to remember the pain that he'd felt when it had begun to work through him, but it was difficult for him to think of much else.

His foot slipped again. Henash was there—but not Henash.

Wind lifted him ever so slightly, propping Lathan up so that he didn't fall. It was a faint swirl of wind, little more than a slight torrent that circled around him before fading again, but when it came, Lathan felt something else. It was the cold. It surged again within him, a reaction that felt almost involuntary—or like the shadow hadn't left him completely.

He looked over to Henash, who remained fixed on the valley below them, continuing to make his way down. He'd used the wind to help Lathan but then hadn't paid any more attention to him—or what he'd needed.

Lathan stepped forward again, rubbing his hands on his arms. It did nothing to warm him up, though the cold seemed to fade. Now that cold felt like it was a part of him, some place buried within him, but it was definitely there.

He waited for Henash to turn or for him to say something, but he didn't. Instead, he continued to pick his way forward, leaving Lathan wondering if there would be anything more he would need to do to make sure he didn't end up slipping—or surrounded by the cold again.

They continued walking in silence. Lathan was more careful, making sure that he didn't slip, following Henash, but increasingly finding his way along the narrow path. He saw no sign of other elementals, though the cold sense lingered inside of him.

"It's not much farther," Henash said.

Lathan looked up. They had gotten closer to the floor of the valley, and now he could see the figures up ahead. They were close enough that Lathan thought he should be able to make out their features, but it was difficult for some reason, though he wasn't sure if that was the distance or if they used some connection to the wind to make it so that they could hide.

The valley itself had started to shift. Now there were colorful flowers spread all along the valley, different daisies and a few meadow flowers. Their fragrance carried to him, but not as much as he would have expected. That had to be the wind. For whatever reason, the wind kept the smell of the valley from reaching them. The ground had changed from a rocky path to a hard-packed dirt path, though occasionally, they would step in a soggy section of the pathway that Lathan had to pry his boot free from.

"Are they waiting on us?" Lathan asked.

"I suspect Marin has known that we're coming."

The wind fluttered a moment, as if in answer.

Lathan looked up to where it gusted from, though he

didn't see any elemental there. He could feel it, and he suspected that the elementals were active, especially given what he'd felt, but the more that he stared, the less that he noticed, other than the wind.

"She doesn't store the elementals in the bond, so what's she using?" Lathan asked.

"You know the answer to that without asking."

"She's just *asking* the wind to help?"

Henash paused, looking to Lathan for a moment. There was a strange light in his eyes as he regarded him, and he reached toward his pouch, withdrawing one of the binding stones and holding it close to himself. He didn't point it at anything, but just held it as if he were concerned that he'd need to use it to bind some dangerous elemental. Did he know—and feel—the strange cold that Lathan did?

"There are ways of asking the elementals for help that don't require a binding stone. Not many are capable of doing it, mostly because they don't have the patience to listen, but if you can listen and if you learn the way to ask, you never have to have the elementals working against you. I don't know with any certainty, but I suspect that Marin long ago learned how to listen. The question that I've always had was whether the elementals were willing to answer." He turned away. "That had been my question before this journey. I think Marin and the elementals have decided to answer that question quite definitively."

He smiled, seemingly pleased with the comment.

As they pressed forward, there was a hint of the wind

that persisted, and it continued to push against Lathan. It was more than pushing against him, though. It seemed as if the wind were trying to press through him, the same way that he remembered the shadow seeming to try to press into him. As he felt it, the wind seemed to react with the cold buried within him, squeezing down into something painful and tight, the shadow hiding from the wind.

They reached a section that looked as if it were stone cut away into stairs, and they stepped down it. Far below, the ground had a faint haze, a bit of fog that swirled with the wind. Then Lathan noticed something else.

Binding stones.

There were several down below as well, much like the binding stones that he and Henash had come across in the clearing in the forest where they'd harvested some of the stone. The more that he watched, the more that he realized that the binding stones seemed to be the source of the swirling haze, the energy within the stones pressing out and radiating into the air around it.

"It's another place like the last one," he said in a whisper. It felt right to whisper here, as if doing anything else would disturb the quiet of this place and the quiet that belonged to the elementals.

"I wondered if they might find themselves drawn to it," Henash said. "And I can't say that I'm surprised she would have been drawn here if she has a true connection to the elementals."

"You've known her for years. How is it that you never really knew what kind of connection she had?"

He glanced to Lathan. "You've known her for years as well. Did you know what kind of connection she had, or did you think that it was nothing more than someone who *wanted* to have a way of speaking to the elementals?"

Lathan supposed he was right. With Marin, it was more that he had thought she was a little odd, but only because of how she claimed she could speak to elementals that others couldn't even see.

They reached the bottom of the valley. The ground was much softer than it had been, and as he made his way forward, he kept looking around for any sign that the earth might start to try to pull them down. It was soft enough here that he wouldn't be surprised if the earth attempted something like that, though there wasn't anything.

The air smelled damp, and the floral fragrance that had been flirting with his nostrils faded, leaving a hint of a heavier scent, something like that of wet earth and grass. The haze was less down in the valley itself than it had appeared from above. Stepping into the valley made it so that they were no longer subject to the strangeness from above.

The cold was there.

It seemed to know that they were near the other elementals, those that were bound to this place. The elemental reacted.

Lathan thought of it in those terms. The elemental

was there, and it was within him, as if the elemental were somehow filling him and reacting to the things that were around him. It was a trace of cold, little more than that, but that trace of cold lingered within him in a way that left him thinking that it would eventually keep pushing through him.

Henash stepped forward, raising his hands, one of the binding stones still in the middle of his palm. The wind swirled around him, lifting the haze in reaction to Henash and seemingly listening to his command as he brought his hands above him to try to banish the light fog.

"We know you're here," Lathan said, stepping forward.

The cold seemed to bury itself inside of him.

The haze thickened a moment.

Lathan looked over to Henash, who had started to frown.

"What's the problem?" Lathan asked.

"Something is not quite right."

He swirled his hands around, the wind lifting with his movement, the haze starting to part but not so much that it disappeared altogether. The more that he swept his hands around him, the more that the haze started to climb, but it was still there.

"Do you feel anything?" Henash asked.

Lathan started to respond, wanting to tell him that he felt the cold, though he didn't know if that meant anything or not. At this point, the cold that he detected could be nothing more than just a surge that flowed from the air around them. They *had* dropped lower in the valley, though, so Lathan thought that it should be warmer, not colder.

None of that was what he felt, though. What he felt was a different surge. This was a faint stirring. It seemed to come from somewhere up ahead of him, though he didn't know if he should be concerned about it or if he should just pick his way toward it. When he took a step, the cold that seemed to be buried deep inside of him flared then flowed out to his arms and legs, finally up to his head, the same way that it had before.

Lathan gasped.

He took a step back.

"I don't think we should go that way," he said carefully.

Henash frowned, the stone in his hand swirling. "There should be nothing here other than these stones. We could borrow from them, but we need to be able to see what we're doing. All we need—"

The wind lifted the fog.

When it did, Lathan saw the clearing of the stones. They were staggered around them much like they had been in the forest clearing before, creating something like a circle of the binding stones that had some seeming pattern. But that wasn't all that he saw.

Several men were on the outside of the stones looking toward them.

They were dressed in all black. Each of them carried an unsheathed sword that looked to be made of the same material as the binding stones. And each of them watched he and Henash, as if they had known that they were coming.

Derithan.

That wasn't what really caught his attention, though.

It was that the Derithan had Jef, Marin, and the others.

And each had elementals holding them.

CHAPTER 16

L athan didn't move. "What do we do?" Lathan asked.

The lead Derithan stood with his blade in hand, watching them both. There was no expression on his face. Nothing other than the binding stone sword in his hand. There seemed to be a strange drawing sense from the sword, though Lathan didn't know if that was his desire to run over to the others and see if he might be able to rescue them, though knowing that he couldn't.

"We stay here," Henash said. "The binding stones of this place are offering us a measure of protection, which I think he's aware of, but it's more than that protection we will need."

"We have to help them."

"They haven't harmed them, so I doubt they will. They want something." Henash looked over to Lathan then. "I think they're after that binding stone for shadow that you now have."

Lathan still held it in his fist, though he was no longer certain that there even was an elemental for shadow in it. When the elemental had surrounded him, he had felt it flow out from the stone, so he questioned whether he would even find shadow anymore.

Henash started forward, slipping his hands into his pouch. Lathan noticed him withdrawing several different binding stones and tucking them between his fingers as he headed toward the Derithan.

"These lands are protected. You aren't permitted here."

Lathan looked to Henash, and it was his turn to frown. They weren't *permitted?* These were the Derithan. As far as Lathan had heard in stories, they did whatever they wanted, regardless of whether they were permitted or not.

"You will hand him over to us and we will leave these lands—and these protections. If you do not..."

The ground surged.

Lathan braced himself for another attack of earth, but it never came. Instead, the sense of power surged. When it struck the ring of binding stones, they took on some of the power that had been sent at them, and it washed away and over them.

"You will find that this land doesn't tolerate your kind. You are not permitted."

Lathan was more confused than ever. Their kind? The Derithan—or was there more to what Henash was saying?

The lead Derithan approached the stone, but he

didn't step too close, as if he didn't want to get near it. "We no longer fear what you have placed. Do you think you can hold us back indefinitely?"

Henash raised his hands, and he motioned around him at the stones. "I don't hold you. This place, these stones, and these elementals hold you. Why should I worry about what I must do when everything else has already offered what is needed?"

What was Henash doing? They needed to get to Jef and Marin and the others, but Henash was making threats to the Derithan. Lathan stepped closer to him, but Henash held his hand behind him, motioning with a hint of wind that seemed to push him backward. The cold surged within him slightly as it did.

Henash seemed to move forward, positioning himself so he put himself in front of Lathan, as if to block the others from getting to him. Lathan could feel the wind radiating off of him, though what he detected was faint compared to what had been there before. Henash continued to send a swirl of wind, but the swirl wasn't as patent as it had been before. Now it served as mostly some sort of a message—and mostly to Lathan. A warning, if that was what it could be called.

"Move aside. You can't stop this."

"You'd be surprised at what I can stop," Henash said.

The Derithan regarded him a moment, then he started laughing. The ground rumbled, the steadiness of it picking up with intensity and carrying out and around them. Lathan could feel that rumbling, felt how it seemed to reach toward the binding stones, and then faded again.

The other Derithan spread out around the perimeter, each of them taking a position near one of the stones. Lathan thought about what they might be able to do. If they had some ability with the binding stones—and the swords they carried suggested that they did—then they might be able to use the stones. If not use them, then it was possible that they would be able to influence them in a way that would lead to the stones struggling. Maybe even shattering.

"Henash?" he whispered. "What's going on here?"

"I'm going to help you as much as I can, but you might need to run."

Without looking back at him, Henash sent a swirl of wind at him. At first, Lathan thought the wind was an attempt to just push him back, but the more that he felt the wind—and heard Henash in the wind—the more that he started to understand the purpose in the way he pushed Lathan back.

"You bonded shadow. I think that's why they're here."

"Then we can let them have the binding stone. I don't need it."

The comment got a reaction from Henash, though not the one that Lathan would have expected. He pushed on the wind again, then cast a quick look over his shoulder at him, a deep frown crossing his face.

"If that's what they're after, then we can't let them have it. There are reasons that we need to protect it as much as possible. I don't have the time to explain now, but I will when—*if*—we manage to escape."

Lathan didn't need for him to tell him that, for them to escape, they'd be leaving the others behind. That wasn't something that he was willing to do. Not for Marin, and definitely not for Jef.

"You want the binding stone?" Lathan said, stepping forward and ignoring the way Henash looked over at him. "You can have it."

The Derithan regarded him with a hard edge to his expression, one that Lathan didn't know how to react to. It was almost a sneer, but there was something else that struck him as commanding—and powerful. He felt the cold within him begin to surge again, then it sat there, staying deep inside of him as if it would collect some of the shadow and try to ball it up and force him to react.

Lathan took the binding stone that he'd gathered, then he tossed it.

He threw the stone over the Derithan's head.

The other Derithan turned, and three of them went running after the stone. The Derithan that stood across from him didn't move. He stared at Lathan. The cold continued to constrict deep within him, which left Lathan wondering *why* it would react that way. Increasingly, he felt as if the elemental had burrowed into him and now it was there just waiting to attack.

The ground started to rumble again. This was a different kind of trembling energy, one that reminded him more of the way that the earth elemental had attacked before, but this time, he didn't think that it was entirely the earth elemental. As he looked, it seemed to be something different.

The Derithan were slamming their binding stone swords into the ground.

They did it in a rhythm. That was the rhythm that he felt and detected. It came steadily, and the earth seemed to respond. Wind as well, whipping around the clearing.

The stones held back the power of the wind, but it seemed as if the stones had grown weaker—or the wind they used against them was getting stronger. A dampness hung in the air that hadn't been there before, along with a heat that started to press through him.

Lathan recognized each of the different kinds of elementals, even if he didn't know *which* elementals they had used. That they had binding stones for each—and binding stones of such a size—suggested that they were powerful. Likely *incredibly* powerful.

Henash waved another binding stone at the Derithan. The wind swirled, though this time it was from inside of the clearing. It felt as if the stones around them responded to what Henash had done, and he tried to push outward. The combination of power started to swell, and though Lathan was in the center of a place that should have offered him a measure of protection, he felt like the wind started to lift him again, much like it had when he'd been carried upward before.

The cold inside of him squeezed. Lathan felt that surge of cold energy, and he could feel the way that it started to constrict around his insides. It took his breath away, and he nearly staggered and fell.

Henash caught him.

The Derithan watched him.

Marin struggled to sit up. She was bound, and none of the Derithan were paying any attention to her. As she started to get up, she locked eyes with him and tried to get his focus. She was whispering something, though Lathan didn't know if she did that to try to talk to him or if she were trying to talk to the elementals the way that she believed that she could. And maybe she could.

"We can't let them take you, Lathan," Henash said.

"I don't think they should take any of us," Lathan said.

"They don't want the rest of us." He sighed, then spun quickly, hands outstretched, and the binding stones sent a wave of wind energy sweeping away from him. "It seems they want you." He sounded calm, but that was only because he was speaking softly. The torrent of elemental power continued to rage around them. The wind hammered. The earth rumbled. The heat and dampness were still there. None of that had changed. Henash continued to try to blast at the attackers, using his connection to his binding stones as he did, but that wouldn't be enough. Lathan could see that now. "I hadn't really understood why they had come out to this part of the world. We barely have any elementals, so they should not have come here. Then you mentioned binding to shadow, and I thought that was why."

"You don't anymore?"

Why were they simply standing there and having a conversation?

The elementals raged around them. The power continued to build, and though he wanted to stop it, to step away from it, he didn't see how it would be possible. That power was too much. The Derithan who had chased after the binding stone he'd thrown had already returned.

One of them had given it to the Derithan leading the attack.

He held onto the stone. Cold squeezed through Lathan.

He tried to ignore it, but that cold was too much to ignore. It was too much for him to do much of anything other than try to think about how he might be able to think his way past it—if something like that were even possible.

"I thought so until you threw the stone." Henash glanced in his direction. "I see the shadow, Lathan. It has marked you. Perhaps you've always been marked, and I wasn't wise enough to see it. That would explain many things that I should have been paying attention to before now. But that is why they want you."

"Marked? I don't understand."

"Unfortunately, we don't have the time to discuss. You need to run. I will do all that I can to ensure you have a chance to run, but you can't be caught. The rest of us will stay and fight, and will make whatever sacrifice is necessary for you to get free."

"No one is sacrificing for me," Lathan said.

How many different binding stones did he still have?

Several that might have some elemental power in

them, he thought. Let him use one of them, and he might be able to get them to safety. Henash was more concerned about getting Lathan to safety than getting the rest of them out.

Lathan grabbed one of the binding stones.

It was one of the long, slender pieces of stone that Henash had sheared from the binding stone circle they'd first encountered. Lathan didn't know how to empty the power from it, though there would be some power in it. Likely stored earth, though he wasn't entirely sure if that was what he'd find when he went to try to use it.

There were others—including a binding stone crossbow bolt.

That's what I need.

He hurriedly took the stone bolt, brought it to the crossbow, and readied it, aiming at the Derithan leader. Henash shook his head, but Lathan ignored him.

And fired.

The bolt streaked toward the Derithan. In the moment when it was about to strike, the Derithan raised his hand, and the bolt changed direction, shooting harmlessly behind him.

"This does not need to be difficult. The others needn't suffer because of you."

"They needn't?" Lathan asked.

Another binding stone, then. He took another, one of the long ones that Henash had drawn off the circle, and tossed it. When it cleared the boundary of the circle they were in, the stone suddenly exploded. That wasn't what Lathan had expected, but he'd take it.

Fragments of the stone struck the other Derithan, but not the leader.

He stood motionless, like a statue that didn't mind the sudden eruption of rock that Lathan's binding stone had caused. The others wiped the stone fragments off them, pausing briefly in the rhythm of slamming their sword into the ground, with some of them smearing blood as they did.

"You can't get past this," Henash said. "Like I said, you need to run. I will hold them off as long as possible."

"How am I supposed to be able to run if they've got us surrounded?"

He didn't plan on running, but he would ask the question. Henash seemed to have something in mind for him, which Lathan wanted to understand.

"I can call the wind long enough to lift you. It will not be as effective as it would be if they weren't here, but I think that I can hold you. Only you." He was again talking quietly, and Lathan realized he used the wind to carry his words to him. "Are you ready?"

"Henash—"

"They can't grab you."

"At least tell me why."

Wind swirled around him. Lathan could feel the way the pressure was starting to increase, and suspected that if he were to linger here too long, it would start to lift him the way it had when it had carried him before.

"Shadow marked," Henash said, his words clipped now. Whatever he was doing seemed to take a considerable effort. "That means *you* are shadow marked. A shadow elemental. It's rare. Few have the potential any longer. A shadow marked can call elementals—all elementals. That's what they want from you, and why they can't get to you. They would call truly *dangerous* elementals."

"What kind of dangerous elementals?"

Lathan suspected he knew what Henash meant. The wind continued to swirl beneath him, the lift starting to guide him upward. Much longer, and it would carry him above the clearing. Then where? Out. Because Henash thought that he needed to save Lathan.

"Draasin, for one. There are others that are equally dangerous, but the Derithan have long chased the power of the draasin."

Creatures of fire that were unlike anything seen in generations. Most believed the draasin were lost, though Lathan's father had never really believed that. He thought elementals couldn't disappear. They would hide, the elements protecting them when they were in any sort of danger.

"That would be the only reason that they would have come out here."

The wind started to *push* on him.

"And that's the reason they can't have you, especially if they believe you are shadow marked. As I now suspect as well."

Wind sent him surging upward.

He slammed into another surge of wind.

The rhythmic hammering of the Derithan persisted. The air surged with heat. And cold burned in his belly.

That sense seemed to explode through him, but uncontrollably.

He tried to ignore it, but that radiated through him. Something unexpected happened then. The strangeness of the cold flared, but then he felt the wind *call* to him. Heat and dampness came to him. And the earth sense seemed to fill him.

Could he actually be shadow marked like Henash said?

Lathan didn't have the time to think about it—or what it might mean.

The cold drew in that power.

Then another surge struck. It was like a bell rang.

The cold shattered.

The elements—and perhaps elementals—that had been filling him suddenly failed.

And he fell.

He found Henash lying motionless on the ground when he collapsed.

The Derithan leader was there, looking down at him with something of smug satisfaction. "You are the one we've been looking for."

With that, the Derithan surged around him and grabbed Lathan.

CHAPTER 17

Lathan heard voices around him. That was the only thing that he was really aware of. There were several of them, and they spoke with a sharp accent, though one of the accented voices was even more heavily accented than the others. It sounded thick, as if the person speaking had a mouth full of rock —or had burned their throat.

"I saw what he did," the first voice was saying.

Lathan *thought* that was the Derithan—the man who'd battled and attacked him—but couldn't be entirely certain. There was certainly something in the tone that struck him the same.

"Had you been there, you would have seen it as well."

"Had I been there, it's possible that it could have been used on me." This was the other—the one with the thick and burned tongue.

"He's neutralized for now. He should be held here without any difficulty."

They were talking about him.

Was he neutralized? He tested his hands and could move them. He felt for his arms and then legs, and everything worked. As he started to shift so that he could sit, that was when he felt the pressure on him.

The voices went quiet.

They knew that he was moving.

And they had fallen silent.

Lathan relaxed again. The tension did him no good and only served to draw more attention to him. He focused on his breathing, thinking he needed to find a way to slow it down, the same way that his father had once talked to him about his breathing when chasing elementals. If he could find that calm, then he could use it to help him pay attention to what was around him.

It took a moment, but Lathan managed to get control of his breathing. As he did, he could feel the steadiness start to come over him, a quiet sort of calm that began to work through him slowly.

"And the other?"

Lathan suppressed a sigh of relief when they started talking again. Let them think that he was still unconscious. In a way, he might as well be. He didn't dare reveal that he was awake for fear of what they might do to him.

What other were they talking about?

Could it be Marin and Jef—or had something happened to Henash? The last that Lathan had seen, Henash had collapsed. Lathan didn't think that he'd get up quickly after that. He'd been facing off against the elemental energy, and that power had been considerable. Probably enough that they would be able to deal with him as easily as they had with Lathan.

"He escaped. It doesn't matter. We have the one that we want. The others are with him, so we can use them to our benefit."

Why would they be after him?

The only answer he had was that it was tied to the shadow.

"I will test him myself when he is fully awake. We must know with certainty before we bring him back. I will not have this go wrong."

"I told you what I felt."

"And I'm telling you what will happen."

They fell silent. Lathan had a sudden sense of the wind whispering past him. One of the others—probably the Derithan that had attacked him in the first place—must have been using the elementals in such a way that they brushed against him. Lathan ignored it as best as he could, though the sense of the elemental blowing past him made it difficult. There wasn't a rumble or anything to suggest that the earth had been used, but it seemed to him that the ground *might* have started to get just the slightest bit softer. Even the air had taken on more of a warmth.

They *were* using the elementals against him.

More than that, as they did, he could feel something else. The cold that he had noticed deep within him had started to intensify, and as it did, that power made it so that he could feel the cold pressing all the way through him, as if the shadow elemental were reacting to what had happened to him—and rebelling.

That had to be his imagination, only that *was* the way it seemed to him.

"Not now," he whispered, trying to keep his voice low and to himself. If they could feel the shadow elemental the way that it sounded like they could, he didn't want to give them anything they could use to know what he might be doing to oppose it. For that matter, he wasn't sure there was anything he *could* do, at least with any real control. He was aware of that cold, but it seemed to react to what was taking place around him, and not at all to anything that he wanted.

Surprisingly, the cold began to ease.

It started slowly, but Lathan could feel the way that the cold no longer surged around him as it had before. It was almost as if the shadow elemental—if that were what he had detected—had begun to retreat.

The ground stopped sagging beneath him. The heat in the air faded. And everything started to fall still.

Not entirely still. The different kind of powers that were used around him made it so that everything wouldn't fall completely still. The cold fluttered from time to time, as if a reminder that it was still there. Though it didn't attack as it had before, so nothing was as targeted as it had been.

A shadow—a real shadow and not elemental—loomed over him for a moment. Lathan feigned sleep until it was gone.

Shadow marked.

Lathan remembered the first time that he had tracked shadow with his father.

He and his father had been collecting. Fire this time. His father always loved fire, and believed that even elementals as small as saa had uses that Lathan had only pretended to believe, knowing that it didn't matter to argue about such things. Saa was usually little more than a spark, that tiny flame used to light a lantern or kindling, but his father claimed to know places to find saa where it was more than that. They were at the edge of the cliffside looking down upon the water far below, waves crashing beneath them as they trekked along a trail that had long ago overgrown.

"You can feel it if you pay attention," his father said, keeping his voice soft. When they were out collecting elementals, his father often kept his voice soft, as if he were afraid of speaking too loudly and chasing off any elemental. Other than the wind, Lathan didn't think that it mattered how loudly they spoke. The wind always seemed as if it minded, though, something that Lathan had found amusing. "The heat is out there. If I close my eyes enough, I can find it."

His father stopped. They were near enough to the cliff edge looking out over the water, and there was a slight stirring of a breeze. Barely enough for him to feel, but it did come in from out over the water, carrying some of the salty scent with it. Nothing that left Lathan thinking that there was elemental power within it, but that didn't keep him from clutching the binding stone that he had on him tightly anyway. It was better to be prepared. Another lesson that his father had taught him about dealing with the elementals. If you weren't prepared, they would surprise you.

Lathan closed his eyes to match his father, but even as he did, he didn't feel anything the way that his father made it seem like he should. There was the warmth of the sun, but that hadn't shifted. That was something that he'd been taught to keep track of. While chasing fire, one needed to be present and needed to be able to detect the faintest shifts of the heat in the air so that you could be clued into a time when the elementals might be moving through.

There wasn't anything here.

"I think we should keep going," Lathan said.

"Are you sure?"

The slight rising hint at the end left him thinking that perhaps his father had detected something and was disappointed that Lathan had not.

Maybe he *wasn't* sure. It would be a mistake to tell his father that he knew what was going on around him if he didn't take the necessary time to know if there were any elementals. He'd focused for the briefest of moments, barely long enough to be certain that there wasn't anything else out there.

Focus.

That meant getting back to the basics about detecting the elementals. Since they were after fire today, it meant paying attention to the gradations of heat.

Wind made it difficult, but wind made many things difficult. They often had to deal with the wind when they were out chasing elementals, so that it seemed as if his father had practically asked the wind to come and serve as a distraction. With the right binding stone, that *might* be possible.

Warmth. Heat.

They were both there, but the warmth hadn't shifted.

Lathan opened his eyes and looked over to his father. "I don't feel anything. If there's something there that I'm supposed to feel, just let me know."

He was almost thirteen, and it was things like this that ended up with him more irritated than he should be. There were times when he wanted to be tested, but there were other times when he thought that his father pushed him for the sake of proving how skilled he was— and how much Lathan still had to learn. He knew that he still had much to learn. Lathan didn't need for him to make a point of showing that every time.

"There's the warmth of the sun. Start with that. Close your eyes, and you can feel it. On a day like today, it's almost like feeling the warmth of a draasin flying overhead."

The comment made Lathan open his eyes and look to his father. "You've seen a draasin?"

He doubted that. His father liked to claim knowledge of many different elementals. Most of the time, Lathan believed that he had the experience that he claimed, but there were a few elementals that were just too difficult to believe that his father had any experience with. The massive draasin—beasts of fire and wind, and some claimed even a hint of earth—were one. They were too large to be overlooked.

"Only once," he said in a sigh. "It was... like magic. There's nothing like seeing those creatures."

"Did you collect from a draasin?"

His father started to laugh, a sound that was unlike him normally. It was almost too high, a little nervous, and uncomfortable. "You don't collect from one of the draasin. Even if you could, the binding stone would not hold that kind of power. The draasin are powerful enough that they would simply destroy any attempt at binding their power."

Lathan thought about what he'd read about the draasin. The winged creatures were massive, but were only known to hunt around the Tolath Mountains in the far east. Even then, the draasin were said to be rare enough that none had even seen one of them for years.

"I didn't know you traveled so far," Lathan said.

His father turned to him, patting him on the shoulder. "When you're older, I'll tell you all about my youthful adventures. Life is better now. Slower." He smiled, but there was a hint of something that lingered in his eyes. "And far safer." He took a deep breath. "Let's get back to you working on feeling for saa. The elemental is here. I wouldn't deny that truth to you. So what I'd like for you to do now is to feel for the heat. You've paid attention to the sun, but now you need to start paying attention to the heat within yourself. When you do, you can find that there's something more that you can use."

The heat. That was what his father wanted him to find, though Lathan didn't know if he could feel for it any better than he had been. When he closed his eyes, he noticed the warmth on his face. That couldn't be what his father wanted him to detect. If it was only about the warmth, then he would have said it.

As he stood there, he noticed a stirring of heat, though it wasn't where he had expected to detect it. This seemed to come from his feet, as if the sun had begun to heat his boots.

Then it was gone.

"I think I started to—"

Lathan cut himself off.

A shimmer of darkness had flickered across the ground near his feet.

For a moment, he thought that darkness was tied to something that his father had wanted him to detect, perhaps some strange drawing of heat that was different than the usual connection to saa, but his father had his focus on the ridgeline, staring out into the darkness toward the sea. Whatever his father thought that Lathan should have detected was out there.

Then what was this?

He didn't move.

That was a lesson that Lathan had learned early. Don't move too quickly, or you risk scaring away any elemental that might want to show itself. With the darkness, Lathan didn't know if that was an elemental or perhaps something else, but he wanted to know.

The darkness slipped along the ground.

It was almost as if the darkness flowed, a shadow that moved along the ground and forced him to turn his attention upward, half expecting that there would be some creature flying overhead and casting the shadow. After talking about the draasin, Lathan wondered if maybe he might even see one of those creatures, however unlikely it might be for them to encounter them out here and regardless of how much he knew that to be an impossibility.

But the sky was clear.

When he turned back, the darkness still slid along the ground.

"Dad?" he whispered.

His father slowly turned. He must have sensed something in the way that Lathan had spoken and had known that there was a concern about moving too quickly. He glanced to Lathan, saw his attention on the ground, then looked downward.

"Don't startle it," his father said.

"What is it?" Lathan thought about all the different elementals that he had experience with, but none of them looked anything like that. None of them even reminded him of anything like that. "Some sort of strange earth elemental?" It *was* moving along the ground, so there was the possibility that was what he saw, but what earth elemental would move like that? It seemed to slide—and that was only when it moved. "Maybe wind?" Lathan said, though it was mostly for himself.

That didn't strike him as wind, either. Wind could

take on some color, though that was rare enough, but any of the colorful wind—and colorful might be a stretch considering that the wind was rarely anything other than a pale gray at best, though it *was* known to be black or brown from time to time as well—would not have been able to look *quite* like that.

"Not wind," his father said. His voice was tight, as if he were nervous. At the time, Lathan had never seen his father nervous about anything. "Something we haven't had a chance to talk about. Something rare—and dangerous. We call it shadow, but that's not even entirely true. It only *looks* like a shadow, though it's something greater." His voice had fallen to a hush.

"Do you want to try to bind it?"

"You won't be able to bind shadow, son. Much like we can't bind the draasin. Some things are simply not done."

Lathan looked up, but when he saw his father still staring down at the ground, he hurriedly looked down again. His father wasn't looking up, so Lathan wouldn't look up. "All elementals can be connected to the binding stone. That's what you said. You just have to have the right kind of a focus and you can—"

"I know what I said, but I'm telling you something different. You can't bind shadow." He stood motionless, which Lathan modeled, knowing that if his father weren't going to move, then neither was he. "We will wait a little longer. Let the shadow decide what it must do."

That was another first from his father.

They had often spoken of his father's respect for the elementals, but this was something else. Not only a respect, but could it be fear?

Lathan had never seen his father afraid of anything, so that didn't feel quite right.

Concern, maybe.

The shadow started to move again, this time sliding along the ground and heading toward Lathan. He shifted the binding stone in his hand, holding it away from his body. His father looked up then shook his head once. There was a hardness in his eyes that hadn't been there before.

Lathan relaxed.

No binding stones on the elemental.

The shadow continued to slip toward him but didn't reach him.

It circled him.

There was a strangeness about it. Lathan could feel a hint of heat from it—the same heat that he'd felt through his boots. Whatever the heat he'd been detecting was, it had come from this elemental. But it was more than just heat that he felt. There seemed to be a hint of cold as well. That was strange and surprising. And the way that it moved, gliding as it did, reminded Lathan of the wind.

"Is it using other elementals?" he whispered.

His father looked up briefly. "Why do you say that?"

"It's just something that I can feel, along with what it looks like. If I'm wrong—"

"You're not wrong. At least, not entirely. Shadow is

different. That's why I said shadow is not exactly a shadow. It's an elemental, but it's one that has aspects of each of the elements. *All* of the elements."

All of them.

The earliest lessons that he had with his father had taught him all about the elements—and the elementals. In that way, Lathan had a better education—at least a more thorough education—than even those in the Saval. Fire. Wind. Water. Earth.

But there was another. That was what his father suggested.

Spirit.

"It has spirit?" he whispered.

Lathan's father nodded. "That's the belief. That's what makes it powerful—and dangerous."

The shadow slipped along the ground, and he could feel the cold within it. That was new, and he wasn't entirely sure that was what he had felt or if it was something else altogether. Maybe what he detected had been the fire elemental that they'd been chasing—or maybe they'd been after shadow all along.

"Just watch for this a little longer," his father said. "If you pay attention to what the shadow is doing, you can see that it's not going to harm you. It won't harm you, Lathan."

Those words stuck with him, even after he had stopped seeing the shadow. That had been the last time that he'd been aware of the shadow elemental until he'd seen it with Jef—though he'd gone looking for it many times and had failed at finding it.

The cold struck through him again. This time it was a ball of cold that was buried deep within him, and when he focused on it, he could feel the burst of cold, though there was something almost hot about it, much like he had felt when he had first encountered the shadow the very first time.

Something struck him in the side. Lathan resisted the urge to cry out, wanting to feign that he was still unconscious, but couldn't. The pain struck like a boulder slamming him in the side, a burst of pain that bloomed through his body, washing away everything other than the pain.

The voice that spoke was the same accented voice of the Derithan that had been there before, though not the one that he'd been dealing with all along. This was the leader. And he was there. Near him.

Energy radiated from him.

Power.

Elemental power.

Lathan felt the heat in the air. The rumble of the ground. The wind swirling around him. Even the dampness that was there around him. All of the elements—and an elemental for each one.

Controlled.

The kind of power that was there was more significant than anything that he'd felt before and seemed to be building around him, squeezing him.

Not only that, but it was overwhelming the cold within him.

That was gone.

The sense of the shadow was no longer there and trying to protect him the way it had seemed like it had attempted to before.

Because the Derithan cut it off from him.

"You're awake. You will come with me."

CHAPTER 18

L athan sat inside a massive tent, lanterns glowing with the light of elementals surrounding him. The ground had been smoothed over using the power of earth elementals to flatten it and shift it. The air was calm, but there was a balled-up sense of energy that was there within him, leaving him thinking that it could explode around him at any moment. Dampness hung there as well, bound to the air.

Lathan was bound near a tall metal pole, his hands tied behind him. He wanted to pull them free, but the elemental energy that was there held him far more tightly than he'd been able to overwhelm. Wind, most likely. Henash would be able to break free of the wind elemental that they used on him, but he didn't know the trick.

If only he had some way of speaking to the elementals the way that Marin had, he might be able to find something that would work for him the same way. Even if he could *feel* something the way that his father had always suggested, it might make a difference.

"Let's talk about what you've done with the shadow," the man said.

He stood across from Lathan in a long black cloak. A thick black beard covered his face, and his eyes matched the color of his beard. Lathan imagined an angular jaw beneath the beard, or perhaps some scar, or maybe another deformity. Regardless, he felt nothing other than the power of the elementals coming off of him.

"I haven't done anything with the shadow," he said. His voice was weary, though some of that was because he'd been beaten by the elementals periodically, making it difficult for him to stay alert.

He felt like he'd been saying the same thing over and over now, and this man still hadn't come to believe him. All he wanted was to have a chance to rest but doubted that he'd be given that opportunity. They were going to assault him until he told them what they wanted to know.

At this point, Lathan was tempted to lie. Not just about the shadow—though he could feel the elemental there within him, so thought that there was some part of that power that he might be able to draw upon eventually—but about what he'd experienced. They wanted an answer, and it might be time that he provided an answer for them, regardless of whether it was the *right* answer or not.

"You have something of the shadow. You were seen with it. Do not deny that."

Lathan didn't know how much of his experience with the shadow they'd seen. As far as he knew, they hadn't' managed to see much of what he'd done, but it was possible that they hadn't needed to see it. With the binding stones and the other elementals, it was possible that they would be able to feel it—and that might be enough.

"As I said, I don't know anything about the shadow. I know there are shadow elementals, but nothing else."

"What do you want to say about *this*?" The man crouched down so that he could look Lathan in the eyes, holding a piece of binding stone.

The one that he'd used on the shadow.

Lathan had actually let himself forget about that. He shouldn't have. He knew that the binding stone would potentially betray him, especially as he had felt the power of the shadow in it before. When he'd been trapped by the wind, thrown up into the sky, he'd thought that maybe he'd used enough of the shadow so he wouldn't have revealed what he'd been doing.

It seemed as if that weren't the case.

The binding stone still held the shadow. Probably enough that they would know that he *had* seen the shadow elemental before. Maybe enough that they could use it to track the shadow.

If that were true, why did they need me?

They had held him. The man kept questioning him. The other elementals battered at him, using that power to try to attack him, so that he couldn't do much of anything. But that didn't mean that they were going to be able to do anything to him.

"I don't know what you want me to say."

The man regarded Lathan for a few moments, then he straightened. "You will talk. You will have no choice but to talk."

Wind sucked out of his chest.

The pain was immense. He tried to ignore it, but the wind felt like it was drawn completely from him, making it so that he couldn't even try to take a breath.

It was followed by another surge of heat.

This one wrapped around him, radiating around his wrists and ankles, squeezing with a burning pain. Lathan tried to fight it, but the pain was too much and he cried out.

He lost track of how long he'd been like that. There was a switch to each of the elements, going from heat to wind to water to earth, each one taking a turn to batter at him. None of them eased, though he didn't expect any of them to ease off.

When it all ended, tears had been streaming down his face, dripping into his mouth. He spat, getting rid of the salt, and tried to look up at his tormenter, but he wasn't there.

Hands grabbed him, jerking him to his feet.

"You're to rest before we try again," a harsh voice said. Lathan had heard that person before. It was the Derithan that he'd first encountered. "Darint wants you fresh."

Lathan didn't look up at him, but he could practically feel the malevolence in his words. *Fresh.*

That meant another round of torture, but maybe they'd give him a break for a little while to recover. Lathan thought that he *could* recover, especially if he had a few moments to do so. Longer would be better, but he doubted they'd give him that much time.

His mouth was dry. When he licked it, he tasted dried blood.

Darint.

He had a name, though that didn't mean anything to him. He'd never heard of Darint.

What if I didn't know anything?

The problem was that he *did* know something, it was just that what he knew wouldn't be enough. Lathan had to find a way to hold out.

Not only that, but he was going to need to find a way to draw upon the cold shadow. That sense fluttered in him from time to time, as if the shadow were there, wanting him to know that it was there and tormenting him for a different reason.

Had he only told the others about the shadow...

They would have continued to torture him. He suspected that nothing would have changed. They wanted to know about the elemental and had sensed that Lathan had the experience with it.

He was dragged outside of the lighted tent and back out into a dark night sky. The wind was calm, though he had a sense that it fluttered high overhead, as if the wind were drawn here. Henash might be out there, or maybe Marin worked with the wind.

Those thoughts drifted through his mind before fading. Were either of them able to speak to the wind, why wouldn't they have done so before now? He could feel the wind, but he couldn't feel anything more within it.

The Derithan dropped him on the hard ground. "You'll wait here."

The man started away from him. Lathan looked up. His vision was blurred, but the man seemed larger than he should. "What's. Your name?"

He had a hard time getting the words out. Lathan's mouth didn't work like it should. The dryness in his mouth made it hard for him to say much of anything, but he was determined to learn more about his captors. He'd start with this one.

The man turned back to him and laughed. "A spine in you. I like that. Kohl Volrath. That's my name. You'd do well to remember it."

"You'll. Not learn. Mine."

The man regarded Lathan, then he started laughing. "Oh, we've already learned yours. Did you think those friends of yours would hold out on you?"

The man started laughing as he headed away from Lathan, leaving him wondering what they had told the others.

Lathan hadn't considered that they would have questioned Jef or Marin, though he should have. Of course they would. Jef knew about the shadow, and

Lathan wouldn't be surprised if he had broken. Marin would probably try to hold out, but how much could someone like her tolerate? She was no fighter. She just wanted to speak to elementals, nothing more than that.

"Lathan?"

The hushed voice came from his right. He rolled, already starting to tense up and think there might be something that he needed to be ready for, when he saw several shapes outlined against the darkness of the night.

"Jef?"

He coughed, and Jef was there, reaching for him.

"What did they do to you?"

"Wanted. Shadow."

"Then give it to them," he said. "There's no reason for you to suffer like that."

Lathan wanted to argue with him but didn't have the energy to do so. He knew what would happen if he were to let the Derithan know about the shadow. They would use it. He didn't know *how* they would, only that they would find some way to use it against them. Against him.

Then what?

They wouldn't need them anymore.

What would happen to him at that point? What would happen to any of them?

He shivered.

"Henash?" Lathan whispered.

He thought that he knew. He'd overheard the others talking but didn't think that Henash would have run away. That wasn't what he'd seen from him in the time that they'd been racing through the forest.

"Gone."

"Gone?"

"Not like that. Fiery Skies, I hope not at least. He's just gone. Marin said that he was here, but the wind took him away. I don't know how that's even possible but if that's what happened, then maybe it's for the best for him. He doesn't need to go through the same thing that you're going through."

"Hurt," Lathan said.

Even saying that much was hard. Everything hurt. And as much as he tried, he couldn't get the words out any better. He wanted to tell Jef to leave him alone, to tell him to give him a chance to rest, but nothing came out the way that it should.

"I'm sorry. Can I get you anything?"

"Water."

"Just a minute."

Jef left him.

Lathan hated being alone again. He stared up at the sky, paying attention to the wind that was there. If that really was tied to Henash in some way, he wanted to pay attention to it so he could feel for the wind and the way Henash had used it. Having experienced wind capable of lifting him, he thought that the wind was going to be the key to escape, but that was only if they could summon enough of the wind.

Or bind it.

Without a binding stone, he wouldn't be able to do

that. Darint and the others had taken his stones, so Lathan didn't have anything that he could use any longer.

Shadow.

He was shadow marked.

Lathan didn't know what that meant, but he had been shadow marked his entire life. At least as long as he'd been aware of the elementals after working with his father. Before that... he wouldn't have been.

Could the shadow somehow help him?

He could feel the shadow, though that was only in the cold that worked through him, buried deep inside. There was nothing more than that. If he could somehow find a way to use that cold, maybe he could find a way to escape.

That would mean discovering some way of controlling the shadow.

What he felt of the shadow was bad enough. That cold lingered inside of him, burning deep within him. There was a power there, though he had to find a way to use it—and control it if possible.

What had his father said about those things?

Feel the elemental.

Let the sense of that come through him.

Lathan focused on that. He let the cold be a part of him.

Then he closed his eyes.

That was what his father had done as well, and the way that he'd wanted Lathan to be able to feel for the power. As he listened to the power that was there, he thought that he might be able to feel it, but then it faded. It was fleeting, before the cold burrowed deeper inside of him, the shadow trying to hide.

Shadow marked.

What did that mean for him?

Lathan didn't have any answers before Jef returned, setting something in his hand. It was hard and cool.

"A stone?" he managed to get out.

"For water. That's what they allow us. Nothing more."

That would be one way to get water, and at least they'd know the water was clean, but it felt like a waste. He'd seen elementals used for something similar in the past, but it always struck him that they were overusing the power of the elementals. Then again, if others didn't do anything like that, then Lathan and Jef wouldn't have a paying job collecting. They needed for others to want that power so that they could justify the fees they charged for their services.

Lathan traced his hands along the stone and could feel some of the coolness that was in it. That gave off a sense of the water that was bound to the stone. What elemental might this be? From the time that he'd been around the Derithan, he'd seen that they had a connection to various elementals, and he didn't know what others they might be connected to—or if they only harvested from the same ones repeatedly.

"How?"

He couldn't get much else out, though wanted to try to ask how to make the stone work. There had to be some trick to it, though as he traced his fingers along the stone, he didn't feel anything inside of the stone that would help him know what it might be.

"You just have to bring it to your mouth and press. There's not much to it, not anymore. We didn't know that we'd need to hold out for you. I'm sorry, Lathan."

"That's. Fine."

He lifted the stone, squeezing his hands around it. When he'd been trying to free elementals before, there had been a trick to it, though Lathan wasn't even entirely sure that he knew what that trick was, only that he had needed to find some way of releasing the elemental.

As he squeezed, he found that he didn't need to do anything. Water just formed along the binding stone and dripped down into his mouth. He licked his lips, trying to pull all of the water into his mouth. It had a slightly mineral taste, one that should tell him which of the elementals this was, but Lathan wasn't of any mind to figure that out. He continued to squeeze, letting the water roll into his throat. Then he swallowed.

When he had enough, he closed his eyes, relaxing his hold on the stone. He didn't know if that would stop the flow of water, but it seemed to work. As soon as he let go of the stone, the water stopped, drying up.

He looked over to Jef. "What happened?" His mouth wasn't nearly as dry, and neither was his throat, so he could get the question out more easily than he had before.

"We got into the forest. I'm not sure what Marin was following, but she seemed to know what she was doing and where she was going. We didn't object. Heard the wind, something strange whistling through the trees, then a rumbling. It came too often to be anything other than the elementals, but Marin told us that we were fine, we just had to get deeper into the forest."

Which meant that she had likely known about the protective circles of binding stone that were in the forest. Lathan hadn't known about them, and he had known more about the elementals than most people in Gorawl.

Lathan had no idea what had happened to the soldiers, but considering that he saw no sign of them, it couldn't be good. Would the Derithan have executed them?

"You should have been fine," Lathan said, trying to sit up. He still hurt where they'd been using the elementals on him, but it was better. The cold in the center of his chest had loosened as well, easing until it was nothing more than a steady knot though it didn't disappear altogether. "There's a part of the forest that should have kept you safe. Henash showed me."

"Binding stones," Jef said.

"That's right."

"Marin showed us. Said they were older than most of the forest, and certainly older than the kingdom. They were here from a time before the kingdom and were used to create places of safety, whatever that means. She seemed to know something more about them and how they kept the people safe from the elementals."

Lathan frowned. Safe *from* the elementals?

That wasn't what Henash had led him to believe.

"Where is she? Others?"

"They're over there. There's a barrier that keeps them from getting here. I managed to get past it. I had a binding stone on me," he said, his voice dropping to a whisper. "They don't know I have it, so they didn't try to confiscate it, and I used it to try to get closer so that I could see what they were doing to you. I wasn't going to sit back while they tortured you."

"How did you know?"

There was a moment of silence that hung between them. When Jef broke it, Lathan already suspected what he would say. "We could hear it, Lathan. The whole camp could. You were... well, you were screaming plenty loud. I'm sure you tried to hold out, and no one would blame you for cracking and giving them what they wanted."

Lathan sighed. He hadn't cracked. At least, he didn't think that he had, though he still didn't know what they wanted out of him. Pain. That was what it seemed like they wanted, but they had been after something else as well. They needed the shadows, though Lathan had been certain that he'd held out from that. He didn't know what they would use the shadows for but doubted that it would be anything good. If he could keep them from accessing power that would let them draw upon more powerful elementals, then he was going to do it.

He finally managed to sit up. The tent in the distance glowed with the soft light that he'd seen when he'd been there, though it seemed to flicker, as if the elemental light that they used wasn't as potent as it needed to be.

Maybe the Derithan had been drawing on too much of the elementals and they'd weakened them. That seemed a bit much to hope for.

There were other tents arranged neatly around them, which he suspected represented the other Derithan soldiers. Lathan counted six separate tents, but he didn't know how many of the Derithan would be in each one.

Too many.

At least for them in the shape that they were in. None of them were fighters, which was what the Derithan were. If Henash returned, they might have a way of getting out of here, but without him, Lathan didn't think they stood much of a chance, leaving them at the Derithan's mercy—such as it was.

"Are you… are you going to be okay?" Jef asked.

"It hurt," he said. "They used some of the elementals, and the binding stones, against me."

He closed his eyes again, thinking about the cold that was in him, staying buried deep within him. It hadn't moved, though the longer that he focused on the cold, the more that he could feel elements of it starting to work its way out through him. There were aspects of different elements within it when he paid attention to it.

Cold, but cold so biting that it was almost hot. There was even something almost *damp* about that cold as well. It was potent enough that he couldn't help but feel as if there was even an aspect of earth within it, given the way that it filled him. Could wind be there as well? *Maybe in the way that it flows through me.*

Shadow… but all the elements.

What he needed to know was how the shadow worked, and perhaps even how it seemed to fill him the way that it did.

What if I could use it?

The shadow hadn't been that hard for him to detect, and now he could still feel it within him. If he could somehow coax it out, he might be able to use it in some way. If that were the case, then they might have something that could be used against the Derithan.

"Where is he?" a voice said from near one of the tents.

Lathan recognized the voice.

It was Darint.

"Go," he whispered to Jef. "Don't let them know that you made it here. Keep the binding stone to yourself."

"I could help," Jef said.

"Not like this," Lathan said.

Then he slowly got to his feet, positioning himself in front of Jef, and ambled toward what he'd heard of the Derithan.

They wouldn't beat him.

CHAPTER 19

Lathan thought that he knew pain. He'd been wrong.

They hadn't moved the camp. It was almost as if there were something important about the camp location that they needed. Perhaps it was the binding stones, or perhaps it was simply that they were still waiting on Lathan to prove that he knew the shadow. Whatever the reason, they had stayed.

And he'd been tortured.

For the most part, they used the elementals against him.

Lathan strained to try to know *which* of the elementals they were using. Some were easy. Saa had been simple to detect. The heat off of it was directed and distinct, and painful. Surprisingly, not as painful as he had expected, especially as he'd come to know which of the elementals they had used against him. That made him wonder if the shadow was somehow holding on to protect him.

Why would shadow protect me?

The answer came, though he didn't know if there was really anything to it.

Shadow marked.

But that might mean that an elemental stayed with him, and that was unlike anything that he had ever known about the elementals. Still, it seemed like there was something there with him, and that something seemed as if it *were* trying to help him. When he felt the trembling of earth, and the way that it constricted around him, nearly suffocating him, there was something else that seemed as if it reached out to try to assist him. That something else had to be the shadow, pulling away just the faintest amount of the earth elemental that would otherwise have overpowered him. It had happened when water and wind had been used on him, though the effect had been difficult to detect.

Lathan knelt with his hands bound behind him, tied to a tall pillar of stone. The Derithan used that so they could try to squeeze the bands around his hands, which made it difficult for him to maintain his position, but he managed to withstand the suffering... because of the shadow elemental.

"Where did you hide it?" Darint asked.

He stood across from Lathan. They were out in the open, the sun dipping in the overcast sky, and the other prisoners just barely visible to him. Lathan suspected they were all too aware of him, as well, though probably more because he'd been yelling.

"I didn't hide anything," he said. "There's no shadow."

Darint crouched down, peering into Lathan's eyes. "We both know that's not true. Now," he said, standing and turning away from Lathan, "you could make this far better for yourself, were you interested in doing so. There is no need for you to suffer. No need for your *friends* to suffer."

Lathan had been forced to listen to the others tormented by the Derithan. It had not been nearly as long as what they did to Lathan, but he suspect that they used it as a way to try to convince Lathan to speak.

At this point, if he *had* a way to tell them about the shadow, he might, but the shadow was somehow *inside* of him, as if *he* were the binding stone. There wasn't anything that he could share with them.

Darint stood across from Lathan, holding onto one of the binding stones. It was one of the first times that Lathan had seen him holding onto a binding stone ever since they had begun to torment him. For the most part, Darint had not needed it. It was almost as if he could call upon the elementals without using the binding stone. Something that Lathan wish that he could learn.

That would be too much like what Marin claimed she could do. And Henash, for that matter.

"We will speak about your connection to the shadows. You have one. I can feel it. You claim that you do not, but each time that we influence you, you use the shadow to protect yourself." He leaned close, and Lathan could smell his breath. There was something minty about it, which surprised him. It should be foul, much like him. "Where is it?"

The cold balled up within Lathan's belly. The elemental, if that was what was with him, seemed as if it tried to constrict down deep inside of Lathan.

Help me if that's what you're going to do, but don't torment me.

He doubted that would make a difference. He had tried talking to the elemental before, but each time that he had attempted to do so, the elemental had ignored him. Were the situations reversed and were Lathan somehow able to hide inside of the elemental, maybe he would have remained silent as well. Better that than to suffer with this torment.

He had long ago decided that even if he told the Derithan leader what he wanted to know, it wouldn't make much of a difference. They were still going to torture Lathan.

And though holding out put his friends in danger, he didn't know what telling him would do, either. There was a real possibility that, if he were to tell Darint what he wanted to know, then they wouldn't live much longer. In Lathan's mind, he protected his friends by letting them suffer. Their suffering was temporary. He knew that, and he knew that if he could hold out long enough, maybe the elemental would come around, or perhaps Henash would return and finally help them.

He needed to help them, didn't he? He would come

for them. Lathan believed that he would. But he had not. So far, he had remained absent, as if he didn't care what would happen to them.

Darint straightened again, and he ran his hands along the fabric of his jacket.

When he did, it rippled. The ground rippled with it.

That was the binding stone? The fabric?

Pain constricted within him. It felt like the earth was trying to crush him, squeezing his legs, his arms. The only part that was not constricted like that was his head, but even that was not for long periods. He doubted that he would be able to withstand this torment for very long if it were to persist.

But the fabric. That was what he had seen. It had rippled, and then Darint had used that rippling to torment him with a constriction of earth.

Were all of his binding stones like that?

Not all. He was holding one in his hand, and that was the one that Lathan had been concerned about, thinking that he had to watch that more than anything else, but maybe he was wrong. There was another stone, or something akin to it, woven into his jacket.

It seemed nearly impossible to believe that something like that was even possible, as binding stones were traditionally actual stones, but he had seen plenty of impossible things when it came to the Derithan. They had proven themselves masters of what should be impossible.

The pain lingered, but it was not nearly as acute or as sharp as he suspected Darint intended. As that pain coursed through him, the cold constricted again, but it was a protective sort of constriction, one that offered a measure of safety. Lathan bit back a scream, but didn't need to bite it all the way back as the torment lingered, though not quite as severe as it had been at first.

Darint stood impassively, waiting. Lathan made a point of shrieking, thinking that was expected, but gradually, as the cold washed through him, even the pain began to ease to the point where it wasn't all that bad. It was still awful, but it wasn't intolerable.

It began to ease again, which Lathan suspected meant that they were relaxing their grip on him so that they could ask him more questions.

Darint turned back to him. His jacket rippled again, and the squeezing stopped altogether. That was how he used the trapped elemental power, but it seemed almost as if he were not using elemental power so much as he was using an actual elemental.

Darint looked down at him. "We will talk again. Shadows. You don't deny that you know of them, which tells me that you have some experience with them. You know how many are familiar with the shadows?"

This was a new line of questioning for Lathan. And surprisingly, he found himself intrigued. He didn't know the answer. Henash, along with Lathan's father, had known about the shadows, but Lathan also had the suspicion that it wasn't common knowledge. Shadows simply weren't well known by most who dealt with the elementals.

"I don't know," he said. "I learned about them when I was young."

Darint stopped. "Where were you raised?"

"Gorawl." There was no point in denying that he was from there. They probably knew all about it. He wouldn't be able to stay ahead of them, nor would he be able to stop them, but if he could tell them something to keep them away...

He would do that.

"No," Darint said. "There would be none there that would know about shadows."

"My father did," he said.

Darint stiffened again.

Lathan realized that he had said too much.

This was something that he had been trying to keep from Darint, and up till this point, he had succeeded. Through little more than a slip of his tongue, Lathan had shared something that he had not intended to. That his father had taught him about the shadow.

He ignored Darint, instead focusing on how he could keep something from him. He tried to focus on the cold within him, that sense of the shadow that he believed was still there. He couldn't reach it. It had to be there, somehow, but as he strained to feel that cold within him, it felt almost as if it were trying to hide from him. Perhaps that was what it was. Perhaps the shadow nestled deep within him, avoiding him.

He looked over to Darint, seeing him watching Lathan, an amusement glittering in his eyes that had not been there before.

"We will talk about this father of yours," he said. "You will tell me his name. What you remember of him. And where he is now."

"He's dead," Lathan said. That much didn't matter. "He died a long time ago. And I don't know where he's from, so you asking me doesn't make it any easier. All I know is that he helped me come to learn the elementals."

"That's all that you know?"

"I told you. He helped me learn about the elementals. But he's not the only person who knows about elementals in Gorawl."

There was nothing in that which would betray anyone. It was easy enough to prove to others, especially as it wasn't just him who knew about the elementals, not just his father, but there were plenty of people. Including Henash and the others who worked with him to try to teach about the elementals.

Darint ran his fingers along his jacket. When he did, the jacket rippled. Wind began to squeeze, and pulled the breath out of Lathan's lungs. He struggled, trying to hold his breath, trying to be prepared for that pain, but everything pulled free of him, making it nearly impossible for him to ignore it.

Darint looked down at him, the same impassive expression in his eyes. He never changed. He didn't care what he did to Lathan. All of this was his way of finding information. Torture was a part of that.

"You told me nothing. The only thing you have shared was that you know about shadows, and it's time that you tell more about what you know."

Lathan couldn't breathe. It felt as if his breath had been ripped free of his chest, and though he tried to fight the sensation, he could not. He struggled, straining against how it pulled the breath from his lungs, but he was determined to keep fighting. Gradually, the shadow kicked in. He was thankful for it. He could feel the cold blooming within him, and as it did, he used that cold to help ease his difficulty.

But that wasn't what happened. It wasn't as if he used the cold. It was more that the cold gradually, slowly, began to relax him so that he could draw in a breath. He didn't do so rapidly, not wanting to reveal to Darint that he could breathe, but he didn't need to, either. The shadow pulled the wind toward him.

Silently, Lathan thanked the shadow. For the first time, it seemed as if the shadow answered. It was faint, vague, little more than a tremor that surged through him, but he could've sworn that there was some response this time.

Had he imagined it?

He was meant to suffer, and he feigned that agony, but it wasn't quite what Darint wanted for him. He wanted Lathan miserable.

Gradually, the wind began to ease, loosening in his chest to the point where Lathan could once more suck in a deep breath. As he did, he made a show of trying to act the part of suffering.

"Tell me about your father."

"He taught me about the elementals," Lathan said. "He taught me how to collect them. That's what I am. A collector. We collect elemental power. We use the binding stones, like the one you have in your hand."

Darint glowered at him. That was the first time that there was emotion in his eyes. "Do not speak of what you can't understand," he sneered.

What had Lathan said wrong?

Heat burned along his skin. He cried out, unable to contain it.

Gradually, the cold pulled some of that heat off. Not all of it, but enough that it wasn't as agonizingly painful.

All he had said was something about the binding stone. Why did Darint care about that?

He traced his hands along his jacket again, and the heat faded, no longer quite as brutal as it had been before. There had to be a pattern to it, only it was a pattern that Lathan could not decipher. Not yet. If they continued tormenting him like this, maybe he could figure it out. He watched the next time Darint touched his jacket, tracing his fingers along it, and noticed that he touched a specific part of his jacket.

Once again, the wind whipped through him, jerking the air from his lungs.

Lathan resisted moving.

Darint leaned over him, watching him. "Answer questions, or this only gets worse."

The shadow had helped him, though how much would the shadow be able to protect him from if the Derithan pushed even harder?

Lathan needed to keep his mind off of those questions so he could focus instead on the pattern.

Darint used some pattern to activate the binding stones in his jacket. If Lathan could identify what that was, and if he could somehow get over to him, grab the jacket...

I wouldn't be able to do anything.

Not on his own, but if the shadow helped, it was possible that he just might be able to do something. That assumed that the shadow elemental wanted to help.

The wind faded again.

"This will persist until you provide the answers I need."

Darint turned away.

Lathan was fully prepared to struggle, knowing that he might be able to withstand the pain, but didn't know if he might be able to hold out indefinitely. There might be limits to what the elemental would protect him against. Lathan didn't know if those limits would be more than what *he* could withstand.

Another of the Derithan approached.

Lathan had seen this person before, though hadn't interacted with him. He was tall, dark of hair, and had deep-brown eyes that seemed to dismiss him.

And he wore a jacket similar to Darint.

Let them torment him.

Lathan would find a way past it.

Then he would fight.

CHAPTER 20

Tears streamed down his face. Most of them were real.

The pain had been tremendous. This Derithan—a man named Rolth—didn't have the same level of control as Darint, and Lathan didn't have the impression that he wanted to. It was almost as if he were eager to lose control, use the elementals against him, and torment him.

Lathan still hadn't said anything more, though increasingly he wondered if that wasn't the point. They didn't necessarily need for him to tell them what he knew. They were trying to break him.

The shadow lingered deep inside of him and wouldn't let him break.

Each time the pain nearly became too much, it seemed as if the shadow called on something more, draining some of the danger of the elemental used on him at the same time. It gave him a reprieve but more than that, it seemed to irritate Rolth, which only served to make him happier.

"Why do you want the shadow anyway?" Lathan asked in a break from the torture. He hadn't bothered to hide that he didn't suffer as much as Rolth wanted. He was the muscle, Lathan decided, and that meant that he wouldn't think too deeply about how Lathan withstood him. Even better, Rolth hadn't hidden his pattern. Lathan didn't know if that helped or not. He had to get ahold of the binding stone jacket, but if he could...

"Shut up," he said.

Lathan smiled to himself. He'd gotten under Rolth's skin, which he figured was a good thing. It was the second day of getting tormented by him, with Rolth eventually giving up in the evening with Darint returning long enough to see if Lathan would give up anything more. "You don't even know?"

"You know so little. You claim this is your land, but you know nothing about it."

Lathan couldn't deny that. He had lived here as long as he had known and had come to see that whatever he had thought he knew about his lands had been incomplete. He had never known that there were binding stones in the middle of the forest that would hold onto some power that would protect the forest. And he hadn't known that the shadow shouldn't have been found in this land.

That was the one takeaway from what Rolth's torment had taught him. He was blunt. Earth and fire mostly, two elements that didn't work well together, so that it actually helped Lathan to a certain extent. And it seemed to help the shadow as well. The bluntness was easier to counter.

"I know that you've been trying to find the shadow." That part he'd teased out. When they'd been chasing him, Lathan had thought that they already *had* the shadow, but that wasn't it at all. They had been looking for it—and failing.

That made him even happier.

"You know nothing."

"Don't I?" He sat up. Rolth had gotten closer to him. He was larger than Lathan, and he had the binding stone jacket, but there was a possibility that if Lathan managed to get to the jacket that he might be able to use it against him. That was Lathan's hope, anyway. "You've been looking for the shadow and haven't found it. You think to use the shadow to summon elementals that you can't get otherwise." He started laughing.

Earth squeezed him.

The shadow reacted. It seemed as if the shadow knew what he was trying—and seemed to approve. That was surprising to him but not as surprising as what happened next. The cold started working through him. It filled him.

Now?

"What elementals do you think you can find? Draasin, probably, but you wouldn't even be able to handle one of the draasin."

The earth squeezed harder, but with the cold

coursing through him, it didn't hurt the way that it could otherwise.

He was right.

Draasin.

But maybe that wasn't all.

What other of the powerful elementals might they want?

"You want to bind them," Lathan said, gritting his teeth to make it seem like he struggled with the torment, though the shadow still offered him a considerable protection.

"Like I said, you know nothing. You can't bind the draasin. You can only link to them."

Then that was what they wanted the shadow for. To link the draasin.

"And the binding stones—"

He lunged at Lathan, anger filling him. "Do not speak of them that way."

It was the same reaction that Darint had. *Why, though?* They were just stones.

It didn't matter. At this point, the only thing that mattered was that he had to find some way to draw Rolth to him.

The ground squeezed him again. It actually took his breath away for a moment before shadows reacted, pushing outward, the cold giving him enough of a buffer that he could catch his breath.

He focused on his hands. They had them bound behind him, and Lathan began to work at his wrists, rubbing them together to free himself. It was difficult, and his wrists were rubbed raw as he worked on them, but he began to feel a loosening of the bindings, until they popped free.

He held his hands together.

He waited a moment. Let Rolth think that he was still bound.

"Binding stones," Lathan said again.

Rolth ran his hands along his jacket.

Lathan took that as an opportunity.

It was growing dark, the clouds overhead making the sky even darker than it would've been otherwise, and Rolth had not expected him to do anything. For that matter, Lathan hadn't expected to be able to do anything. When he lunged, he managed to connect with Rolth right as he touched his jacket, tracing his fingers along it. Lathan slammed his hands down, cold blooming within him, coursing all the way through him, as if the shadow wanted him to stop Rolth.

Lathan squeezed. The cold began to do something different.

It flowed from him. That was surprising.

Rolth squirmed, but Lathan pressed his hand on his binding stone jacket and traced his fingers, before pushing it forward. He understood how to activate binding stones and how to direct it, so when the earth crushed Rolth, already beginning to squeeze him, Rolth's eyes widened.

Lathan punched Rolth in the side of the head, driving his fist into his temple, then into his jaw, and once more into his temple. Rolth stopped moving.

Lathan drew his hand back from the binding stone jacket and freed it from the earth. The cold still worked with him, rolling through him in a way that left him feeling as if the shadow wanted him to take action now, though Lathan wasn't exactly sure why it would have chosen this time for him to do that. He hurriedly jerked the jacket free and was surprised to feel how heavy it was.

Why *should* it be surprising, though? It was a binding stone jacket, and he should not be surprised that there would be some weight to it. Binding stones were generally heavy.

He slipped it on.

He scrambled toward the other part of the camp, reaching the strange barricade that had held him in place, and pressed on the binding stone jacket, tracing his hand along it, feeling the earth line that was in it. The ground trembled, and the barrier that had been there parted, giving him access to the inside of the camp.

Jef came toward him. "Lathan?"

"We need to get moving," he said. "Get the others. Are they all in this part of the camp?"

"Most of them. They tried to separate us, but—"

"There's not the time for us to talk about this right now. I attacked one of the Derithan, stole his binding stone jacket, and I don't know how long we have before they realize what happened. So we need to move before they come for us."

It wasn't well thought out, but after having been tortured as long as he had, Lathan didn't think that he could plan very well at all. It was a wonder that he had been able to come up with any sort of plan. A plan, such that it was.

He looked around, searching for the others, and found Marin crouched on the ground, eyes focused off into the distance. As he headed toward her, she turned to look at him. Her eyes widened for a moment.

"We need to get moving," he said.

"How?" she breathed out.

"I'll explain later, but we need to go. Gather the others. We're going to need to run. Are you able to run?"

"I might have a better idea," she said.

Even in captivity, she still looked as if she were perfectly content. She turned her eyes up, murmured a few words, and Lathan began to feel the drawing sensation. It was happening slowly, but he detected what she did. She was whispering to the wind.

And the wind answered.

"I might be able to help," he said.

Lathan probed for the wind section on the Derithan jacket. Then it began to swirl around him. Marin murmured something, and the wind began to gust even more.

"I tried to let Henash know that we need him, but I'm not sure that he will hear."

"He's gone," Lathan said. "I doubt he's going to return."

"He only left because he couldn't help us, but he's been sending word." She looked up at the sky, murmuring to the wind once again.

Henash intended to return?

Lathan didn't know why that surprised him, but it did. Maybe because he hadn't expected that Henash would return.

"What's the wind telling you?" he asked.

Marin barely turned toward him. She kept her head tipped upward, looking toward the sky, lips moving as if she were speaking to someone. "The wind tells us many things, Lathan. You just have to know how to listen."

He traced his fingers along the binding stone jacket again, feeling the strangely smooth and slightly warm fabric, and made a point of touching one particular line in the fabric so that he could try to trigger one of the elementals. When he did, he felt a hint of the soft energy that came from water. An idea came to him, and he added a bit of heat.

Marin watched him. "What does that do?"

"As far as I can tell, the jacket is somehow a binding stone—but don't call it that to the Derithan. I don't understand it, but they don't like the term."

"They probably have some sacred term for it."

He shrugged but wondered if maybe she were right. The Derithan had seemed unusually upset about the idea of him calling it a binding stone. What if the stones had some religious significance to them?

That would suggest that the elementals had some religious significance to them, and he wasn't convinced that was the case with the way that they had hunted and used the hyza elemental. Whatever else they felt, it wasn't something where they honored the elementals.

He traced his fingers along the fire elemental band in the jacket. Now that he knew what to feel for, it was much easier for him to know where to touch and trace the jacket so that he could feel the energy in it. A twinge of power surged, and this time it seemed as if the cold inside of him responded, as if the shadow elemental were reacting to the way that the heat began to build.

By combining fire and water, he hoped that he could create a layer of fog to hide what they intended to do. He didn't know if the elemental energy trapped in the jacket would be enough, but as he worked his fingers along the fabric, billowy fog eased away from him, spreading out.

"Try earth," Marin said. She had gotten close to him. "If you can somehow make all of the elements work, see if you can't mix earth in with it."

"For fog?"

"All you're trying to do with it is to see if you can mix some of the elements together so that it will create something that we can use to hide our passing, right? The fog will mix with the earth and should push it up. Otherwise there's a possibility that the earth will end up absorbing it. You don't want that. You want the fog to carry as far as possible."

"In that case, I could mix in the wind."

"You could, but let me. You don't know how to whisper to it yet."

He wanted to argue with her, but she turned away from him and began to murmur quietly enough that the wind seemed to respond, carrying the growing fog up and away from her. Lathan wouldn't have thought that she had some way of actually speaking to the wind, but what else could it be?

"Now we should go," Marin said.

The sounds from the Derithan part of the camp had started to shift as they seemed to be aware of what had happened. He followed Marin as they crossed a narrow path, and they came to the edge of the forest. A collection of the massive binding stones circled here. The arrangement was significant in some way.

"Where are the others?" Lathan whispered.

He kept his hands near the jacket, thinking that if it came down to it, he'd want to use the binding stone jacket. The fog persisted behind him, flowing up from where he'd activated the fire and water with a hint of earth thrown in to make it even more difficult for the others to see through. With a wind activation, it might not matter how much fog he'd caused to come in. The Derithan might be able to push out the fog with a powerful gust.

"Not far from here. We move over this ridge and we should find—"

The ground shifted.

Marin struggled to compensate for it. She staggered forward, and Lathan hurried to catch her, though didn't manage to get to her quickly enough. When she fell, earth started to swallow her.

Lathan lunged for her, diving to the ground.

He caught her wrist before the ground swallowed her altogether. When he pulled, a flare of absurdly painful cold washed through him, far more aggressively than he'd felt before. Lathan cried out and hated that he did. All that would do was reveal their presence.

A sudden surge of cold seemed as if it helped Marin, allowing Lathan to pull her free. She sat up and gasped. Wind whipped around her, and Lathan could *see* the elemental that she somehow summoned, though he didn't know what elemental of wind she used.

"Thanks," she muttered.

He tried to release his hold but couldn't.

Marin pulled his hand away, trying to pry it free. "You can relax," she said. Something in her voice had changed. There was a tinge of a soothing note mixed with a hint of a command. "You've helped."

When she said it, the cold within him started to fade, retreating deep within him. Now the earth began to change as well, less rumbling coming.

Behind him, there was a distinct sense of energy from within the camp. Lathan could feel what the Derithan were doing and how they attempted to push the fog that he'd released, but some held despite what the Derithan were doing.

"We need to hurry," Marin said. "Something is building."

As soon as she said it, he knew that she was right. Something *was* building, though he didn't know what it was. It seemed to be a combined power from each of the elements, something that was far more powerful than anything that they'd dealt with before.

Lathan traced his hands along the different lines in the jacket.

They seemed to reflect the power that was out and around him, as if whatever they were doing built with the similar kind of power.

Not similar.

The same.

The jackets were connected.

And he could feel it—whatever it was—building from within him.

What was more, the cold seemed to react to that, pulsing through him. Burning.

As if the shadow attempted to consume all that power.

If it did, what would happen to him?

CHAPTER 21

L athan scrambled to get the jacket off him. It burned in a way that he could scarcely even fathom. But it wasn't the jacket that was causing the problem, he knew. It was the shadow elemental buried within him that reacted to the power of the jacket, whatever that might be. That jacket had each of the elementals activated at this point, and the shadow attempted to absorb all of them.

Marin reached for him, and Lathan jerked his hand away, afraid of what would happen if the cold began to try to consume her, as well.

"You have to relax," Marin said, her voice soft. Once again, it was something of a command. Was she commanding him, or was she aware of the shadow elemental and somehow commanding that?

She had always been odd and it always seem to have some understanding of the elementals. She'd claimed to have an ability to work with them and speak with them in ways that were different than him, but he had not expected that she truly had this ability.

"I'm trying to relax," he said, his voice tight. "I'm trying to get this jacket off. It's tied to each of the elementals, and they're doing something to it." Not just to it, he thought, but through it. He wasn't exactly sure what that was, only that the longer that he wore the jacket, the more that he could feel that shadow elemental attempting to try to swallow everything that came.

"And you have to relax."

She reached for him again, and when she grabbed his wrist, he didn't fight. She was stronger than she looked. When she looked in his eyes, it seemed as if she were looking, not only at him, but at the elemental within him.

"I can see you. Relax. You don't have to fight now."

The shadow began to retreat, withdrawing to where it no longer attacked him.

"How did you do that?"

She shook her head. "I've told you. Sometimes you just need to know how to talk. Other times you need to know how to listen." She pulled him with her, and they headed away from the campsite, toward the edge of the forest.

They reached the trees.

An explosion of heat blasted. Marin squeezed his hand, and she dragged him forward.

Light bloomed where they ran, carrying them farther and farther from the campsite.

And then the wind gusted. It swirled around them

but then seemed to take up a position behind them. It was odd. Lathan was distinctly aware of how the wind seemed to create a rippling, shimmering blanket barrier behind them.

He slowed, glancing backward.

"Was that you?"

"I don't command the elementals," she said.

"You could've fooled me," he said.

She smiled tightly. "Well, sometimes I try to instruct them," she said, her smile widening. "But only when they need it. Most of the time, I simply try to talk to them. The elementals have needs, you know. It takes the right kind of person to know how to listen."

"So if it's not you, then who is it?"

"I think Henash decided to return," she said, flicking her gaze upward. "Then again, I don't think he's been gone this entire time. He's been watching, mostly because I think he worried about getting too close, but now that he knows that we managed to escape, I'm not terribly surprised he returned."

The wind rippling behind them could be Henash. They hurried forward. How could the others have gotten away from here so fast?

"Just a little farther," she said. "The wind is telling me that something is up here."

Increasingly, he felt as if her comments on what she felt of the wind were more and more likely to be true. It was a strange thing to accept and acknowledge, but it would have been stranger for him to deny it, especially after what he had seen from her.

The cold blossomed within him. He still had not yet taken off his binding stone jacket, but he no longer had the same pain that he had before, as if whatever she had done when she had used her comments to the shadow elemental had somehow convinced that to retreat. When it blossomed, it didn't have the same all-encompassing sort of hunger it had before, as if the shadow understood that it did not need to push quite as hard as it had.

The wind whistled.

When the light blossomed, Lathan didn't feel the pressure of heat bursting behind them. Marin guided him, and he followed gladly. Ever since they had left the city, he felt like he had been following someone else's direction all the time, but this time, he felt as if she was the one he should be following. If she truly had some way of speaking to the wind, then he should pay attention to her.

They reached a small hillside that wound down into a wider darkened ravine. Darkness had begun to fall in full, and without any light, they would have to go by feel, something that neither of them seemed particularly eager to attempt. As he followed Marin, he realized that she wasn't going completely by feel.

"Is the wind guiding you?"

"If you focus on it, you might be able to let the wind guide you, as well. It's not like it's whispering. Talking pretty loudly, in fact."

Lathan thought the comment odd, though how was it any odder than some of the things his father had once said to him about the elementals? He had shared a very unique view of elementals and the way that people could communicate with them. It wouldn't be altogether different than Marin's belief that she could speak to them. Perhaps it wouldn't be all that different than Henash's belief in what he did with the elementals.

He focused, wondering if perhaps he might listen and hear something from the elementals. As he did, he found the soft whispering of the wind. Not anything loud the way that Marin claimed, but there was a murmuring quality to it.

He rested his hands on his jacket, tracing his fingers along the wind line for a moment. The wind whispered around him as he traced his fingers there, giving him a sense of what was out there so Lathan thought he *could* listen as Marin wanted.

There was no further sense of the elementals behind them, though he believed that the Derithan were still after them. Marin whispered to the wind. That seemed to cause it to gust upward, as if the wind answered her.

"There," she said softly. "Can you feel it?"

He felt as if he *should* be able to feel it somehow, though could not.

"The wind. The earth. Even a hint of water and fire, though they're faint." Marin turned to look around her. She held her hands up, as if she could touch each of the elements as she spun in place. Maybe she could. "I don't know how to speak to the others as well as I do to the wind. You know that each of the elementals has a unique voice, and I don't have a way of getting to the others as well as I'd like."

They stepped down into a narrow valley.

Light surged.

It had been dark—or at least dim—and then it brightened up.

The sudden change was jarring to him. Lathan rubbed his eyes, trying to make sense of what had happened, but couldn't tell anything other than how the light had changed. Cold blossomed in him, and there was a hint of the shadow elemental trying to reach to him, though he wasn't exactly sure what the elemental wanted right now. Maybe nothing more than to alert him that it was there.

"Lathan!"

He heard Jef's voice, and knew he had to be nearby.

Every so often, cold bloomed inside of him, and he felt the other elementals around him.

"I wasn't sure what happened to you. Marin disappeared, but she's been doing that from time to time."

"I've been trying to reach Henash," Marin said.

The brightness eased a little bit.

That wasn't quite right. It wasn't that the brightness had eased so much as it was that the cold seemed to surge within him to swallow some of that brightness. The shadow elemental worked to try to help him, absorbing some of the other elemental energy nearby.

"You keep saying that you have been trying to get a hold of Henash, but if you really wanted to talk to him, wouldn't you have used the wind?"

"You know?" Lathan asked, turning to Jef.

There were other shadows behind them. Lathan counted several others.

More than he would've expected. Where had they come from?

"Well, she's been telling us all about her ability to talk to the wind, and we tried to believe her." He started to laugh and squeezed Lathan's arm. Where he touched, the shadow elemental bloomed again and cold surged through him, as if the shadow elemental were trying to swallow even that amount of touch.

Jef jerked his hand back. "What was that?"

Marin stepped closer, frowning. Lathan could see her frown, but more than that, he could see a swirling of energy around her that was new.

"Where are we?"

"She called it the Heart of the Forest," Jef said. "She says the wind wanted us to come here."

"The wind *did* want us to come here," Marin said. "And I can't help it that you can't listen. You could, but you're too stubborn."

Jef started to laugh, and he looked over to Lathan. "Do you hear that? That's the kind of thing I've been dealing with while you've been... Sorry. I know you've been preoccupied."

"A bit more than just preoccupied," Lathan said. He traced his hands along the binding stone jacket, feeling the cold blooming through him as he did again. That couldn't be a coincidence. Whatever it was that he felt as he touched the binding stone jacket, it surged through him, giving the shadow elemental some sort of a boost. "Is it safe for us to stay here?"

"For now," Marin said. "We need to wait for Henash. That's what the wind is telling me."

"And if the wind is wrong?" Jef asked.

"Has it been wrong yet?"

"I suppose not." He turned to Lathan. "She knew when you were going to break free. Can you believe that?"

"What do you mean that she knew?" Lathan asked, and he turned to Marin. "You knew that I was going to attack the Derithan?"

"The wind told me that you had enough," she said, and then she shrugged. "I don't blame you. With everything they put you through, I can't believe that you managed to hold out that long."

Lathan licked his lips. The cold seemed to be intensifying, and he had to try to ignore it.

Then it flared before falling quiet.

Wind whipped around.

Lathan looked up. Within the swirling of wind, there was a translucent energy, the shape of some wind elemental he didn't recognize. And a figure.

At first, he feared that it was one of the Derithan, but he recognized the dark-brown cloak.

"Henash," Marin said, striding over toward the clearing where Henash dropped. "It's about time. I've been told you were coming, but I didn't know it would take you this long to get here."

Lathan looked over to Jef. "She actually *can* talk to the wind."

"I know. I have to stop giving her a hard time." He frowned at Lathan. "What are you wearing?"

"A Derithan jacket." Lathan traced his hands along the surface of it. "A binding stone jacket. What do you think?"

"What do you mean that it's a binding stone jacket?"

"It took me a while to figure out how they had access to so much elemental energy," Lathan started. "At first, I thought they had a collection of binding stones. After what we saw them due to the hyza, I wondered if they might have consumed the elementals, but then I started paying attention while they were torturing me."

"I think I would've been more focused on the pain."

"I was," he said hurriedly, realizing how that sounded. The shadow elemental had protected him enough that he couldn't feel the pain as badly as he would've otherwise. But telling Jef would raise some questions that he didn't necessarily want to answer. "But after a while, you start to get numb. At least, I did. And it gave me a chance to let my mind wander and focus on what they were doing to me." He touched one of the earth lines in the binding stone jacket. "Can you feel that?"

The ground trembled slightly. Jef's eyes opened wide. Seeing that, Lathan realized just how much his vision had improved. He traced another line, using fire. He was careful with that. There was considerable power in the binding stone jacket, and he had seen how tracing too much fire could cause a surge of heat that would explode outward. He didn't want to catch Jef with that, but he also wanted him to feel the heat.

"Are all of the elementals wound into that jacket?"

"I don't think spirit is."

"And shadow?"

"I don't think shadow is, either," Lathan said.

"They kept asking about you and shadow and all of those things," he said. "We told them everything that we could. I hope that's okay. I tried to withstand it, but I couldn't. It hurt too much. I don't know how you managed to go numb and ignore it."

"It hurt," Lathan said.

They fell quiet. Lathan traced his fingers along the binding stone jacket, feeling the various lines and noticing the rippling of earth or the flash of heat or even the swirling of wind that came around him as he did. With each place that he touched, the elementals flowed.

"You might need to be careful with that," Henash said. "It's possible that they have some way of detecting it."

"Great," Jef said. "He's stolen the best weapon that we've ever found, and now they can use that to track us?"

"I don't know," Henash said. He looked past them. The others in the clearing were gathered together, and Henash frowned as he looked over to them. "We can stay here for a little while. There should be enough of a connection to wind that we can use it, but I may need to do it with one person at a time, as I don't know if I have the strength to do it in a group."

"Your plan is to carry us out on the wind?" Jef asked.

"We can't all stay here," Henash said. "They don't necessarily care about the others." He locked eyes with Lathan for a moment. "I hate to say it, but you need to go first. You might be enough to draw them away."

"I'm not leaving the others behind," he said. "If there after me, then the obvious answer is for me to stay behind." He held Henash's gaze. "Take them away. I stay here, keep activating the binding stone jacket, and maybe draw them."

He didn't like the idea of the Derithan catching him again, and certainly didn't want to let them torture him again, but he also didn't want anything to happen to people that he considered friends. Jef and Marin deserved better.

Henash grabbed Lathan, and he pulled him off to the side. He dropped his voice, but he didn't necessarily even need to do that. Wind swirled around him, which Lathan could see in a steady translucent swirl. "You know what they're after," he said, his voice harsh. "And I know you are trying to be strong, and Fiery Skies, I want the same thing, but in this case, I don't know that you need to be strong. The reason that they want you isn't so much because of the shadow, but because of how you can use the shadow. Shadow is rare."

"I know that. My father taught me that."

Henash grunted. The sound was muted, the wind tapping it down. "Of course he did. But you haven't even questioned why your father would even know about the shadow or why he would know how it was rare. The shadow was rare enough that he shouldn't have been aware of it. That is, unless he had some experience with it."

"What are you saying?"

"I suspect your father was shadow marked as well."

"So?"

"You don't understand, do you?" Henash frowned at him, cocking his head to the side. The wind swirled, and the strange translucent wind elementals continued to swirl around him, which didn't help Lathan at all. He could see them, but he couldn't tell what it was that they were. If he had a binding stone—more than the binding stone jacket, that was—he might've been able to hold the wind elemental, and he might've been able to use that to determine just which one it was. "There are only a few people who are shadow marked, and those who are have great potential."

"You've already told me that, Henash. Shadow marked means that I can call to some of the greater elementals using the shadow." That was what the Derithan wanted from him and the reason that he had held out. If they had managed to get a hold of some of those greater elementals, he didn't know what they would do, but he suspected that they would torment the people of his village and perhaps even of the kingdom.

"It's not just calling to them. You can control them."

"I'm not controlling an elemental."

"No. Not yet, at least. But you could learn to. That's what they fear."

"Why?"

"Because the shadow marked are descendants of the Asiran line."

It took a moment for him to piece that together and to come up with where he had heard that term before.

Asiran.

They were a line of people that had lived long ago, and had once controlled much of these lands, though their kingdom had faltered generations upon generations ago. Long enough that none still remained.

"I don't understand why that matters."

"I've told you why it matters. You can control the elementals."

"And?" Lathan felt as if he were dense, but he wasn't exactly sure why.

"And if you can control the elementals, you can use them to rule."

He started to smile. "Like some sort of elemental king?"

Henash nodded, his face serious. "Just like that."

Lightning crackled around them overhead, shooting from someplace high above them.

As Lathan looked up, Henash groaned.

"I thought we had more time."

CHAPTER 22

Henash and Marin made quick work of getting the others gathered, neither of them speaking as they tried to convince everyone to gather in the center of the clearing. Lightning crackled somewhere in the distance. Henash had a large, elongated binding stone clutched in his hand, and he pointed it to each person, as if he were going to use it on them.

Jef stayed close to Lathan. "What's going on with the lightning?"

"The only thing that I can think of is the Derithan have used a different elemental on us," Lathan said. "I'm not exactly sure which one, though, so don't ask."

Normally Lathan was the one to know about the elementals and to identify any of the different ones that they might end up dealing with. Lathan had a good mind for the elementals, and combined with everything that his father had taught him over the years, he had an advantage in that he knew them better than most.

But not this time.

Lightning didn't strike him as any of the elementals.

It could be a combination of something like a fire and water elemental, but how would those function? There were many different elementals that had access to more than one of the elements, something that had been difficult for Lathan to understand when he'd first been learning about the elementals, but water and fire were simply incompatible.

Maybe a mixture of wind?

"They will breach the protections of this place soon," Henash was saying. "If we move quickly, the wind should offer enough protection to carry you away. It's going to hurt. There is no way to do this with anything short of a burst of wind. You'll have to hold yourself in such a way that you make sure to protect your head. I can't guarantee that you'll land safely."

Lathan started to pull on the binding stone jacket, but when he did, the cold within him surged again. The shadow elemental seemed like it didn't want him to remove his jacket.

"It could help the others," he whispered.

Jef looked over, seeing how Lathan pulled on the jacket, and shrugged. "If you say so."

There was no point in telling Jef that he wasn't talking to him. That wouldn't matter to Jef anyway. Instead, he turned his focus to the jacket, tracing his hands along the surface of it and trying to press on the different lines that worked in it so that he could activate the different elementals. It was time that he figure out whether they would be able to help.

The cold flared again.

This time it was even more blindingly cold than it had been before. The cold surged, starting someplace deep within him before spreading out and stretching toward his head, where it seemed to linger the longest.

The wind whipped around, carrying one of the others up into the sky. Henash didn't go with them.

"I'm not sure that I want to travel that way," Jef said.

"It's not that bad so long as the wind doesn't beat at you too much," Lathan said.

Jef looked over to him. "You've done it?"

"Not intentionally. The wind... well, it just sort of lifted me."

Another gust of wind came, and this one carried another into the air. They were sent to the west. Lathan couldn't think of what would be out there, only that it wasn't toward Gorawl. Was he sending the people out of the forest—and possibly closer to the capital? That would be one way to get the others to safety, but he didn't know if that would even be enough. How fast and how high would the wind be able to carry the others?

Marin turned back to Lathan. "Can you use that jacket to help me summon the wind?"

"It's a binding stone jacket," Lathan said, tracing his hands along one of the lines that was worked into the fabric.

"Maybe it seems like that but it works more like a

summoning jacket. When you activate it, you're calling elementals to you, not forcing them to work with you. At least *you're* not forcing them to work with you. I suspect that the Derithan *had* been forcing the elementals. That's probably why they come chasing them the way that they do. Force them to serve so that when they want to call to them they have a ready supply of elementals they can draw upon." She stepped to him, reaching out and tracing her hand along the line for wind. "If you use this, you should be able to summon more of the wind elementals to us faster. That might help us get some of these others out of here before something comes." She looked up, turning her attention to the upper part of the valley, frowning as she did. "I can feel that it's coming, though I can't see them. Can you see them?"

Lathan shook his head. The lightning continued to strike, the steady streaks shooting brightness through the sky, though they never managed to reach the forest floor. There was no thunder, nothing to suggest that a storm was coming. Only the steady and rhythmic nature of the lightning.

"What do you want me to do with this?" he asked.

"I think if you use the summoning portion of it, you should be able to call to the elementals. I can't say that it's going to work *exactly* the same as it does when I call to the wind, or when Henash does, but I think there's enough similarity."

Another burst of lightning struck. This one came near where they'd been standing.

It was close—too close.

It never reached the ground.

Lathan didn't see what it was that Henash had done, but it seemed to him that Henash had to have done something. He twisted his hand, and the air above him seemed to thicken as he did, turning into something different.

The lightning struck the thickened *something* and then began to dissipate, but not completely. There was still a considerable amount of power in it. Smaller sparks stretched out to either side. The air hummed with the energy that came off the attack.

"You can help," Marin said.

Lathan doubted there was anything that he would be able to do, though energy continued to crackle around him. He pressed his hands up against the jacket, feeling for the different lines of power within it. He could summon the elementals with it, if Marin was right.

Lathan pressed on the lines.

There came a swirl of wind.

This time was different than when he had used it before. That had been a surge of power around him, as if there truly had been some power that was stored in the jacket, but this time Lathan could feel that the power that answered to him didn't come from within the jacket but from around it.

And it seemed to erupt from the binding stones that were gathered around this clearing. The lines in the jacket didn't hold the power—it did exactly what Marin had suggested and summoned it.

Now that he could feel it, he wondered how he

hadn't noticed it before. That was how they had managed to use the power of the binding stones on them. They had been using the summoning in the jacket, drawing on the power already in the clearing tied to the binding stones of this place, and pushing that outward in a way that was overly powerful for them—and something that they couldn't even overpower.

"That's it," Marin said. "Keep doing it."

Lathan traced more.

Henash sent more people off and out to the west.

When he did, Lathan was acutely aware of some elemental power involved while he traced the lines on his jacket. Another person went. Then another.

Lightning struck again but didn't manage to get quite as close to the ground as before. Whatever was out there—whether it was elemental or something else—managed to push it back and keep it firing above them.

"Quick," Henash said. "We don't have much time. You can go next."

Lathan realized that he was now talking to Jef.

Jef looked to him, a question in his eyes. Lathan shared that concern. Leaving meant that Jef was at the mercy of wherever it was that Henash sent them, though neither of them knew what it was that he did or how he could push them away.

"Go," Lathan said. "If he can get you to safety, you need to take it."

"If he's going to send me without you, I'm not going to do it."

It was a nice sentiment, but they'd been traveling

separately in the forest since the attack, and he didn't think that Jef needed to try and offer him any sort of protection.

Lightning sizzled again.

It streaked down from above, a lance from someplace high overhead. This time, Lathan could feel it as it came streaking toward him, as if there was something in the lightning that he reacted to.

Not him. The shadow elemental.

That surged. Cold bloomed through him.

Everything that happened next came in a jumble. There was a blast of wind. Jef cried out as he was *pushed* by the wind, sent flying to the edge of the clearing. Marin chased after him, though she did so far more gracefully, as if she were gliding on the wind—which she might have been.

And the lightning struck him.

When it did, the cold surged into something he'd never felt before.

He had been aware of the shadow elemental and the cold that came with it, but this was something altogether different. This was a surge of blinding pain, followed by a powerful blast of light that made everything brilliant white around him.

The light faded first.

Gradually, he could make out elements in the forest around them.

There was Henash, standing not far from them, his face twisted into one of overwhelming concern. Marin watched him, though she did it with a different expression. Was it surprise or something else? He couldn't tell.

Jef wasn't far from him, but when he looked to him, he found him lying on his side, facing out and away from the center of the clearing, as if he couldn't stand to watch whatever had happened here.

"What happened?" he asked.

The cold still hadn't faded, though it wasn't as painful as it had been. There was a tracing of it that coursed through him, and now that cold felt like a rhythm, as if it were constricting something through him. Each time that it did, there was a coursing of power. That coursing started to squeeze, practically sizzling through him.

There was no *practically* to it.

The coursing *was* sizzling through him.

He looked down and felt the strangeness that was still there, an energy that filled him—and realized that it seemed like the lightning was still flowing through him. It didn't hurt. Somehow. It seemed as if the lightning were drawn into him, absorbed by the shadow.

"Do you see what's happening?" Henash said.

Marin watched him, keeping a distance away from him as if she were concerned that he might hurt her—or the elementals that she spent so much time talking to.

"I felt the lightning strike... and then nothing. I don't know what to make of it."

Henash approached him. He moved carefully, with Marin watching, saying nothing, though Lathan could see the concern etched in her eyes. "Can you still feel it?"

"I can feel something. The cold, mostly."

Henash looked to Marin before turning back to Lathan. "The cold." He laughed nervously, a strange sound coming from Henash. "I've been trying to figure out why they were so convinced that you had something that they wanted. The shadow binding stone might have been something, but that wouldn't have been enough for them. No. They would have chased it, but they wouldn't have pushed so much power at something like that."

Henash took another step toward Lathan, cocking his head to the side as he regarded him. "How long have you known?"

"About the shadow?"

Henash nodded. "You *do* know, don't you?"

"I think it was when the wind carried me up. Something happened at that time. I tried to use the shadow elemental binding stone but it didn't work."

"Because you hadn't bound part of the shadow. You'd bound the *shadow*. And then you called it to yourself." His voice dropped toward the end, and he shook his head. "What did you do, Lathan?"

The air crackled, and it seemed like another attack was about to come, but never did. There was a quiet in the air otherwise.

"What's this about?" Jef asked. "Why did *someone* push me like that?"

"We need to get moving," Henash said. He looked at Marin. "Do you think that you're ready to call the elementals?"

"I've had Lathan using the summons. That seems to

be directing more of them here. I think that with his help, we should be able to call even more of them than we had before."

"It's not anything that I've done," Lathan said. "It's the stones." He pointed to the binding stones that created a small circle around the clearing. Most of the stones were quite large and all of them were irregular, creating a strange contour to everything. The power they trapped seemed to call on even more energy than what they'd been drawing before, enough that Lathan could feel how that power seemed to radiate outward. "They're holding onto some of the elemental power that's here. I can feel it."

Henash nodded slowly. "As they should. Perhaps it's for the best that we aren't asking too much of them. We don't want the stones to have to pour out too much of their potential with a pending attack."

The air started to crackle again. Lathan felt it *before* he saw anything.

It was almost as if some part of him reacted to that crackling. The energy that coursed within him flowed upward, a cold that mixed with some aspect that struck his mind, leaving a sense of the power that bloomed there, as if the shadow elemental wanted him to know it was there...

Then the cold seemed to shoot *out* of his mind.

That was a different sense than he'd had before. When it did, it streaked upward. A part of it remained connected to him, but he could feel how the cold went upward, chasing after the lightning that he knew would come at any moment.

Then the cold struck the lightning. There was a flash. The lightning faded. The cold withdrew down and *into* Lathan. When it did, he detected the same surge of power that he'd been feeling before, the coursing of energy that started from deep within him and then began to flow outward.

"What was *that*?" Jef whispered.

"That is what the Derithan are after," Henash said. "And *that* is what they cannot obtain."

CHAPTER 23

Henash spoke softly at the edge of the clearing, leaning toward Marin. The air hung with a hint of fog. That had been Lathan's doing, though now it seemed as if the fog just began to slowly ease away, as if there was something that were pushing the fog from the ground, mixing the elementals the way that he had when drawing on the binding stone jacket.

Or the summoning jacket.

If that was what it was. Lathan didn't know whether that was what it did. Maybe it was nothing more than a strangely woven binding stone, but if that were the case, why did it seem like he could feel the shifting movement of the elementals coming from the *actual* binding stones near him?

"What do you think the two of them are talking about?" Jef asked, leaning close to him. "Is it the way you're suddenly able to absorb lightning?"

Lathan stared into the distance. There hadn't been another strike, but he could still feel that energy within him. It was as if the shadow elemental and however it bound that power left him charged.

Why would it do that to him?

"I'm not doing anything," he said, "and don't you let Henash make you think that I am."

"I saw it, Lathan." He kept his voice soft. "Now, I don't know what it is that I saw, but I saw the way you seemed to catch the lightning. Then you pulled it down into you."

"That was—"

The elemental?

Him?

Lathan didn't know.

The one thing that he *did* know was that whatever it was had definite power. He'd felt the way the elemental had swung up so that it could catch the lightning before it did anything to him. Without it, he would have been destroyed.

"It doesn't matter. We can't linger here any longer."

Jef shrugged. "I don't care what it was. Regardless of what they tell you, it was amazing. Don't let them make you think otherwise."

He snorted. "Thanks."

"Just think about it. We've been chasing—and collecting—elementals for as long as I can remember and now you have some way of simply drawing it to you? What would it have been like if we knew that all along?"

"I don't know," he muttered.

He stomped over to Henash, who looked up when he neared. The wind swirled around him, creating a thin, barely visible barrier that worked its way around him. Lathan could feel the wind and could feel the way that it was holding him back. Out of irritation, he traced his fingers along his binding stone jacket. Wind surged, and it slammed into the protections that Henash had placed around he and Marin.

"I don't know what the two of you are discussing, but if it's not about getting out of here, then I don't want to know. The Derithan *will* attack again."

"They will," Henash said, turning to Lathan. "But I think they need to regroup to decide what the best approach might be. Given what you've now demonstrated to them—not only escaping with one of their summoning items, but now catching one of their greatest weapons—I think they'll hesitate. They still want the shadow so that they can use it to draw out another weapon, but they recognize that you have posed a different danger than they had probably anticipated."

Lathan looked up the slope heading out of the valley. He couldn't see anything up there—only more of the trees. Some of the fog hovered above them as well, drifting upward and slowly starting to thicken, which he didn't know if he needed to try anything with the elementals to disrupt.

"What do you suggest, then?"

"I've been talking to Marin about what happens if I don't make it out of the forest." He looked upward. The wind once more circled around him, a steady and drifting energy that continued to flow near him. "Not that I'm preparing for failure, but one of the things that I learned long ago is that you must prepare for the possibility of failure. In this case, given what we're dealing with, one of us needs to get to the king to let him know what the Derithan have done. We should have been safe from them."

"Even with what you know of them?" Lathan asked.

"What do you believe that I've told you about them that I should know differently?"

"That..." Lathan thought about all the different things that he'd started to learn about the Derithan. They hunted elementals, but that didn't seem to be the complete truth. They had hunted the elementals, and when he'd seen them chasing the hyza, he had feared for the safety of the elemental, but not because he worried about the elemental so much as that he worried about what someone like that would be able to do once they trapped that kind of power. They obviously had something that they could do to deal with it. They had drawn the elementals to them.

What would happen if they were to access even more powerful elementals?

That wasn't the question he should be asking, though.

Lathan started to look around. "Why here?" he whispered.

"Exactly."

"There's something in this forest that they're after. Not the binding stones, though that is a part of it, isn't it?" Lathan hadn't been sure what it was. They had gone under the assumption that the Derithan had been after the shadow elemental and had chased Lathan into the forest because of it. Once they had him captured, they hadn't done anything other than wait—as if they needed him and the shadow elemental here so that they could use it for whatever it was that they intended.

He headed over to the nearest of the binding stones.

Lathan could feel the stones, and he could feel the energy that seemed to be trapped within them. Elemental energy. That was obvious as he approached, though he didn't know if that was because he had somehow been drawing upon the jacket as he approached or if it was a different reason. Maybe it was simply that there was significant power here. Lots of elemental power.

Jef stood next to him. "I can feel it. It's like a stone that has trapped too much. You know what it's like when we bring some of our stones into the Saval, and they take the bonded elemental energy? That's what this feels like. It's like the stone itself is filled. Almost too much, though I don't think that something like that would ever be *too* much. Just enough that we can feel."

Jef crouched down, holding his hands above the stone. He let out a soft sigh as he did, tracing his fingers above the surface of the stone, and Lathan wondered if there was anything within it he could feel that Lathan could not.

Rather than mimicking Jef, Lathan used the jacket. If it served as a summons, then he could draw that out. If there was something else to it, then maybe he could take advantage of that, as well.

When he hit one of the lines—not wind, though he had been tracing wind quite a lot recently—he noticed that the air started to shimmer. Heat. Fog.

Lathan looked around.

That fog had been a constant presence since they'd come into the forest, though for the most part, he'd been convinced that the fog was tied to what he and the others had been doing with the elementals. What if there was something else going on?

When he touched the jacket, tracing his hands along the surface and feeling the way that everything seemed to surge, he was more alert about the fog—and could feel the way that power seemed to linger within it.

"What do you feel?" Henash asked.

He stood separate from Lathan, with Marin standing near him. Neither of them spoke, as if they weren't sure what they could say. At this point, Lathan didn't know what they needed to say. There was a hint of the energy all around him, but that energy seemed to come from the forest as much as it came from anything.

"I feel the pull that's here," he started. "It seems drawn to the jacket."

"Is it the jacket or is it drawn to you?" Henash asked.

The shadow.

Was it that?

As he stood in place, he could feel the cold, but ever since he'd been introduced to the shadow elemental in the way that he had, he had been aware of the cold. That sense had grown to be almost a part of him, if something like that could be a part of anyone.

But did it draw on the energy that he detected?

It was almost as if the shadow was trying to call to the elemental and it was working with the jacket.

Was the jacket some sort of shadow elemental as well?

Lathan trailed his hands along the jacket, his fingers pressing into the fabric, attempting a summons.

Henash was quiet, and Jef was looking at him, concern in his eyes.

"Parts of the forest are old," Henash said. "We've talked about how those who came before once used the forest as a way to offer a measure of protection. But it wasn't protection *from* the elementals. It was *for* the elementals."

Marin stepped forward. "If you listen, you can hear the whispers. They still speak of it. The elementals love to talk, if you're willing to listen."

Jef started to smirk, but when Marin shot him a hard-eyed stare, he fell silent and shook his head. "What do I know?"

Lathan had tried listening to the elementals since she had made that claim, much like he had tried listening to the elementals when his father had wanted him to know how to feel for them. There was power to be found, his father always believed, and if he could find that power, and if he could understand it, then he'd be better equipped to bind it.

"What elementals?" Lathan asked.

Was that a murmuring that he started to hear?

That had to be his imagination. There wasn't anything whispering above him—was there? The cold within him persisted, though. That was definitely there.

"There was a time when the elementals were chased for a different reason than how we use them," Henash said. "There are those like Marin who still feel that we've overused the connection to them, but the elementals have not restricted what we draw from them—though they could."

"You're talking about what people used to do *with* the elementals," Lathan said.

His father had shared that with him as well. Before Gorawl, and before the kingdom, there had been people who chased the elementals to the point that they were destroyed. That was hard for him to imagine now, especially as it seemed difficult to believe that the elementals *could* be destroyed. At least, he would have said that before having seen the way that the Derithan were willing to hunt.

"That. And something that came before. Long ago." He looked to Marin. "Records of that time in the Great Library are sparse, and even the elementals don't speak of it much. They might not even remember, though the elemental memory is much greater than that of mankind. They called it the Bonding. That's all we know."

Lathan leaned down and looked at the binding stone nearest him. The name was too similar to binding stone to be coincidence, but what was this binding?

He held his hand out, reaching for the stone, when a surge of faint coldness began to work through him. It was a subtle sort of energy, but he noticed that the shadow elemental seemed to react to his hand here, as if there were something about this place—and this binding stone—that it didn't like.

Lathan pulled his hand back.

"So the elementals came here to be... what? Safe? Protected?" Jef asked.

He turned to Marin. Lathan could see the confusion on his friend's face. He wore it openly, though when it came to Jef, he often wore his emotions openly.

"The Derithan are not the first to think that they would control them," Marin said. "We do it to this day."

"Not like that," Henash said.

"Not like that, but close enough that it doesn't even matter. Not anymore. The elementals *let* you draw on them because they know the alternative is worse."

"Or because it doesn't harm them."

"Do you really believe that, Henash? After what you've seen, and what I know you can feel, do you really believe that what they"—she shot Lathan and Jef irritated glares—"do to them that they would simply not care?"

"My father always said that what we do isn't to the elementals," Lathan said. Marin looked over, seemingly still angry. He shrugged. "Well, that's what he said. We didn't do anything *to* them. We connect *through* them. The elementals tap into something greater, and that's what we're trying to reach."

"To be just like the Derithan," Marin said, waving her hand.

"What?" Jef said.

Henash frowned. "What makes you say that?"

"What makes you not able to see it?" She looked to the binding stone, then to the jacket that Lathan wore. "That's what they're doing, after all. They don't *need* the elementals to draw on the power of the elements. Oh, they have ways of summoning them, but they don't need that for what they do."

"They reach the elements themselves?" Jef asked. "You think the Derithan are some sort of elemental?"

She turned and jabbed him in the chest with her finger. "It's not a matter of *them* being an elemental. There are powers of the elements in the world. You don't need to be one of them to reach it. You just have to have the right kind of connection in order to do it. The elementals, especially the wind, talk about it. They say that was once common. Now everyone tries to just use the elementals—because they think it's easy."

"It's *not* easy," Jef said. "It's just that it's the only way to do it. Tell her, Lathan."

Lathan didn't have a chance to tell her.

The ground started to shake.

The energy of the trembling was more than what they had felt before, this time seeming to come from all over. He could feel something through the jacket and through the shadow elemental within him, but he didn't know what it was the shadow tried to tell him.

A warning?

"We need to move," Henash said.

Trembling came from everywhere around him. How much of this was elemental, and how much of it was tied to the binding stones here? He traced his hands over the jacket. Wind swirled. Earth rumbled. There was even a hint of heat, that fire that seemed to come from someplace buried.

"Go," Henash said. He came toward Lathan, and he whipped his hand around him, creating a circle, as if he were commanding the wind. Perhaps he was. Lathan didn't exactly know how Henash used the wind. Some of it seemed to be different than a binding stone. "If they get you, they will be able to do the very thing they wanted to do. They will be able to control the elementals. I will try to get word to the Saval. If I can get word there, Tolinar should be able to help us."

"I don't know that I can." Lathan wasn't sure why Henash trusted Tolinar, though he suspected that it was the same reason that the kingdom trusted him, and why he had been sent to the city in the first place.

"You may not, but the shadow connection that you have should be able to help."

The cold surged within him. He could feel that cold washing over him. It came regularly. Rhythmically.

Somehow, Lathan was going to have to use that shadow connection. He didn't know what that was going to entail, though.

Wind suddenly whipped around him.

This time, Lathan had a distinct sense that the wind was from Henash and not from anywhere else. Marin had started to drift, floating in the air. Jef watched her, and it seemed to Lathan that the wind started to tug at him as well.

"How is she doing that?" Jef whispered.

"As far as I can tell, she's probably talking to the elemental. Maybe elementals. I can't tell."

"Do you think you could do that?"

"I don't have the same ability to talk to elementals."

Henash floated as well.

But now the wind was tugging at Lathan, even more forcefully than before. It was doing the same to Jef. The two of them were floating. It wasn't unpleasant, not the way that it had been when the wind had attempted to lift him before and the shadow elemental had surged within him, reacting as if to protect him. This was soft, almost comfortable. Lathan could even imagine traveling like this.

Not just imagine it. He *was* traveling like this.

They were carried up, above the trees, and then even higher. Somewhere he could see Marin and Henash, but it was difficult to make them out clearly. The wind swirled, and Lathan pressed his hand over the wind lying on the jacket until the wind wrapped around him and then around Jef. Jef cried out, though maybe he'd been crying out for a while and the wind was just tearing his yells away from him. If only Lathan had a way to control all of this.

But didn't he? He had the shadow.

That cold was there.

"Help me," he whispered.

Lathan had no idea if it would make any difference to talk to the elemental, but it felt like the right thing to do.

Cold began to bloom through him. This was different than it had been before. When he had felt the cold in the past, there had been surges of cold, not this steady growing sense of it. This did not hurt. And it began to steady them.

"I need you to help him, too," Lathan said.

Was he really talking to an elemental?

After all the time that Marin had suggested he talk to the elementals, here he was, doing exactly that. And it seemed to him that the elemental listened.

They stabilized.

"Keep us with them," Lathan said.

The cold pulsated within him. It was faint, but that was definitely what he felt.

They were flying on the wind.

But where were they flying *to*?

CHAPTER 24

Lathan and Jef seem to have an easier time with the wind than Henash and Marin. When he looked over to them, there was almost a tremulous quality to the way the wind was swirling around them, unlike how it was swirling around he and Jef. Could the shadow have made such a difference?

Lathan wasn't exactly sure how he felt about that. He didn't want to control the wind. He didn't want to *harm* the wind, though it seemed as if the shadow were guiding him.

Henash and Marin began to descend.

"Are you able to control this?" Jef asked.

Lathan ignored him while focusing on the shadow, along with the binding stone jacket.

"Bring us down after them," he said, not knowing if he could talk to the elemental that way. It had seemed to work the last time, though.

And it worked this time. The elemental began to

steadily lower them, so that they were descending gradually. The wind still whistled around them, but Lathan realized that he hadn't been feeling that whistling nearly as much as he would have expected. It was as if some buffer around them offered a measure of protection.

When they came to land, they did so near the shoreline.

He took a few steps, pleased he was back on solid ground, while Jef dropped to his knees, leaning forward and kissing the ground. Henash and Marin both turned to watch the other two. Behind them, the forest stretched. Lathan could see the trees, a swirling of what looked like a fog that hung over it, but he could not tell if there were any other elementals that were active in the forest.

The cold remained with him.

He strode toward Henash. "Why did you bring us here like that?"

Henash frowned. "I didn't. I started to, but I didn't have any command over it."

Lathan glanced to Marin, but she was shaking her head as well.

"I didn't have anything to do with it. I can talk to the wind, as you probably figured, but I've never managed to coax it into carrying me. If I could have, we wouldn't have been trapped in the Derithan camp for as long as we had been. But why here?"

Where was *here*?

This wasn't a part of the shoreline that he was familiar with. He made his way over to the cliff's edge, and looked down. Waves crashed far below, but he didn't need to approach in order for him to have an idea of what to expect down there. He could hear the waves, he could feel a bit of spray in the air, and what was more, it was almost as if the connection he had with the shadow had permitted him to *feel* it as well. That was the strangest part of it.

Marin joined him, looking down. "It's almost peaceful. Except when you start to think about how the water would crush you if you were to fall into it. Some people think that the waves have an elemental within them, but I don't think that's the case. I think the elemental is beneath the waves."

"My father claimed the spray is the elemental."

Marin nodded. "I've heard that, too."

They had gone down to observe it one time, and Lathan had looked at the waves as they crashed but had not been able to identify any sort of elemental within them, despite his father's prodding.

Lathan turned back to Henash. "Let's say that this was the shadow." Henash nodded. "I'm not exactly sure if that's what it was, but assuming that it might have been, why do you think that the shadow elemental would have carried us here?"

"Probably to call more elemental energies to it," Henash said.

"That hasn't been my impression." He wasn't exactly sure how to describe what impression he had, only that when he felt the shadow blooming within him, it did not seem to try to call different elementals to it. Then again, he had felt how the shadow had seemed to absorb some elemental energy, as if it were more than happy to try to swallow some of that power, consuming it.

He stood on the edge of the rock, looking down at the water. "Why did you bring us here?"

Marin looked at him, but she didn't say anything. She probably approved of his attempt to speak to the elemental. She always had wanted others to use the same techniques she did, presumably to affirm that she was not nearly as touched in the head as some claimed.

The cold flowed through him, but it didn't surge the way that it had before. Perhaps the cold and the shadow elemental that was tied to the cold had come to connect to him in a different way.

"We can't stay here. I don't know how long it will take the Derithan to realize that we are gone, but I suspect they will know pretty quickly. If they have any way of tracking us, we don't want to remain someplace out in the open," Lathan said.

He didn't know if the Derithan could track them. They had proven formidable, and they had found them already, so Lathan couldn't help but feel as if it were incredibly likely that they had some way of following them. They had to stay ahead of them somehow.

Even though he felt the shadow elemental, Lathan couldn't tell what the elemental intended. It seemed to him there was something to what the elemental tried to tell him. There was cold that bloomed within him, though the cold was not a burst as it had been several times when he had been stealing the elemental energy.

This was a steady, almost soft sort of feel. It wasn't unpleasant. In fact, there were parts of it that felt almost comforting.

"Let me get this straight," Jef started. "You've got some shadow elemental that is connected to you in a way that you now can feel it? And it's somehow absorbing other elementals, and... What? Using them?"

Lathan shrugged. "I'm not exactly sure if the elemental is using them, collecting them, or simply absorbing them. It felt as if the shadow guided us while we traveled."

"It wants something, though, right? The elemental is asking you to do something to help it."

"I don't even know if the elemental knows what it wants," Lathan said.

"Well, think about where we were when we first came across it. Do you think that matters?"

"Possibly. I don't really know."

"We were chasing hyza. So if the elemental was after fire..."

Lathan chuckled, and he shook his head. "Again, I'm not so sure that it's quite that simple."

"But why wouldn't it be?" He looked over to Lathan. "Isn't that what you've been trying to figure out, anyway? The shadow has to be after something. It might be using you in some way, but it's after something else." Jef snorted. "And here I am talking about an elemental having some intention, as if it was some intelligent and sentient creature."

Marin turned then. Had she been listening the entire time?

"Do you really think elementals could live as long as they do and not be intelligent? They aren't simple mindless creatures, Jef."

He raised his hands, as if to hold her off. "I wasn't trying to upset you."

"And do you really think there are no elementals here now? They are listening. They know what you're saying about them."

Jef tipped his head up, looking around him. "If the elementals are here, and if they are listening, then they know I don't mean them any harm."

"They also know that you have enjoyed using binding stones to try to hold and control them."

"Again," he said. "It's not about me trying to control them. I'm just trying to collect one aspect of their power. Is that so bad?" He looked over to Lathan. "And why is she targeting me here. You've done the same sort of thing. And I would think that would mean that we both are at fault, at least if were going on the belief that the elementals are intelligent and should be protected, and maybe even respected." His voice trailed off a little at the end, as if he couldn't believe what he was saying. Maybe he couldn't.

Marin let out a sigh and glanced over to Henash, who was standing on the shoreline. He looked out over the water. "They aren't wrong. We've been coming at this the wrong way. We've been trying to figure out what the

Derithan are after, but what if the better question is what the shadow elemental is after?"

"I've been trying to talk to it but haven't been able to find anything."

Jef nodded. "There you go. He can't talk to the shadow elemental. But you were saying something about me being right. I'll be honest, I do like hearing that sort of thing. The problem is that I'm not exactly sure what I'm right about. Are you talking about me trying to understand what the elemental wants us to do?"

"We came across the shadow while we were chasing hyza. We thought that it was the Derithan chasing after the shadow which caused it to run, but what if the shadow chased hyza?"

"I don't know. What reason would an elemental like that have for catching a fire elemental?"

"But it's not just fire," Lathan said. "That's the thing about hyza. I remember when my father told me about it. They are fire and earth. It's a strange combination, to be sure, but when you collect from hyza, you are really accessing two elements at the same time." It was part of the reason that he had been intrigued by hyza. Along with other elementals that were like that. Hyza wasn't unique in having that sort of connection, but such multiple element-bonded elementals were fairly rare.

"Perhaps the shadow was chasing hyza because it was hungry," Jef said.

"Elementals don't eat elementals," Marin said.

"You're an expert on that?"

"More than you."

"Elementals have to eat. At least, if they aren't the mindless beasts that you claim them to be."

"What do you think ara eats? More of the wind?"

Lathan smiled at the suggestion.

"I'm sure there's dust or small creatures that float in the wind. Maybe that elemental eats another elemental of wind. Sort of a predatory cycle, if you will. I don't really know."

"The elementals are fed by the elements. That's what you collect from."

"And you get all upset when we do, because you think we're hurting them, but if all we are doing is disrupting their eating, we're just making them hungry, not much more than that."

Lathan turned away from the two of them.

His mind worked through what he had encountered with the Derithan, along with what he had encountered with the shadow. If the shadow elemental had not been simply running from the Derithan, what was it after?

Better yet, where was the hyza elemental going? They still didn't know why the elementals had been migrating. That seemed significant for some reason.

And the Derithan had been after the hyza, though Lathan didn't know if it was for the same reason the elementals had been migrating, or if there was something else to it.

"I don't suppose either of you can talk to fire," he said, turning and interrupting Marin and Jef's argument. Henash looked up at him. "That's assuming that any of us are right on what was taking place. Assuming that any of us knew what the shadow was doing. Maybe chasing hyza, or perhaps... I don't know. Something else. If we could speak to fire, or one of the elementals, we might be able to get some answers."

It seemed impossible to even consider.

"I can only speak to wind," Marin said. "I'm still working on other elementals. Most don't like to talk to me the same as wind does. But when it does talk, there are many things I can learn."

"You can't learn how to talk to fire."

"But I can talk to elementals who can," Marin said.

She tipped her head back, and looked up at the sky. She started moving her lips, but she didn't say anything that Lathan could hear.

"I doubt this is going to do anything," Jef muttered.

"I don't know. Maybe we need to give her a chance."

"To do what? To keep making us believe that she actually can speak to the elementals? I did see her flying, but if that was the shadow, and not her, maybe she wasn't doing anything anyway."

Marin kept her head tipped back, lips moving soundlessly. The longer that she did, the more that Lathan began to question whether or not she truly could speak to the wind.

Then she looked over. "I know where to look."

CHAPTER 25

They had been walking for hours. Lathan wondered why they chose to walk if the wind could carry them, and when he had asked Henash, he had been told that they only traveled by wind when they had no choice otherwise. It seemed a bit ridiculous. If the wind could carry them, why not take the fastest approach?

The blackened rock raised in an outline before them, reminding Lathan of when they had come across the hyza. It felt as if it had been weeks ago, though it had only been a few days.

The landscape had shifted. Much of it was scrub plants. Dried, often thorny, and if they had any leaves, they were waxy and thick. There was no water, and Lathan wondered whether that might be a problem, though he still had his binding stone jacket, and suspected that if it came down to needing water, he could simply trail his hand along one of the lines, summon some water, and they would have what they needed. Food was a different matter, though. In a land like this, there didn't appear to be much to eat.

At least, there hadn't appeared to be much to eat. Henash didn't seem to be bothered by the bleakness. He had stopped at one plant, crouched down in front of it, looked at the leaves, and then carefully pulled one off. "You have to watch for thorns, but the leaves are edible. And it stores water, so if you don't have connection to a water elemental," he said, glancing to Lathan and nodding, "you can get some that way. It's not ideal. And it doesn't taste the best, but it does provide some sustenance."

Lathan had avoided plucking his own leaf for as long as possible, but when his stomach began to rumble, he had grabbed one as carefully as he could, barely managing to avoid one of the thorns that Henash had warned them about, and took a careful nibbling bite.

It was bitter. Chewy. As he chewed, the pulp lodged in his teeth unpleasantly, and he tried not to think about it too much.

Jef had chosen the same time to take his own leaf. "Well, this is just awful. I hope we aren't stranded out here too long. I'm not looking for gourmet, but I certainly wouldn't mind a little meat."

"If you can catch one of the mice or squirrels that live out here, feel free," Henash said, waving his hand out into the rocky, bleak scrub that surrounded them. "Even if you catch it, though, they don't taste much better."

Marin chewed on her leaf without saying a word.

Gradually, the landscape shifted again. The scrub plants ended.

All that was left were rocks that piled up, many of them black, and heaping mounds of stone as if some massive battle had been fought here at one point. He'd seen glimpses of this when hunting with Jef and had been to the border of it with his father when he'd been younger, but that had been a long time ago.

There had been no sign of the Derithan since they'd left the forest. Lathan thought that was somewhat reassuring. The Derithan had no shortage of elementals they could call upon for them to pursue them, but the further they went, the more he started to question if it meant they had the wrong idea traveling this way.

What if the Derithan weren't after the shadow?

"They aren't going to stop pursuing us," Marin said. "Until they have what they want."

Henash had nodded.

Lathan couldn't help but wonder what the two of them knew that he did not. It seemed to him that there was something more they had not yet shared. "They might've gone after the shadow in a different way," he said. "Maybe they decided that it was too difficult for them to acquire coming this direction."

"Perhaps," Henash said. His tone suggested that he didn't believe it.

Lathan didn't believe it, either. With as much as the Derithan had pursued them, he had a hard time thinking they would have abandoned them so quickly. There had to be another explanation.

"What do they want?" Lathan whispered.

This time, it wasn't to Henash. The question was directed toward the shadow elemental, and he didn't think that the elemental would answer him. Surprisingly, a wave of cold began to flow through him, starting steadily and building within him. That energy began to swell upward, then stopped somewhere in his belly before it continued upward, reaching a place that lingered in his head.

His breath caught.

It was more than just the cold. It was a sense of movement. Wind. A rumbling, though he didn't know if that came from outside of him. Heat? That couldn't really be there, could it? A surge of understanding flooded him, the heat washing through him. And lastly, he could swear his heart hammered more heavily, though it wasn't anything that he controlled. It came from beyond him.

Was that the shadow?

The shadow controlled all of the elements. He believed that. And now he wondered if the elemental tried to tell him something.

What is it?

Move.

Lathan's heart hammered again.

That had come from within him.

From the *shadow.*

Are you talking to me? Lathan asked, not sure how such a thing would even be possible.

Marin warned that he should try to listen to the

elementals. And his father had spoken of something similar. Was this it?

You have taken too long.

"Lathan?" Henash asked.

His voice seemed to come from a distance. A great distance. Lathan didn't want to ignore him, but he wanted to focus on the elemental as much as he could now. He felt like he needed to focus on the elemental because it was there, waiting on him. And he seemed to *know* that the elemental *had* been waiting on him.

"I'm fine," he whispered.

But was he?

You should move.

The elemental guided him. Not just guiding him. *Directing* him.

Where do you want us to go?

Not us. You.

Where do I need to go?

Black Rock.

That was where they'd been going. That was where he had thought they needed to go anyway, and he'd been right. But why would they need to go there?

Gathering.

It seemed as if the shadow was having a hard time getting out what he wanted to say, though that might only be his imagination. The elemental spoke to him.

And Lathan could talk back to him.

All of that seemed... impossible.

What kind of a gathering?

The questions came deep in his mind, and there was

something about talking to the elemental like this that was strange, though it was also natural. How could he talk to the elemental like this? Marin actually spoke out loud. And Henash had seemed to do the same thing.

Something touched his arm.

Lathan jerked his arm away before realizing what he did.

"What's going on here?" Jef whispered. He looked over to Henash, who stood off to the side of the path, watching them both. Did he know? Probably not, but this *was* Henash, so Lathan wouldn't be surprised if he somehow suspected.

"I can hear it."

Henash pursed his lips.

"You hear what? This elemental?"

Lathan nodded. Now he even had a sense that the elemental waited on him, trying to give him a chance to gather his thoughts before he pushed him even more. Why would Lathan know that?

"He—it?—started talking to me. I can hear it," he said, touching one hand to his temple and rubbing at it for a moment. "I know how that sounds. But I can hear him. He tells me that I need to go to Blackstone because there's some sort of gathering."

"The elemental told you that?" Henash asked.

"That's what it said. I have a sense that the elemental wants to tell me more but is having some difficulty doing that."

"If the shadow has not spoken to another in a while, it might be difficult. Not all elementals have that ability, or have that interest. They need to practice, much like you—or I—would need to practice if that were us."

That was what Lathan would need to do, then. Practice. But what was he to practice doing? Talking? Trying to understand the elemental? All of that seemed impossible for him to even consider.

No time to consider. You focus.

I'm trying.

There seemed to be something more in what the elemental was saying. He heard the words, but there was something more within it as well.

Lathan had said the elemental didn't understand him, but it was him as well. He didn't understand everything that the elemental tried to tell him, either.

Move faster. You.

What about the others?

You. Faster. They come.

How will they come?

They come.

Lathan didn't feel like he was getting where he needed. "The elemental wants me to—"

Wind whipped around him.

What are you doing?

You go. They come.

"What's it doing?" Jef asked.

"I don't know what it's doing. It's trying to tell me that I need to go with it, but I'm trying to stay here." *I'm not ready to go with you. I need to stay with them.*

You come.

Then the wind picked up even more. It was swirling

with considerable power, enough that Lathan detected the power that was there and how it began to build.

Then it carried him.

Don't. I can't do this.

You come. They follow.

That was what the elemental had been saying over and over.

They follow.

"Follow us!" Lathan shouted.

He didn't have any idea if they reacted in time. The only thing he knew was that the elemental had lifted him, sweeping him above the ground and back into the air so that he was flying. Again.

This time, Lathan had no control.

When he touched the binding stone jacket, it felt as if the shadow took that power and *swallowed* it.

There was laughter.

Actual laughter.

What's so funny?

You. Not swallow. Taking the bond. No swallow.

Isn't that what you're doing? You're taking the elementals and absorbing them.

There was more laughter. The sound of it came from deep inside of his mind, and it was enough that he felt as if the elemental was actively amused by his ignorance. They were flying high above the ground now—and it was definitely *they* more than it was him. He could tell that the elemental had the control in this situation, even if he didn't understand what it was that the elemental did to him.

Not absorb. Know so little.

There weren't many times when he would agree that he knew little about the elementals. His father had made a point of ensuring that he knew the elementals, knew the difference between them and knew how to connect to them. He had studied under his father's tutelage so that he could master the connection to the elementals and had worked to the point where he could do things that even those who studied in the Saval could not. That was how he and Jef had convinced themselves that they didn't need the Saval for them to understand the elementals.

But this was something that *was* beyond him.

And the elemental had made a point of sharing with him how little he knew, and there was nothing that Lathan could do to prove otherwise. He *didn't* know nearly enough. Marin had talked about speaking to the elementals, and he hadn't known whether that was something that he could actually do until now. For a long time, he had thought that she was speaking to the elementals in the same way that his father had taught him to speak to them, trying to connect so that he could understand what they might want and need from him. Little had he known that it was nothing like that.

Where are you taking me?

Black Rock.

The others had started to pursue them now, so he felt a measure of relief. Knowing that he wouldn't be traveling alone—though he wasn't exactly sure that he'd ever be alone with the shadow elemental in the back of his mind—helped him with the anxiety that he felt about what the elemental wanted out of him.

Why? What's the Gathering?

It felt formal. He wasn't sure why that was, only that it seemed to him that the Gathering was something significant for the elementals.

Gathering.

Lathan couldn't get a sense of what the elemental was trying to tell him, though it seemed important.

They traveled quickly. This time, there was a sense of the wind, but there was a sense that they were traveling even faster than he would have imagined possible. When he'd flown with the elemental in the past, he had known the speed, but there had been a sense of the wind and the energy and the power that was there. This time, there was something that seemed to surround him in a way that felt almost protective, but the more that he focused the more that he didn't know whether this was anything that he could actually connect to. The elemental created some strange power.

There was something more to it though.

As he focused on it, he became aware of how the elemental seemed to connect to the binding stone jacket. At first, he had thought that connection was not real, but the more that they traveled, the more that he understood the power of the elemental and how it was drawing on some aspect of the jacket. It was coming through that connection, and it was doing so in a way that left him trembling with the power.

You are swallowing that power.

Not swallow, the shadow said again. *Connect. Bond.*

Could the shadow be doing the same thing that he had been doing when he had been working with the elementals? Why wouldn't it be able to do much of the same? There would be no reason that the connection he made with the elementals would be unique. He had to use the binding stone, but he also understood the elementals likely had a way of ignoring that kind of power.

And perhaps that was what the elemental was able to do. Maybe the elemental formed something that *was* a binding stone.

Could the shadow elemental *be* a binding stone?

Know so little.

The elemental was aware of his thoughts.

Lathan wouldn't be able to keep anything from the shadow.

But the shadow *had* helped him.

Unless it hadn't.

Lathan had no reason to believe that the elemental would help him if it had any other possibility. What if the elemental only offered to help because it was connected to him and not because the elemental was some benevolent force?

And having those thoughts would be dangerous, if that were the case. If the elemental *wanted* to harm others, then there was a possibility that even thinking anything about the elemental would be dangerous to him.

How could he handle something that was buried in his mind and seemed to know everything that he knew?

How could he avoid it if there was something the elemental intended to do that would harm those he wanted to protect?

Know so little.

Then prove to me that you're not going to try to harm me. Or those I'm with.

Black Rock.

What is there?

There was a long moment of silence. Blessed silence, Lathan decided. Having the elemental active in his mind left him thinking that he might be better off with silence, but he couldn't shake the feeling that he needed to have some answer.

What you want. Answer.

CHAPTER 26

It took much longer to reach the Black Rock than Lathan would have expected. He didn't know what to make of the travel, only that he'd been trying to connect to the shadow elemental during the journey but hadn't been able to get him to speak again. There was a near perfect silence that would be somewhat reassuring though he didn't know if that truly *was* reassuring or if the fact that the elemental had been quiet was something that should concern him.

So far, the elemental had done nothing to make him feel like he *should* be reassured. Knowing as he did that the elemental had the ability to practically listen to his thoughts left him in a difficult situation. It was... more than disconcerting. It left him concerned. There wouldn't be anything that he'd be able to hide from the elemental, even if the elemental didn't want to harm him —which he wondered about now for reasons that he hadn't had before.

When they started to land, Lathan attempted to reach the shadow again. *I know that you're still there. What are you doing?*

Silence.

He waited.

There would have to be some sort of a response, but nothing.

The air had changed during the journey. That was the only thing that he really had. When they'd first started off, there was a swirling of energy that was around him, but the longer he traveled, the thicker the air had become. He couldn't quite tell why it would feel that way unless the shadow wanted him to feel that way.

They pierced what seemed to be clouds, but then he didn't know if that was what it was. The cloud swirled. That seemed to be thicker than he had known before. He struggled to breathe, trying to keep up with the sudden change. He'd been feeling like it was a thickness to the air, but now it felt as if it were almost dangerously thick. It felt painful to take a breath. Heat seemed to press on him, and he gasped, sucking in mouthfuls of heat.

What are you doing?

This time it came out in a panic.

It was the only way that he could communicate, though. He couldn't speak so wouldn't be able to say anything to the elemental in that way. Just mental gasps.

You wait.

I can't breathe.

Everything had started to go black around the corners of his eyes. It was as if the darkness that they travelled through in the clouds had started to squeeze him.

Not clouds. Shadow.

That was what he felt, wasn't it?

He could feel the shadow. He could feel the darkness that was swirling around him. He could feel the pain of the energy that was there. And there wasn't anything that he could do about it. He tried to hold his breath, but pain surged in him. That pain flooded him, but it was mixed with something more. Almost as if the wind were pried out of his lungs, squeezed out from him.

Were the Derithan attacking him?

Not the Derithan, he didn't think. This was something else. This was a burst of a different kind of power, and it seemed to him that he could feel the source of it. That energy was there deep within him. Cold.

The shadow did this to him.

Help.

Everything started to go black.

Pain flooded through him.

Cold worked through him.

When he'd thought that he understood the shadows before, he had been wrong. What he'd known was something different than this. What he'd known had been cold and painful, but it hadn't been anything quite like what he felt at this point.

It was almost as if he could feel the shadows squeezing down and through him.

Then everything went black.

Lathan panicked.

Was this how he'd die?

He had chased dangerous elementals before and had known that there was always the possibility that he might come across something that could push him, but he'd never expected that he'd find anything that challenged him like this. He wouldn't have expected the shadow to attack him in this way.

I don't know the shadow.

But didn't he?

His father had been talking about the shadow from the moment that he was born.

Lathan had chased that as long as he could remember. He had never really expected to find the shadow, and he certainly hadn't expected to have bound the shadow with the binding stone, but now he had. And now he didn't know what that meant for him. It was a dangerous power. He could feel that power, even if he couldn't fully understand why or what that meant for him.

Then the darkness started to clear.

He could breathe.

It took a few moments for the haze around his vision to clear, but when it did, he could make out a bleak landscape around him. There was darkness.

Night?

It hadn't been that long that they'd been traveling, had it?

He didn't think that it was. If they'd been moving that long, he thought that he would have known about it, but this seemed as if it were something different than that. Not night.

Black Rock.

Lathan had seen glimpses of it before.

The elemental was there, still swirling around him and leaving the energy of the elemental inside of him in a way that he could feel almost trying to overwhelm him. Cold lingered.

When a gust of wind swirled near him, Lathan was surprised that he could feel it.

The shadow didn't try to pull on that gust and no longer attempted to absorb it. Swallow it.

At the thought, there was a hint of laughter, but it was less than it had been before and quieter. As if the elemental weren't able to keep communicating with him.

Then he saw Marin floating above the ground.

She looked... majestic.

There wasn't any other way to describe it. The wind whipped at her, pulling at her hair, but it did so in a way that it floated around her almost regally. She lowered slowly, the power of the wind holding onto her but not the way he had seen her doing before. Had she somehow changed how she was connecting to the wind? He'd believed that she used the wind by speaking to it, but maybe she had a way of directing it.

Lathan landed.

Heat wafted off the ground toward him. The air slipped past him, billowing against his cheeks every so often. There was a faint rumbling from a distant place, though he didn't know where it came from, only that he could feel the wind as it began to shift past him. The thickness that he'd detected before began to make a different sort of sense. Humidity. there was a real density to the air that he hadn't understood before now.

All of the elements.

That shouldn't surprise him. When he paid any attention to the shadow elemental, it seemed as if there were each of the elements in it. Perhaps even spirit, though he didn't know if he would know whether spirit was part of it.

The shadow released him.

The sense of shadow remained, but it wasn't as significant as it had been before. There was still some of that power, but when he started to try to focus on it, the energy of the shadows began to fade from him.

Marin stepped free and made her way toward him. "That was unexpected. Did the shadow guide you here?" She looked around her, as if expecting to find an answer.

Lathan didn't have anything to offer her. How could he explain what he had been feeling and what the shadow had done to him? Lathan didn't think there was any way for him to explain it. The connection that the shadow had formed to him—and the way that it spoke to him—seemed to defy any explanation.

"I don't know what the shadow was after. Is after," he added. "Black Rock. That's what the shadow says." Lathan looked up. "What happened to Henash and Jef?"

"I doubt they'll be long. Henash will push to move quickly but he doesn't have the same connection to the wind."

"He can't talk to it?"

"He can talk to it," she started, tipping her head to the side and listening as if she would find some answer, "but he doesn't know the truth of the wind the way that those who can *feel* it know." She regarded him for a long moment. "I can tell that you're more aware of it than you had been before."

Lathan tried to feel for the cold within him, though there wasn't anything that reacted quite as well as he had hoped. There was a sense of the cold, but that was it. Nothing more than that, and certainly nothing that would help him know what the elemental wanted from him. Unless the shadow spoke to him again, he wasn't sure that he would even have a chance at knowing.

Why aren't you talking to me?

Black Rock.

That's where we are. Now what?

He looked around, thinking that there had to be some answer about what the elemental wanted from him, but as he looked, he didn't see anything. From the cold through him, he didn't think there were even any elementals. So why would the shadow elemental, an elemental that seemed to absorb other elementals, want to be here of all places?

The sense of the elemental laughing at him came again.

He'd heard it enough now that he recognized it and knew that there wasn't anything that he could do to counter the amusement in the elemental. He *was* amused, but this time there wasn't the same amusement that there had seemed to be before. The elemental laughed softly enough that he had to strain to hear it, but he could most definitely hear it.

"I'm trying to understand what the elemental thought that we should find here." Lathan turned. There was a swirling of wind above him and he suspected that was Henash starting to make his way down, though he remained high above him. "The shadow has seemed to absorb everything that comes his way. He doesn't want me to think that's what he's doing—but that's what he's doing. Or she." He looked to Marin. "Are elementals gendered?" That might be why the shadow was equally amused at him. Lathan didn't even know whether he was connected to a male or female elemental.

"I think it depends upon the elemental. Some of them are. When you think of some of the great elementals, things like the draasin, they are definitely gendered. There are some who think that they might have been among the first of the elementals to break free of the initial connection to the elements, but that's nothing more than speculation."

"What connection?" Henash—and Jef, he saw—were starting to descend. They were about fifty feet above the ground but coming down slowly.

"The elementals and how they connect to the elements. I forget that you never studied these things. You know as much as we learn in the Saval, but..." She frowned slightly. "Anyway, the precursor elementals. Like everything, there had to have been something that came before, right? The elements themselves. Some think there's something beyond even that, but as we don't have any way of reaching the elements without the elementals, we can't really know."

"And the draasin are considered the first?"

"Among the first. Creatures that might have been something else and became elementals over time and through their connection." She shrugged and looked to Henash. "I know how that sounds, but when you study the way that we do, it doesn't sound quite as strange."

You come.

The voice came more loudly this time, tearing through his mind. It lingered there for the better part of a few moments until he closed his eyes and strained to try and focus on something else. At this point, he wasn't sure that he would be able to let go of the strangeness that he felt, but he believed there had to be something that was happening that he might be able to work with.

What are you so concerned about? You brought me here because you wanted my help with something, so what is it?

There was a long silence. Jef watched him, but he didn't say anything. Henash had been quiet ever since they had landed back in this space, but it was more than just the silence. It was the emptiness that he felt as well.

Concern. You.

Lathan tried to focus on the elemental and wanted to know more about why it would be concerned about *him*. When he tried to connect to the elemental, there wasn't any sort of response other than a hint of cold that flowed through him, suggesting that the elemental remained active—and trying to connect to him in some way.

Concerned for him—or about him?

That would be a different response depending upon which it was for the elemental.

"Where is the elemental telling you to go?" Marin asked. "I've been trying to talk to the wind, but it has grown silent. I suspect that whatever you've done with the shadow quieted my connection to the elementals."

"I haven't done anything."

Not that he knew of, at least. But there was the fact that he had connected to the shadow, and that he had to feel that connection, that seemed to be significant to him. If he could keep drawing on that connection, he might be able to find a way beyond what he'd been doing so far.

"You've done something. Even if it's just about what you've done with the shadow..."

But what did he do?

There was a cold that flowed now with him. It began to get deeper, colder, and he noticed how it started to work all the way from his toes up into his mind. As he focused on it, he let the cold work through him, thinking that if he could work with it enough, he might gain a better understanding of the shadow.

Concern you.

What did that mean?

Why do you need to be concerned about me?

He took that approach, thinking that it would be easier to lead down that pathway, though he wasn't completely sure that was what it was.

Shadow. Heart. You.

What does that even mean?

You feel it. Shadow heart.

Marked? That's what another said to me.

Though Lathan still wasn't sure what it meant that he *might* be shadow marked. Did it mean that he was tacked onto something of the elemental, or perhaps it simply meant that he had felt the shadow before. That might be all that it was. And he *had* felt the cold of the shadow, so that seemed to be a significant thing for him.

No mark. Heart.

"Shadow heart?" Lathan said aloud.

Henash sucked in a sharp breath. "Where did you hear that?"

He pointed to himself. "The shadow said it. I've been asking where he's leading us and why he's taking this path. He said he was concerned for me, then said it was because I was a shadow heart. You said it was shadow marked, but you've not said anything about this shadow heart."

Henash tipped his head back, looking at the sky. When he did, there was a sense from him that he was trying to explain something, though was it to himself— or to the elementals that he seemed able to speak to?

"A shadow heart is something different. When we talk about a shadow marked, that's rare enough. It's considered a blessing to have the shadow marking, mostly because it means the elemental has gifted you with a connection. But a shadow heart is even rarer still, and not something that I fully understand. There are others we could ask, but unfortunately, they are not here."

That was something that he could feel already, so that wasn't the issue. Lathan *had* connected to the elemental, so there was nothing more that he would say about that. He could feel the cold working within him even now, as if the shadow wanted him to find a way to use that cold.

Could that be what it was?

The elemental wanted to provide something to him so that he could use that power? If that were the case, then why not simply let him have access to the shadow and use it in that way? Unless the elemental wasn't sure how to do that. Lathan had been feeling the cold as it worked through him, and he understood that it might be about more than just the cold.

"What would that mean?" Lathan asked.

"I've never known a shadow heart. I don't even know." Henash looked to Marin. "Have your elementals said anything about that?"

"They wouldn't know anything. They are aware, but it's different. I struggle for them to have full awareness of what's happening, though the elementals are trying to get me to know what they are doing—and how to help."

Lathan focused on the shadow. *What are you trying to do with me?*

There was silence.

Cold flowed, so he knew the elemental was still there and still trying to be active within him, but there wasn't the same answer that he had before. He strained for it, wanting to feel that cold that came through him so that he could know what the elemental wanted for him to do, though the longer that he felt that cold, the less that he began to think that he might be able to find any sort of answer.

Shadow. What are you trying to do to me?

Not to you. Save.

Save me? But save me from what?

Darkness.

CHAPTER 27

As Lathan strained to know what it was that the elemental tried to tell him, the earth began to tremble once more. The trembling picked up, and the steady shaking that started began to intensify, leaving him thinking that it was all earth but might be more than just earth. They hadn't felt anything quite like that before.

Then the binding stone jacket began to squeeze.

It was painful, and he struggled to try to ignore the pain.

"What's going on?" Jef asked. "You look like you're trying to swat away a nest of flies, sort of like that time when we came across the—"

"Jacket," Lathan said. "Squeezing. *Hurts.*"

And that was all that mattered. It *hurt*, and though he tried to ignore the way that the jacket squeezed him, he couldn't get past it. It seemed as if it were using all of the elements at the same time, the blast of the different elemental energies flowing all at one time and in such a way that he could scarcely ignore it.

"I see what's happening," Marin said. She had approached, and now she had her hands held out and seemed to be trying to pull on the wind, though Lathan doubted that would make a difference. "You have to let the shadow absorb it."

"I can't."

Lathan didn't have any control over it. When he felt that cold, that was about the only connection that he really had. He pushed on the sense of the cold, though he couldn't really use that in any way.

"What's it feel like?" Henash asked.

"Pain. Just squeezing." It was a wonder that he was able to get those words out. He had a hard time saying anything, though the pain that worked through him was intense enough that he thought that he might just pass out.

When he *had* felt that kind of sense before, the shadow elemental had drawn on it. Why not this time?

"Derithan," he said. That was what this had to be, but where were they?

Close enough that they likely were the ones responsible for this. Close enough that they wanted to squeeze him so that they could do what? Take the shadow?

Or was it about him?

Shadow heart.

That was a different thing than a shadow marked.

Lathan didn't know what a shadow heart was or whether that was anything that he needed to be concerned with anyway, but he could feel the cold of the shadow.

When he felt that cold before, it had helped him and begun to absorb some of the other elementals. The shadow might claim that it wasn't absorbing, but he suspected that there was something to it, regardless of what they believed.

"Help. Hurts."

Henash reached for the binding jacket but quickly jerked his hand away. "Not going to be able to do much with that. Can you try something different? Maybe see if the wind will whisper this off?"

Henash had to be talking to Marin about that, but he would have to try to find his own way of getting this off of him. As he focused on the pain, he tried to make a connection to the cold, letting that energy be a part of him.

That was what he needed. That cold was going to be the key for him knowing how to break free of this. He could feel the cold, but that was all that he could feel. That was a strange stirring of energy that he wanted to draw upon. That would be something that he would be able to use. Maybe the elemental would continue to push outward and provide him with enough of an assist that he could...

The ground trembled again.

This time it was even more potent than it had been before, and the cold that was within him started to respond but then faded again. There was a stirring. Nothing more than that, though he wondered if that stirring would be enough for him to find a way to get through the pain.

And the pain...

That was significant.

It surged through him, the cold squeezing, pressing, and leaving him to think there might not be anything that he could do differently to try to ignore that sense. It overwhelmed him.

Lathan dropped.

He could feel the pain worsening. He tried to ignore it. Lathan wanted to find a way to move past the pain, but couldn't.

Wind pressed around him.

That had to be Marin. Maybe it was even Henash. And if that were the case, it might be possible for him to get some protection. If they used the wind in a way that would take away the pain...

But it didn't do anything.

Nothing changed.

Just more of the cold. More of the pain. More trembling.

Lathan shot into the air.

He didn't know if this was something that he had any control over, or if this might be Henash and Marin. If it were them, why would they push him into the air?

They wouldn't have done that.

The air pushed him, battering at him. He was swirling, spinning in place, and trying to hold some sort of a connection to force his way down.

Help me.

Helping. Dangerous.

What can I do?

Use. Cold.

What was he supposed to do with it?

The wind. That was what he could see. That was what he could feel.

There were other elementals. That pain.

The energy. Could he somehow have some way of trying to control that? If he could draw on the cold...

Cold. That was what the shadow elemental gave him, though he didn't know if there was anything more in the cold that he might be able to try to do. When he focused on the cold and the energy that was there, he knew that it was possible. It had to be possible.

Rather than simply feeling the cold, what if he attempted to use it the same way that he would have used the binding stone on elementals?

That might be something that he could do. Lathan didn't know if attempting to do that would make a difference, but at this point, the only thing that he cared about was trying to get rid of the pain.

Cold.

That was what he felt, and almost all that he knew.

Lathan focused on the cold, letting that wash through him.

Gradually, the pain began to change.

It didn't lighten completely, but there was less than there had been before. Slowly, the constriction of the binding stone jacket began to change, wrapping around him but not with the same intensity. The shadow—and the cold—had taken some of that. He tried to focus on the cold that was there with him, trying to think if there was anything more that would work so that he could get past it, but he had to take time.

Thank you for helping. It was better already. *Why did you bring me up here? My friends are down below. They can't help me from up here.*

No thank. Done.

Why did you bring me up here, though? There had to have been a reason.

Others.

Lathan tried to look around, but the wind swirling around him made it difficult for him to see anything clearly. There might be something that was there, but as he tried to focus on it, all he knew was the cold.

What others? You need to help me understand what is going on. You've said that I'm the shadow heart, but I don't know what that means. The others who are with me don't know what it means, either. Can you help me to understand?

It was the most that he'd asked of the elemental at one time, but in this case, he thought that he had to ask. Knowing what the elemental wanted of him was going to be the key, even if he didn't really understand it now.

Others. Come. Hurt heart.

What is the shadow heart?

Can bring together. Shadow. Others. Connect. Heart.

Lathan tried to make sense of what the shadow was telling him. The shadow could bridge the others? Did that mean that he—if he was the shadow heart—could somehow create a bridge to the other elementals?

Why does that matter now? The Derithan are after something, right? That's what you're concerned about but what is it?

Others.

The Derithan? Lathan wished that he had an easier time of communicating with the elemental. There were things that he simply didn't seem to understand how to connect to Lathan. And now they were flying up here, the others that he'd traveled with back down on the ground, and likely trying to understand what they might be able to do.

Others.

We call them the Derithan. They chase elementals. They used this jacket. Is that what you're concerned about?

They want heart.

Which meant that they would want *him*.

What would they do with the heart?

Hold. Use.

How can I stop them?

Hide.

Was that what the elemental was trying to do for him? If the shadow thought that he needed to run and hide, then maybe that was where he was taking him, but that wasn't what Lathan wanted.

The others need me. They can't fight. They need help.

That was how he felt about it, but he didn't know if they would need too much from him. Henash and Marin could use the elementals, and if Jef managed to get ahold of a binding stone, then he might be able to do something more as well.

Bring me down. Let me help.

Not the heart.

I'm not going to run when they need me.

And he was convinced that they did need him, though he wasn't sure how that would work. The pain in him was about the same, not diminishing despite him having a better connection to the cold and the shadow. He had thought that he might be able to gain something more if he could use the shadow, but it seemed to him that even as he tried, the cold wasn't doing what he wanted.

The air cleared just enough for him to see the ground below.

And his heart stopped.

Derithan swarmed the bleak landscape.

As he watched, he thought he could feel the elementals that were involved, but it was more than just what he could feel with the elementals. He saw Marin and Henash, both looking as if they were trying to counter whatever the Derithan were doing.

Please. Help me with them.

The elemental remained quiet.

Lathan could feel the cold, and he tried to use what he could feel to see if there would be any way for him to help. What he needed first was to get back to the ground. The Black Rock.

Why here?

That was something that he should've understood before now, and he hadn't taken the time to ask. There had to be some reason that they would have come here, of all places. What did the Derithan think they would find here?

If Lathan could answer that, he would know what they needed to do to stop them.

There had to be something about this place, and about the Black Rock, that had drawn the Derithan, though he had spent considerable time here and had not come up with any obvious answer. Obvious was what he needed at this point. He had been traveling with the shadow and thought that he understood, but he remained confused.

The shadow elemental had brought him here for some grand purpose.

I need your help. I need to know what you are after. Why do you fear for me?

That seemed to be what the shadow elemental was afraid of, after all. He was the heart. Whatever that meant.

Cold fluttered within him. It was deep, biting, and when he focused on it, he would almost call it blinding, but then it passed. Increasingly, Lathan started to think that he needed to have that cold flowing within him so that he could understand the purpose of it, and there had to be some purpose. The cold had been the most prominent sense that he had of the shadow elemental. Each time that he had felt the cold, he had also known some other aspect and had come to know the strange energy that continued to swirl.

What had he said before?

The elemental swallowed others.

And the shadow had laughed at that idea.

Lathan could still hear that laughter buried in his mind, as if the elemental were there, lingering deep within him and trying to remind him just how ridiculous it was that the shadow would swallow another elemental.

But what had he seen?

The shadow hadn't attacked. Shadow had never attempted to attack. Instead, the shadow had tried to help him from the very beginning. He remembered how the shadow had been there, giving him assistance when he was in danger.

But what about the very first time that he had encountered the shadow?

There had to have been something to that, as well.

The shadow had been racing across the Black Rock. He had seen it running and had assumed that it was simply moving the way that all elementals migrated, but in this case, what if there was another purpose?

Please. Help me understand you.

Lathan didn't expect the elemental to answer and was shocked when the cold surged in his mind.

The cold came from someplace that he had never felt before. It burned deep within him, and the longer that he felt it, the easier it was for him to understand what that cold attempted to do. It tried to show him something.

Lathan simply had to open himself up for it. They floated.

All around him, Lathan was distantly aware of energy. That was the only way that he could describe it.

It seemed to come from elementals that were all around them, and the kind of power that he felt began to bloom from some place deep, almost overwhelming. Lathan tried to ignore it, but he could feel that power, and could feel the way that it swept around him. Each of the elements were represented by the explosion of energy that came from the elementals filling his mind, an awareness of the power that lingered within him.

But the cold came. Through it, Lathan felt something else.

The cold, but also a connection.

As that cold burned in his mind, he began to feel where it flowed. At first, it seemed as if it flowed into his mind, as if the elemental were trying to show him something, but he realized that wasn't what it was. The elemental was certainly there in his mind, but the elemental also flowed somewhere else, out and beyond him, straining out to the elemental power that he continued to feel.

That was what it was. The shadow elemental stretched, connecting him to the others. He found his hands tracing along the binding jacket, and once more, cold bloomed.

It was different, though.

The jacket.

Everything within him seemed to go still. Lathan had thought the jacket was some sort of binding stone. Marin had suggested that it might be some sort of summoning jacket, but it seemed as if binding stone was a more apt description, only not completely correct, either.

He could feel the way the jacket worked, and now that the cold lingered in his mind, burning deeply, Lathan understood it. The jacket wasn't a binding stone. And it wasn't a summoning jacket.

The jacket absorbed the elemental.

Lathan had seen something similar when he had seen the Derithan attacking hyza. He had thought that the Derithan had simply used a binding stone like what he did and how he believed the binding stone merely collected and stored a bit of the element connection, which he suspected was the truth. But in this case, now that he felt along the surface of the jacket, he started to have a greater understanding of what exactly the jacket did. The jacket pulled on the power of the elemental, to the point where it consumed it. The jacket stored the elemental.

And the Derithan had been herding them. That had to be why the elementals were migrating in the first place, but why would they have been pushing them here?

That was how he had come across the shadow.

Lathan had been trying to understand why he would encounter a shadow elemental again after all this time and why the others would have been migrating as quickly and as often as they had been, but understanding that made even more sense.

But what could he do?

Are you wanting to save me, or do you want me to help?

He had no idea which it was, but increasingly, he

thought that the elemental had some purpose in mind and he had only to understand what it was.

There was no answer.

That didn't surprise him. He wasn't exactly expecting the elemental to respond, only the more that he felt it, the more that he began to think that the elemental had to have some purpose in mind.

Save the heart.

Wasn't he the heart?

Lathan focused on what the elemental had shown him, using that connection once again to follow the cold, follow the energy, and to try to feel it, but he could not see anything. There were the strands of energy that connected him beyond where he was, and yet...

Strands of energy.

The elementals.

Lathan could see the elementals somehow.

Some of them were close enough that he could practically feel them, but as he realized what he detected, he knew it wasn't elementals in the sense that he was accustomed to. These were elementals trapped within the binding jacket. These were stored elementals. But they were drawing from something else. They were connected in some way. Faint tracings of power, little more than a pale latticework of energy, stretched away from the elemental and toward Black Rock.

Lathan ran his hands along his binding stone jacket, feeling the contours of it, and then focused on the cold. When he did, the cold seemed to react. It was the first time that it had happened. Always before when he had been trying to focus on the cold, on what he felt with the shadow elemental, Lathan had failed. In this case, and this time, by focusing on the cold, he began to feel the elemental starting to loosen something. It was almost as if the shadow elemental understood what he tried to do. He was not attempting to activate anything. All he wanted now was to push. Call the elements out of the jacket. Release them.

And he would release them to the shadow elemental.

He tried not to be distracted by the tracings of power that trailed to the other elementals all around him, but it became increasingly difficult for him to ignore how that worked.

Derithan.

It was all around him. The power was considerable. *Their* power was considerable.

And he understood. The Derithan had surrounded Henash and Marin and Jef.

Not because of Lathan—at least, he didn't think that it was directly because of him—but because of the others whispering to the wind and perhaps even because of the binding stone that Jef carried with him before his capture.

They wanted those elementals.

He focused. His eyes were shut tight. The cold within him was burning, and yet Lathan could see pale tracings of color that connected him to the other elementals. Almost a glowing orange for fire. A whisper of gray for the wind, mostly translucent if not for a little bit of color to it. A deep florescent green for water. And a thick, rich brown for earth.

But there was another line there.

It was connecting to it all. He had expected it to be dark, the way that he assumed the shadow to be, but that wasn't what it was. Instead, there was a gleaming silver line that threaded through all of them, connecting to them, but more importantly, connecting to him.

The silver was there within him.

What was it?

Another elemental?

Before Lathan had a chance to understand, a blast of elemental power struck, knocking him from the air.

CHAPTER 28

L athan struggled to get control over the power that had tossed him to the ground. It was almost overwhelming, though. He could feel that power whipping around him and the different elementals that battered at him, but more surprising was how he could still see the latticework of connections the elementals shared.

Cold lingered in his mind, but it wasn't nearly as potent or as blinding as it had been before. Lathan actually wished for more of that cold, a greater connection to the shadow elemental so that he could ensure his safety, but that connection seemed to have retreated. Either that, or the shadow elemental had chosen to go quiet. Still, he detected that ongoing sense, and the energy that came with it. If nothing else, he might be able to use the shared connection the shadow elemental had given him for him to understand what was happening around him.

He crashed to the ground.

There was very little that buffered him and little that protected him. The only thing that seemed to cushion the blow somewhat was the fact that he had been pushing on the binding jacket—he still wasn't exactly sure what else to call it, and binding jacket seemed to fit —so that the wind had shielded him a little bit. Not completely. When he struck, pain bloomed within him, and he struggled to even catch his breath and slow that down.

"Get up," a voice from near him said.

"Henash?"

"Get up. The Derithan are converging. We thought the shadow elemental might have been carrying you to safety. It would've been better if it had," Henash said.

"The shadow—"

Lathan didn't have an opportunity to say anything more about the shadow. Another explosion thundered, this one coming on a shooting strike of lightning coursing toward the ground, followed by a rumble of heavy thunder which caused the air to compress upon him, squeezing. As before, Lathan detected the steady squeeze coming from the binding stone jacket and started to question whether that was something that he should actively work against.

The binding stone jacket.

He touched it, feeling the different lines of power there, and then pressed, letting that energy flow outward. That was what he needed, after all. He needed for the binding stone jacket to release the elementals that were trapped within it. And he needed to empower the shadow. Whether or not the shadow elemental swallowed that elemental energy, Lathan suspected that he needed to help release the elementals so that the shadow elemental could gain more power.

He was shoved from behind.

He staggered, and then something else grabbed him, keeping him from tipping.

"Come on," Marin said. Her voice was soft, and she was shielded somewhat by a translucent haze that swirled around her. The wind elementals that she had been speaking to.

Lathan traced on the binding stone jacket and focused on the cold within him, trying to connect the two. There seemed to be a surge, and then the faint silver line that he'd been seeing between them surged again.

"Where are the Derithan?" he asked.

"I don't know," Marin said. "We don't even know what they are after."

"Elementals," Lathan answered. "It's the only thing that makes sense. It's probably tied to the shadow and how the shadow can help them draw more elementals. Especially with the migration." He just didn't know what it meant that they had these binding stone jackets, or how they could use them.

He traced on it again, this time finding one for earth. He focused on the cold within his mind and realized that connection remained there, though it was buried. There was cold, almost blinding for a moment, and then it faded into a soft, burning sort of cold. Then the silvery line formed much like it had before. It seemed to flow deep within him, connecting to him.

That was new, and he wondered why he should see it so clearly.

He staggered again. This time, it wasn't Marin pushing on him, trying to shove him forward, so much as it was something pushing behind him, sending him staggering forward.

"Jef?"

"Henash was keeping an eye on him. Surprisingly, Jef is more skilled than he should be."

"What do you mean?"

"Well, when the Derithan came, he managed to react almost as if he knew they were coming."

Lathan looked around, and when he did, he managed to catch sight of Henash, the wind swirling around him, along with the pale translucent lines that stretched toward Black Rock, along with Jef.

He hadn't expected to see any sort of lines around Jef's chest, and his heart stopped, and he understood what it was that he saw. Several different colors swirled around him when they shouldn't.

A binding jacket.

"Jef stole one too?" Lathan muttered.

Marin caught his arm and looked over to him. "What was that?"

There was another blast, a burst of lightning, and

Lathan looked up almost not in time. The darkness that burned within him bloomed, and it seemed as if the shadow stretched upward, creating a cushion overhead. It managed to absorb the lightning and then did the same thing to the thunder that suddenly rumbled, following afterward. The different bursts of power did nothing to him, thankfully.

The air still hung with the blasts of power, and he waited for another one to follow, but none came.

"Jef has a binding jacket. I can see it. I think it's something the shadow elemental has done to me."

"Why would he have... No."

"I don't really understand it," Lathan said. "They questioned him."

"What if they are using him to get to us?"

Lathan had no idea what had happened. He wouldn't have expected Jef to have willingly sided with them, unless he thought that he had to in order to help his friends. And there was a matter of the Derithan finding them so soon and so easily.

It seemed as if they had managed to catch up to them.

Jef wouldn't have betrayed him, though.

Lathan didn't have much time to think about it.

Power swirled around him. He could feel the different elemental energies that were coming, and he could even see the faint tracings of power as they came toward them. Derithan.

He counted at least seven. Each of them had on a

binding stone jacket, something Lathan could see because of the colors that swirled around it. He wondered if he could use the shadow elemental to absorb those elementals, drawing them away, but he might only be able to do that if they unleashed the elementals at him and the others with him.

He positioned himself near Marin.

One of the Derithan strode forward. It was the same man that he had seen before. "You have fought long enough. Now you will guide us to it."

"I'm guiding you to nothing," Lathan said. He had no idea what it was that they wanted him to guide them to but wondered if the shadow elemental might know. If Lathan were to ask, would the elemental answer?

"You will guide us, or your friends will die."

He heard a quick shout that went silent.

Not Jef. Jef was standing near them, still surrounded by the Derithan, but the elementals on his jacket were obvious, even though Jef tried to hide it beneath his own tunic. It was Henash. He had fallen to the ground, collapsing with his quiet shout, and stopped moving.

Help him. Do whatever you need to absorb the wind elemental that is suffocating him.

That was the only thing that Lathan could think was happening, but how were they able to overpower Henash, someone who had proven that he could command the wind far better than any other?

He needed to find the answers later. For now, he needed to stay alive.

"Let them go," Lathan said.

He had the vague, faint sensation of the cold stirring, sliding away from him. As it did, he had to hope that he had enough time. Henash had provided answers, but it was more than just that. Henash was a friend.

So was Jef.

Henash gasped, sitting up.

When cold bloomed within Lathan, he understood what had happened. The shadow elemental had gone and helped. Not only that, but Lathan could feel the elemental's strength. There was another line of deep silver that flowed, different than it had been before. Now it bloomed in Lathan's mind. Was he becoming aware of the elementals that the shadow consumed?

Henash held his hands out, and the wind continued to stir as he did. There was something about Henash's presence that gave Lathan a sense of reassurance. Lathan had no idea what it was that the Derithan were after, but increasingly, he thought that it was all about the elementals. He wasn't exactly sure what it was, nor whether there was anything in what they sought that he might be able to stop, but it had to deal with the elementals.

Absorbing the power of the elementals.

With the newfound connection that he had, he could practically see the faint tracings all around him. Cold lingered within him, sitting deep within his mind, hovering there, a sense of connection that Lathan could feel and wished that he could use.

Only... why couldn't he use it?

Can you help me find the connection I have with these elementals?

The more that he focused on that energy, the more certain Lathan was that there was a connection they shared with the elementals. He didn't exactly know why, but as the shadow elemental began to absorb the others, Lathan could see the connections form between them, a latticework of energy that bonded him to these others. It was that latticework, that connection, he thought he could use.

Save the heart.

I need your help. Absorb as many of the elementals as you can.

With the thought, Lathan wasn't exactly sure what would happen with the shadow elemental and was surprised when it suddenly seemed to burst free of him. It happened slowly, gradually, building away from him until that energy created a fog all around.

It wasn't fog at all.

Shadow.

The Derithan fought. The fight was nothing like anything Lathan would have ever imagined before. It was energy, elementals, and it was power. And through it all, he was aware of the shadow doing something more.

Consuming.

He had considered it some sort of absorption of the elemental energy before, but he didn't think that fit. Not with what he felt now. Instead, it really seemed to be some sort of consumption of the other elementals. But from what he had seen from the shadow elemental, Lathan no longer believed that the consumption harmed these others. Rather, it seemed as if it shifted them. As soon as the shadow reached the nearest Derithan, the shadow flowed over them. It happened so quickly that the Derithan didn't have a chance to do much more than attempt a minimal resistance.

Lathan did nothing. The shadow elemental worked.

Cold bloomed, but it was a distant sort of cold this time, not nearly as direct as it had been before. There was a part of him that started to question whether the cold was even real, but then a line of pale silver connected to him, and then another, and then another.

Each time the lines of pale silver connected to him, Lathan realized that the shadow elemental had done what it needed. It moved on. But not before Lathan could feel these other elementals. They filled—and fueled—the shadow.

Was he destroying the elementals?

He had to stop the Derithan, but could he do so at the expense of the elementals?

His father would not have wanted that for him.

Another Derithan stepped closer.

Lathan ignored them and focused instead on the shadow. He let the elemental sweep outward, a burst of energy that exploded from the shadow elemental, and swept toward the Derithan. The Derithan cried out. There came another surge of stuttering cold, and lines of pale silver formed between he and the elementals that were suddenly freed—or consumed.

Something pressed against him.

Lathan could feel it.

He wasn't exactly sure what he could feel, only that there was a sense of pressure pushing against him.

Not just pressure, but warmth.

A shape emerged, glowing brightly. At first, Lathan thought that maybe it was the hyza elemental that he had been following all this time, but it was too powerful and much too large. The shape began to slither, slipping out and around, burning through the shadow. The cold began to retreat, withdrawing back into Lathan. The shadow was burned away.

Can you do anything here?

They are too powerful. They have bonded too many.

And whatever it was that they bonded had to be powerful.

Could it be one of the draasin? The massive fire elementals were considered impossibly rare, but he didn't think that they had this form. Lathan wasn't exactly familiar with the form of the draasin. He only understood that they could fly, and they were filled with a powerful, almost all-consuming flame.

Consume them, he said.

Cold began to ball up deep inside of Lathan. It was terrifyingly cold, painful, but there was some other part of it that he thought he might be able to find as well. Maybe the shadow could help him, but only if it separated from him.

Darint stepped forward.

"You have had it the whole time?" His voice was soft,

angry, and somehow curious all at one time. "Quite intriguing. And here I had thought that this assignment was a waste of time." He smiled. "But perhaps reports from this region have proven to be far more accurate than I had ever known. Especially once I bring you back."

They would bring him to the Derithan?

If they did, he had no idea what would happen to him. He had no idea what happened to the shadow.

And he had no control over either. More than that, however, it seemed as if the shadow were retreating deeper inside of him, as if the shadow were worried about what the Derithan wanted of it. The shadow consumed, didn't it? And then what?

Darint strode toward him.

He kept waiting for Henash or Marin to help, but he realized that they could not. Something was holding them.

It was only Lathan and Darint.

And this was a powerful Derithan. Too powerful.

He had seen how the Derithan would take elementals, absorbing them and possibly even destroying them.

If that were to happen to the shadow elemental, what would happen to Lathan in the process?

He needed the shadow elemental to help.

Cold burned inside of him.

An understanding came with it. The lines of silver swirled.

Elementals had scattered. Elementals all around him.

They were there, freed from the binding jacket, but

they were destroyed. They weren't consumed. They were simply freed.

What had the shadow consumed, then?

All this time, Lathan had feared what that connection might mean, but perhaps the elemental had not consumed anything other than the bond that the Derithan had dared to place upon them.

The lines of connection all around him felt familiar. Those silver lines were strangely comforting, but more than that, there was something about the strange lines that he thought he recognized, and had felt before.

Darint strode closer. He was power. Heat and flame radiated from him. He scowled at Lathan, but there was a triumphant expression in his eyes. He thought that Lathan could do nothing. And perhaps he was right.

Cold burned.

The shadow wasn't going to be enough for him.

Lathan was too inexperienced, and the power that the Derithan were able to access was too much. Far greater than anything Lathan could do.

He felt that with an intense certainty, and a wave of sadness washed over him. It wasn't just failing himself and failing the elementals. He felt as if he were failing his father.

And all his father had wanted was for him to understand the elementals and the connections that formed between them.

Power battered at him.

Connections.

Something about that tickled at the back of his mind.

Connections. That was what his father had always wanted, after all. He had wanted Lathan to find those connections, to understand them and to make his own connection to them.

Then, with a flash, understanding came to him.

Lathan pulled on the connections.

CHAPTER 29

Those lines of power formed far more brightly than before, the connections to elementals. He could see them in a way that he had never even imagined, dozens of them now freed and waiting on Lathan to use that connection.

Not only that, but something his father had once said about the elementals came back to him.

"Each of the elementals has an opposite. Not as if it were some sort of natural predator, but merely more of a natural counter. Hot and cold. Light and dark. Fire and ice."

"But fire and earth are opposites," Lathan had said.

His father had smiled, patting his shoulder. "See? I didn't even need to teach you. You already knew."

Lathan couldn't remember when his father had taught him that or when he had come to understand it, but he had known. Earth countered fire.

And the kind of fire that he felt now was considerable.

But throughout everything, he felt a connection to earth as well. He had freed many earth elementals. Perhaps more than he had realized, and that faint tracing of connection that was out there lingered, giving him a sense of it.

And he thought that he could use that.

He pulled on those connections. Threads of energy surged, and the earth rumbled. The flames that the Derithan was drawing upon began to sputter and then finally sputtered out.

Lathan pulled even more. He switched to water, recognizing water elementals all around him, despite the arid air. He added a bit of wind, and it swirled forward, holding still to earth. And lastly, he added his own draw upon fire.

All of the elements were drawn. Elementals for each one called forth.

Darint looked at Lathan, and then lightning streaked down.

Lathan braced for the impact.

Surprisingly, the shadow elemental did something.

Lathan wasn't exactly sure what happened, only that cold burst inside of him, and a cloud of dark energy circled outward, swirling and consuming. It felt as if the lightning were drawn toward that cold. It fortified Lathan.

Another attack, then another followed in quick succession.

The shadow absorbed each one.

Then a massive burst of lightning came streaking.

Lathan braced. He could feel something from the shadow, almost as if it were trembling and afraid of this next burst.

When it struck, it hit where Darint was standing. When the light cleared, he was gone.

The cold lingered in the back of his mind. The lines of power were still there.

He looked over. Henash and Marin stood on either side of Jef, watching him.

Lathan made his way over.

"What just happened?" Jef asked.

Lathan could feel the binding stone jacket whispering, almost as if it were connecting to him and perhaps even connecting to the power that was near him.

"You have one of their jackets."

"I... I didn't know how to use it. I just grabbed it. I shouldn't have. And I should've told you about it."

Lathan wasn't about to argue with Jef, not about that.

"Can I keep it?"

"Only if you can understand it," Henash said, sliding over toward them. "And I'm afraid you will have to spend some time in a more traditional study. You both will."

Jef looked as if he were going to be sick, but maybe it was what they needed to do. Lathan needed to understand the elementals much better than he already did. But there was more he could learn from those in the Saval. That was where he needed to go.

"Thankfully it didn't seem as if they got what they wanted. I'm not entirely sure what happened, but I saw something. Elementals. Dozens of them. One for each of the elements, save spirit. They were all here, and they all attacked that Derithan. You were directing them?"

"I think that when the shadow elemental severed the binding jacket connection to the other elementals, it formed one of its own." At least, that was what Lathan thought had happened, though he wasn't exactly sure whether that was the case or not. As far as he knew, it could have been something else. It could have been simply that the elemental had formed a connection to Lathan. And if that were the case, then he wasn't exactly sure that he understood what it was. "Anyway, we needed to come to the Black Rock."

He motioned for the others to follow, and he moved forward. He felt wind lift him, and he looked over to Marin and Henash, but neither of them looked as if they were responsible for it. Jef seemed surprised, carried up on the wind, and following them with a gust of air. They didn't have to go very far. They reached a bleak section of a rocky black-stone valley. There was nothing below.

Black Rock was known as a desolate wasteland. It was a place where nothing lived. It was a place where none of their people had gone. It served as a barrier between the kingdom and lands far beyond. Why would the Derithan have been coming here?

The shadow elemental had guided him here.

Lathan came to a stop near a rocky ridgeline, and he could feel the cold surge within him. For a moment, that was all he knew. Then those silvery lines began to stretch away from him, and they flowed out toward the ground, sweeping outward, touching the stone and forming something of a connection to it, as if threads were left behind. Some aspect of them lingered within Lathan's mind, but for the most part, those threads stayed here.

The cold lingered. Lathan half expected it to part him, but it didn't.

"I feel... something," Marin said. She tipped her head up, and for a moment, the wind swirled. "The wind is talking. It seems content." She looked back to Lathan. "What is this?"

"This is a place of rebirth," Henash said, his voice dropped to a whisper. "I can feel it. Something has just happened here." He looked over to Lathan. "Was this you?"

"Not me. At least, not really. I think this was the shadow elemental. I'm not exactly sure what it was, nor what the elemental wanted, but this was where he wanted us to be."

"Why?" Jef asked.

"I don't know."

Lathan lingered where he was, surrounded by the others, no answers coming to him. Distantly, he began to feel something. He looked over to Marin, who had her head twisted strangely, looking up at the sky, murmuring to the wind. Henash was doing something similar, though not the same. Jef just stared, and he seemed to be somewhat embarrassed. He should be. He had betrayed them, or had seemingly done so.

After a while, Lathan recognize that something was changing.

Elementals. Dozens upon dozens of elementals were coming this way.

What did you do?

The heart has been saved.

What is it? What did you do? Lathan asked again.

The elemental didn't answer, not at first. Lathan could feel the blooming of power, and he had no idea what it was, only that it was building.

And then he felt a rumbling.

Not just a rumbling, but a stirring. The gossamer threads began to spiral together, twisting and forming. The elementals seemed to have a connection to those thin, silvery threads, and they pushed it forward.

That energy began to pool. The elementals, some of them unseen, some of them obvious, pushed that silvery pool forward. Lathan had a distinct sense of power coming from that, even if he didn't understand what it was. And then everything stopped.

Light flashed. The ground seemed to tremble. The air hot. Wind swirled. And his heart hammered in his chest.

The elementals were active, only for what?

An enormous roar thundered.

It came from deep below the ground. The rock was no longer stained black, Lathan realized. It had taken on some color, though he wasn't exactly sure what it was.

"What is it?" Lathan asked, afraid to speak too loudly.

Marin shook her head, but Henash was looking down.

"It's this place," Henash said. "The elementals were drawn here. But I don't even understand why. I think we need to head back to town and to the Saval. Tolinar may know more, and if he doesn't, then we may need to send word to the king himself, if he hasn't already."

"Great," Jef muttered. When Marin frowned at him, Jef just shrugged. "So much for our quiet part of the kingdom."

Don't miss the next book in The Binding Trials: The Unbound Elemental.

When the truth about his father changes everything Lathan knows, his search for answers brings only more questions.

Having survived the Derithan attack, Lathan must understand his connection to the elementals. There's a power to them, but first he must find the truths of the elementals long hidden from him.

When an ally becomes an enemy, Lathan must act quickly.

The elementals are in danger. If he doesn't learn to use his connection to bind the elementals, the Derithan will claim their prize.

And the elementals will be destroyed.

SERIES BY JASPER ALDEN

The Lost Riders

The Golden Fool

The Binding Trials

Similar Series by D.K. Holmberg

The Dragonwalkers Series

The Dragonwalker

The Dragon Misfits

The Dragon Thief

Cycle of Dragons

Elemental Warrior Series:

Elemental Academy

The Elemental Warrior

The Cloud Warrior Saga

The Endless War

Printed in Great Britain
by Amazon